"I kno ... feeling,"

Tyler said from behind her, his voice low and infinitely gentle.

"You—you do?" Her head came up, her eyes wide open. Was it too much to hope for? That he could have had the same feelings all these years?

"Why?" she asked hesitantly. "I mean, how can you know what—"

"Because I've felt the same way myself."

"You have?" Jerri whispered as she turned to face him. How could that be? she wondered. She had never thought he knew she was alive, much less—

She swallowed the lump in her throat as she watched him advance slowly toward her. "What do you...think we should do about it?"

"That's easy, Smoky," he said, his voice a deep, tender caress as he reached for her.

Jerri closed her eyes. She couldn't speak. Couldn't breathe. She had waited so long for this moment....

Dear Reader,

Each and every month, to meet your sophisticated standards, to satisfy your taste for substantial, memorable, emotion-packed stories of life and love, of dreams and possibilities, Silhouette brings you six extremely **Special Editions**.

Now these exclusive editions are wearing a brand-new wrapper, a more sophisticated look—our way of marking Silhouette **Special Editions'** continually renewed commitment to bring you the very best, the brightest and the most up-to-date in romance writing.

Reach for all six freshly packaged Silhouette **Special Editions** each month—the insides are every bit as delicious as the outsides—and savor a bounty of meaty, soul-satisfying romantic novels by authors who are already your favorites and those who are about to become so.

And don't forget the two Silhouette *Classics* at your bookseller's every month—the most beloved Silhouette **Special Editions** and Silhouette *Intimate Moments* of yesteryear, reissued by popular demand.

Today's bestsellers, tomorrow's *Classics*—that's Silhouette **Special Edition**. And now, we're looking more special than ever!

From all the authors and editors of Silhouette **Special Edition**,

Warmest wishes,

Leslie Kazanjian,
Senior Editor

BARBARA CATLIN
Smoky's Bandit

Silhouette Special Edition

Published by Silhouette Books New York

America's Publisher of Contemporary Romance

To Jerry Dean:
my sister, my closest friend,
my finest and toughest critic.

This one's for you, Jerry,
for your unconditional
love and support and acceptance.

And because without you,
this book never would have been.
Never, ever, ever.

SILHOUETTE BOOKS
300 East 42nd St., New York, N.Y. 10017

ISBN: 0-373-09488-4

First Silhouette Books printing November 1988

Printed in the U.S.A.

Special thanks to Ron Bownds for providing
information—and inspiration—by sharing
the real-life success story of his
Utopia brand bottled waters.

Books by Barbara Catlin

Silhouette Special Edition

Prisoner of Love #303
Smoky's Bandit #488

* co-authored as Miranda Catlin

BARBARA CATLIN

admits to being an ordinary person who loves to write,
a woman whose dream to be published by Silhouette
before the age of forty became a reality "just under
the wire, which is the way I seem to handle almost
everything in life. Doing the two things I love most—
writing and being a single parent to two active, usually wonderful teenagers, a daughter and a son—leaves
little time for heading up civic organizations, growing
and canning my own vegetables or performing brain
surgery on the side."

Claiming to be a realist as well as a romantic, Barbara says one of her favorite sounds is "the roar of
those school buses rolling away each weekday morning, while my back is pressed against the door and I'm
clutching that first cup of coffee." But she also loves
the quiet of the ruggedly beautiful Texas Hill Country she's lived near for several years, and that serves as
her favorite setting—used for both *Prisoner of Love*
and *Smoky's Bandit*.

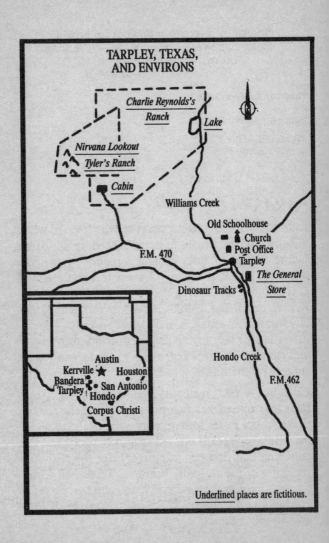

TARPLEY, TEXAS,
AND ENVIRONS

Charlie Reynolds's
Ranch

Lake

Nirvana Lookout
Tyler's Ranch

Cabin

Williams Creek

Old Schoolhouse
Church
Post Office
Tarpley

F.M. 470

Dinosaur Tracks

The General
Store

Hondo Creek

F.M. 462

Austin
Kerrville
Houston
Bandera
San Antonio
Tarpley
Hondo
Corpus Christi

Underlined places are fictitious.

Chapter One

"Here. Let's see if this settles your nausea."

Jerri Davenport watched as her best friend poured hot tea into her cup. "Thanks," she said quietly, rubbing her stomach, hoping the motion of her hand would calm the fluttery, queasy sensation. It didn't.

The homey warmth of Beth's kitchen wasn't helping, either, Jerri decided. She shrugged out of her tailored winter jacket and placed it on the chair back, then wrapped her fingers around the cup of tea in front of her.

"This is all your cousin's fault, you know," she stated flatly, a disgruntled frown on her face as Beth joined her at the big oak table. "I wouldn't be in this predicament if it weren't for him."

"My cousin's fault?" Beth asked, her tone incredulous. "Which one?"

"Tyler, that's which one."

"You mean Tyler *Reynolds*?" Beth asked, as if she had a cousin named Tyler Something-else. "How can you possibly blame your dilemma on Tyler Reynolds?"

Jerri's hand moved to the cigarettes on the breakfast table. She picked up the pack, fished out the third-to-the-last one and lit it. Wrinkling her nose, she glared at the ribbon of smoke slithering toward the ceiling as she put her left hand to her stomach again. On her drive from Houston to Beth's rambling, ranch-style home in the Texas Hill Country on the outskirts of Kerrville, she had smoked seventeen cigarettes, knowing precisely what would happen. It would be simple: she would become deathly ill and never want to look at another cigarette in her life.

Unfortunately her stroke of genius hadn't worked quite as brilliantly as she'd planned. Jerri was sick to her stomach, all right...but not sick of the tobacco habit. At the realization, a knot began to form on top of the nausea.

"Yoo-hoo," Beth said, leaning forward and flagging her out of her temporary stupor. "I repeat: I know it must be horrible, trying to quit smoking, but how can you blame that on Tyler Reynolds? You barely know the man." Her eyes rounded. "What am I saying? I don't think anyone really knows the man. Certainly not me—and I'm his cousin."

"Maybe you don't know him," Jerri said dryly, "but you certainly do have his name down pat."

Beth was still staring up at her with an intensity in her eyes that Jerri had never seen before. Beth Reynolds Ferguson, she realized, was not going to let this one go. Jerri was a good five inches taller than her best friend's five foot two, but it was obvious the fragile-looking woman wasn't going to let that bother her.

"So how can you blame—"

"I can't," she admitted, momentarily avoiding her friend's inquisitive glance. "It was my own fault. I was young and I was foolish, okay?" She smiled innocently and lifted one shoulder, determined to treat her confession with lightness. "But if it hadn't been for trying to impress your cousin with my worldly sophistication, I'd never have started smoking in the first place. Don't you remember the night I had my first cigarette?"

"Heavens, no! That must have been, what, seven or eight years ago?"

"Seven years and—" Jerri stopped for a moment, tilting her head and moving her fingers while her mind worked the calculation "—nine days, to be exact."

"Cut the histrionics, Jerri."

"I'm not just being dramatic, that's exactly when it was. It was our second year in college, the second time you invited me home with you." She picked up her gold lighter, using it to emphasize her words. "Surely you remember. My mother had to work that Christmas cruise to Jamaica and we couldn't be together, so you invited me to spend the holidays with you and your parents."

Still looking puzzled, Beth shook her head.

"It was Christmas Eve, and Tyler let us ride with him when he went to that big country and western dance in Bandera." When her friend mouthed "Ban-*dare*-a?" Jerri nodded and tossed the lighter into her handbag. "I can't believe you've forgotten. That night will be etched in my memory forever."

Beth thought for a moment, then threw her head back and laughed. "Lord, yes. It's all coming back to me now. As I remember, that night was etched in your *hair* for quite a while, too, after you set it on fire—waving that cigarette around."

"Yes. And at the time, I was actually grateful that Tyler was dancing with that . . . that redheaded floozy and didn't see us beating out the blaze." She had laced the words with humor, but the pain that gripped her chest felt a thousand times more intense than the physical pain gnawing at her stomach. She lowered her gaze, then forced a wry smile as she glanced back up. "Thank goodness I didn't singe anything but my split ends."

"Yes, and thank goodness I had those manicure scissors in my purse so we could run to the ladies' room and give you a quick trim!" Beth laughed again as she pressed her fingers to her cheeks. "Boy, I'll never forget that horrible odor. That was the first time I'd ever smelled burning hair!"

Jerri rolled her eyes, then made an attempt at smiling. But this time she couldn't. "So much for showing Tyler how worldly and sophisticated I was. All I eventually managed to get out of the deal was to get hooked on these filthy things." She picked up the cigarette pack and threw it across the table. "Talk about a plan backfiring."

Beth smiled, reaching out to yank on a lock of Jerri's short, light brown hair. "Is that supposed to be a pun?"

"No. Just a Freudian slip, I guess." For all Tyler Reynolds knew—or cared—she could still be that same girl with the strange-smelling hair that was shorter on one side than it was on the other.

Darn it, she thought glumly. He probably had never noticed she had light *ash*-brown hair to begin with—even before she'd put that first cigarette to it.

Beth frowned suddenly and put her hand over Jerri's. "Why don't we skip this little jaunt down Memory Lane? Why don't we just talk about what's really bothering you?"

"Nothing's bothering me," Jerri said, her spine straightening. "I was just—"

"Fine." Beth patted Jerri's hand before she stood up. "Just keep on laughing and smiling and putting up that big brave front. But don't expect me to sit here and go along with it, because I'm not convinced. I've never seen you looking this down—or desperate. Or whatever it is." She gave her a stern look. "And I'll be honest with you, Jerri. You may be hurting right now, but I'm hurting, too!"

"Oh, Beth," she said quickly, "forgive me. I didn't even ask if this was a bad time, and here I am barging in on you, feeling sorry for myself and—"

"You see?" she asked, her voice rising. "There you go again—trying to comfort *me*. And that's exactly what I'm talking about. We all have a right to feel sorry for ourselves every now and then, so why don't you just let yourself do it?'' Her eyes abruptly softened, along with her tone. "I'm hurting because I want to help. You've held my hand through plenty of crises, and yet I don't think I've ever seen you even cry. This time—just this once—I want to be there for *you*." Beth touched Jerri's cheek, smiling tenderly, then gave her another stern look as she handed her one of the two remaining cigarettes. "So why don't you put *that* in your pipe and smoke it? I'll peek in on Chad and be right back.''

Momentarily stunned, Jerri stared as Beth turned and headed for the nursery, where her ten-month-old son was taking his afternoon nap. The thought of Chad made her smile, but it also reminded her of what had been niggling at the back of her mind. She frowned and lit the cigarette, trying to fight the sense of anxiety she felt welling up inside her.

Beth was right, she decided, and perhaps that was why Jerri had come here in the first place. Perhaps instinct had told her that she needed the woman who'd been her closest friend for as long as they'd known each other.

Her eyes fluttered shut. Maybe, for once, she should *allow* herself to need Beth.

"You're right,'' she said, opening her eyes as she heard hushed footsteps approaching. "I need to talk. I . . . I need you.''

"Good,'' Beth said, taking her chair again. "And I'm going to do what you've always done for me. I'm going to listen and ask questions and try to be objective. So tell me. What brought on this mood?''

"It's just that...it finally dawned on me that at this rate, I'm never going to have what I want out of life.''

"You have everything. What could you possibly want?''

"I want—'' Jerri avoided Beth's curious gaze. "All I've ever wanted out of life is a station wagon with wood on the sides. Well, I'm twenty-seven years old, and look what I'm driving!''

Beth's line of sight followed Jerri's demonstrative gesture to the car parked on the opposite side of the wide expanse of windows. "You've got a cute, sporty little car! Why on earth would you want a station wagon with those hokey wood panels?"

Jerri leaped up from the chair, waving her cigarette like a banner in the air as she started pacing across the kitchen. "We graduated from college nearly five years ago, and I've got a cute little car that doesn't mean a thing to me, except that it gets me there and back. I've got a career that most people consider glamorous and fulfilling that doesn't leave me with an ounce of satisfaction. It's not what I want to do, but I can't quit because..." Her voice lowered to a murmur. "Well, because I just can't."

"If you're not happy with your job, Jerri, then I can certainly sympathize with you." Beth's look expressed her concern and puzzlement. "But what's all this got to do with a station wagon?"

Jerri dropped back onto the chair, then put her head in her hands and sighed. "It's a symbol, I guess. From the time I was a kid, it's been something I always dreamed about. From the window of my dorm, I'd see the nonresident kids arriving at school every morning, and a lot of their moms drove station wagons like that. In my silly little fantasies, I always visualized my mother and me living together and her driving a 'woody' when she dropped me off at school every day." Her face grew warm as she continued. "And now, in my grown-up fantasies, I always picture myself driving one of those station wagons. And having a home."

"But you have a home. A beautiful one, too, if you ask me."

"I have an *apartment*, Beth, when what I really want is a home. And a husband and kids!" Her hand flew up from her side again. "I've got a deluxe electric blanket with more settings than—" she pointed her finger at the long counter across the room "—your microwave oven over there, when what I really want is a man to keep me warm at night."

Beth's expression shifted to one of astonishment. "So get out there and find him! You certainly have all the right equipment for it: gorgeous gray eyes; legs that go on forever; nice, full—"

"Beth!"

"I'm not saying a pretty face and a good figure are all it takes, but come on now. How many men have come up to you lately asking if they could open your mouth and check your teeth?" When Jerri rolled her eyes, Beth continued. "And you've got a lot more than physical qualities going for you, so I repeat: get out there and find him! Whatever happened to the Jerri Davenport I met when I started college? The Jerri who graduated magna cum laude simply because she *wanted* to graduate with top honors? The Jerri who always got anything and everything she ever set her mind to?"

"Not everything, obviously." Jerri ran her fingers through her short hair in exasperation. "And don't think I haven't tried. But every man I meet seems to come up lacking. I always start comparing them to—" She clamped her mouth shut, watching her friend's eyes widen.

"To—" Beth's jaw dropped "—my cousin? To *Tyler?*"

"Yes." Frowning in disgust, Jerri reached across the table to retrieve the near-empty pack she had tossed there a few minutes before. "Go ahead and tell me—I've been an absolute fool. Don't think I haven't told myself that plenty of times."

"I'm the one who feels like a fool. A blind, insensitive fool. I had no idea you felt this way about Tyler."

"I...I never wanted you to know." Jerri flipped her wrist, trying to make light of a situation that she realized must sound ludicrous, even to her best friend. "It was my problem. And what with Tyler being sort of, well, the black sheep of your family, so to speak, I never thought you'd be exactly thrilled."

"I wouldn't call him the black sheep. Not precisely, anyway. He's more of an outsider. I think he prefers it that way, although I've never been quite sure why. And if you had asked me a long time ago, I could've told you that."

"You know how I am, Beth. Years of formal training, I guess." She crumpled the cellophane wrapper and threw it down again. "I don't...tend to wear my emotions on my sleeve."

"An understatement, if I've ever heard one." Beth propped her chin against her hand. "But regardless of all that, I always thought I could read you fairly well. I still can't believe I didn't see any signs of this."

Jerri shrugged her shoulders. "You know when I spent spring breaks and long weekends with you at your family's ranch in Tarpley?" She rolled her eyes in embarrassment. "You had pointed out Tyler's gate, so I knew his little piece of property was right down the road. And I was always hoping he'd drop by—even for a few minutes." Grimacing, she flicked her ashes with more force than was necessary. "Why do you think I never dated anyone in college more than once or twice? I fell for your cousin that first time you took me home with you—Easter weekend of our freshman year. After that, no mere man could live up to the image I had of the almighty Tyler Reynolds!"

"I don't mind telling you, I'm dying of curiosity. What did you and Tyler do that weekend?"

"Nothing," Jerri answered truthfully. "Absolutely nothing. I just thought he was wonderful." Self-consciously she studied her polished nails, then stared at the glowing end of her cigarette. "I remember that Sunday afternoon as if it were yesterday. The sun was incredibly warm, and we were all outside, visiting and eating barbecue. I can still picture Tyler standing there all by himself, propped against an old oak tree with his arms crossed in front of him. There he was, towering over everyone, and he had that five o'clock shadow that dark-haired men sometimes have. The kind that simply takes your breath away. He was wearing dark Western clothing, and with that scar next to his eye—" she reached up, grazing the exact outline of it along her own skin "—and the smoke from his cigarette billowing up in front of him, he reminded me of a bandit. I can't explain it, except to say that he looked aloof and tough and mysterious. And *incredibly* sexy."

"And?" Beth asked, stretching out the word.

"And then I saw a completely different side of him, something that intrigued me even more. I went into your house to get something—I don't even remember what now—and when I walked down the hall, I glanced into your bedroom. The door was ajar, and he was putting his daughter down for a nap. Samantha was only about four or five, I guess, and he was leaning over her." Her voice took on a soft, dreamy tone as she visualized the scene. "He was smoothing her forehead, brushing her wispy blond hair away from her face, and his voice was low and husky—but it sounded so gentle. I couldn't even hear what he was saying, but he leaned closer then and kissed her cheek, and she didn't say a word. Before she closed her eyes, though, she gave him this precious, radiant little smile that spoke volumes."

Realizing her lips were trembling, Jerri stopped for a moment to regain her usual composure. "I just thought it was so touching—him and that sweet, beautiful child who obviously adored him. It was as if the two of them had nothing in the world but each other, and yet that was all that mattered."

She touched her mouth and glanced upward. Realizing her friend had remained silent, letting her go on and on, Jerri laughed self-consciously and shook her head.

"I can see how that must have affected you," Beth said, "but I'm still a little confused. I don't want to pry, but has Tyler done anything at all to encourage the way you feel about him?"

"No. Absolutely nothing," Jerri answered in disgust. "Every time I'm around him, I turn to mush inside, and then I seem to freeze up. I can hardly breathe, much less speak!" She tilted her head, her voice taking on a stiff, formal tone. " 'Hello, Tyler. Nice weather we're having, isn't it?' That's probably the most provocative thing I've ever said to the man. No wonder he doesn't know I'm alive!''

Her friend's instant laughter only reinforced her own train of thought. "It's stupid, Beth! It's nothing more than an obsession, some kind of ridiculous hero worship I've been hanging on to for eight long years. I'm probably thinking of him as ... as a father figure or something, since I was so young when my daddy died." Jerri didn't believe that theory for a minute, but perhaps she could latch on to it for the sake of her pride. Perhaps, in the eyes of her best friend, it would pass as a reasonable explanation.

She took a deep, steadying breath before she went on. "I've decided it's a sickness, just like smoking is a sickness. And I refuse to let it go on any longer." She squared her shoulders. "I'm going to stop smoking. And while I'm at it, I'm going to stop hoping that someday Tyler Reynolds will wake up and notice I'm alive. If I ever expect to get my station wagon, I've got to be practical."

"And what exactly does that mean?"

"That means I'm going to kiss both my addictions good-bye, once and for all, and get on with my life. As of this morning I'm on a long vacation. I'm going to lock myself away and go cold turkey." She crushed out the already-cold cigarette and grabbed her handbag. "I want you to keep these for me."

"Ah, yes," Beth replied as she sifted through the pile now laid out on the table. "Car keys, cash and credit cards. The infamous Three Cs of Survival, as we used to refer to them."

"Wait a minute," Jerri said, digging into the bag's side compartment and pulling out another item. "Make it the Four Cs." She dropped her checkbook onto the heap. "I have the car packed with staples and an ice chest full of food, along with everything else I'll need for at least a week. All I'm asking is that you drive me to those cabins near here. And if you'll keep these things for me, I won't be tempted to go to the nearest store and buy a pack of cigarettes."

"I can't just dump you at some rented cabin! We have plenty of room here, so why don't you—?"

"Don't even suggest it," Jerri interrupted. She gestured toward the nursery. "After a few days—a few hours, probably—even sweet-tempered little Chad would end up despising me, and that's the last thing I want."

Jerri reached for her friend's hand then, her eyes pleading. "I've tried everything else, Beth, and I'm convinced this is the only way I'm going to be able to do it. I love you for wanting me to stay, but what I really need is some time alone, some time to think things through." She picked up her car keys and folded Beth's fingers around them. "Now. If I call and ask for money, you've got to promise me you won't come across with it—under any circumstances."

"But what if you have an accident? What if you're really hurt or something? I can't just—"

"That's exactly what I'm talking about! You've got to have your guard up at all times. I'm liable to call and tell you anything. Just because you're my best friend, don't think I wouldn't lie to you to get cigarettes. So even if I call and tell you I'm bedridden, even if I claim I've got a raging fever of a hundred and twelve, I don't want you to do anything more than offer to take me to the emergency room."

"But you'll need money to pay the rental fee."

"No problem. My reservation's made and I've already given them my credit card number."

"What's to keep you from having a pack of cigarettes delivered to your cabin—even a carton—and telling the manager to add it to your bill?"

Jerri shifted positions, squirming against the chair. "I hadn't thought about that."

"Don't think I didn't see that gleam in your eye just now. No, your plan isn't going to work."

"But it has to work. I'm determined that I'm going to turn over a new leaf, and the smoking thing is the first step." Suddenly she sat up straight. "I could tell the manager not to let me charge anything extra, beyond the cabin itself. I could—''

Chad's unexpected, playful yelp interrupted Jerri, reminding her how anxious she was to see him again.

"No." Beth stood, heading for the nursery. "It'll never work," she said over her shoulder, "but I have a plan that will."

"Great!" Jerri called back, reaching across the table for the crumpled cigarette pack.

"Thank you, Beth," she then whispered, a flood of relief washing over her entire body.

She smoothed the paper, then carefully removed the one cigarette left inside the pack. She held it in front of her, staring at it and reminding herself she couldn't light it.

Not yet. Because this would be the last cigarette she would ever smoke. The very last one....

Frantic, Jerri rifled through the last drawer in the line shack's compact kitchen. To heck with the ladylike behavior she'd been taught all her life! she told herself as she slammed the drawer shut and yanked open the cabinet doors overhead. If she could find a tobacco pouch and cigarette papers left behind by some crusty old cowhand, she would gladly roll her own.

She had smoked her last cigarette less than fourteen hours ago. Fourteen measly hours, and she was already a basket case. She had combed every square inch of this rustic little place, and since it was furnished so sparsely, where else could—

"The nightstand," Jerri exclaimed out loud, her eyes wide as she turned on her heel and raced toward the cabin's one and only bedroom. What more likely place?

She jerked on the drawer handle. Nothing. Unless you counted an empty tissue box, a stubby pencil covered with teeth marks, and a red-and-white bandanna.

"Darn it!"

Sinking onto the lumpy mattress, Jerri raked her fingers through hair tousled by a fitful night with precious little sleep. She grimaced as she looked into the narrow, full-length mirror fastened to the wall in front of her.

"You're a pathetic sight," she said disgustedly, taking in the strange, wild-eyed maniac looking back at her. "Really, truly pathetic."

When her scrutinizing gaze moved downward, though, she couldn't help laughing. The warp in the bottom section of the mirror made each of her fluffy slippers look about a foot wide. With eyes round as baseballs and a hairdo that resembled a mop, all she needed to complete the picture was a plastic daisy pinned to the lapel of her winter bathrobe—the one she called "Old Blue." Yes, Jerri decided, if she had a yellow-and-orange daisy with a squirt bulb dangling from it, Barnum and Bailey would hire her in a New York minute.

If she had the daisy... and *if* there were a circus within fifty miles of this godforsaken place!

"Darn you, Beth," she muttered. Why, she asked inwardly, had she let her best friend bring her out here and dump her in this tiny, remote cabin?

"It's perfect," Beth had said on the drive the night before. "You need a place with no people around. This old line shack on Daddy's ranch is just the thing." She'd given Jerri a wry, sidelong glance past Chad, who was strapped in the infant car seat between them. "And in case you're already getting some funny ideas, don't dwell on them. The cabin's a good ten miles outside of Tarpley, so even if you wanted to reach civilization—meaning the nearest cigarette machine—you'd have to hike ten miles through these scenic, treacherous hills."

The plan was for Beth to drop her off and then come back to join her this morning, when her husband would be back from his business trip and could take care of Chad while Beth spent a few days with Jerri.

"You need to have a friend with you," Beth had insisted. "Someone to hold your hand, so to speak. I don't believe this is going to be quite as easy as you seem to think it'll be."

And she'd been right, Jerri admitted as she glanced at her watch. Beth was already thirty minutes late, and if she didn't get here pretty soon, she would have to do a lot more than hold Jerri's hand; she'd have to transport her to the nearest loony bin.

Her spine made contact with the mattress as she fell back and stared at the ceiling. What on earth, she wondered, had made her think this would be easy? It had all seemed so simple when she'd dreamed up her scheme: in a few weeks of long-overdue vacation time, she would forget all those hopes and dreams about Tyler Reynolds. And while she was at it, she would simply rid herself of the nasty nicotine habit that had caused him to tag her with the nickname "Smoky" in the first place.

Jerri rolled onto her side, groaning as the old mattress swayed and pitched her unwillingly into its saggy middle, just as it had a hundred times the night before.

If she'd been able to get a decent night's rest, she thought as she balled up her fist and punched the mattress, maybe she wouldn't be in this state. Instead of sleeping, though, she'd spent half the night tossing and turning and trying to keep her nose away from the musty-smelling sheets.

She had even indulged in a lengthy game of mind over matter, imagining that instead of the lumpy mattress, it was Tyler's hard, lean body pressing against her softness, pretending that instead of the musty odor that surrounded her, the linens actually smelled of Tyler's distinctive after-shave.

But the human mind was only capable of so much, and she had finally given up and searched the darkened room for her perfume atomizer. She had ended up over-spraying the sheets to the point where she was left with two choices: spend the remainder of the night on the sofa in the parlor or choke to death on the gardenia-scented perfume that had always been her favorite. Until now.

The sofa hadn't been much better, but she had managed to get three or four hours' sleep—sleep that had been plagued by dreams of Tyler Reynolds. Tyler standing over her in the dark parlor, his ruggedly handsome features visible in the glow of the burning cigarette he held in his hand. He had leaned closer then, whispering to her, smoothing her hair, telling her to go back to sleep....

Smiling softly, Jerri closed her eyes and felt herself drifting off. Maybe that was what she needed to get rid of this restlessness, she thought as she squirmed into a more comfortable position. Beth would be here soon. And in the meantime, she would catch a few more minutes of—

Her eyes flew open as the overpowering smell of gardenias brought her wide awake. Jerri sprang to her feet with newfound resolve. She had to stop wallowing around in this bed!

More than that, she lectured herself, she had to stop wallowing in self-pity. She was stuck in this deserted line shack, but she would simply have to make the best of it.

Glancing at her watch again, she started pulling jars and bottles out of her makeup case. She had brought a major project with her to keep her mind busy, but what she needed right this minute was something to keep her hands busy. Something that, while she drank her morning coffee, would occupy the one free hand that would normally be holding a—*a you-know-what.*

Reaching into the drawer, she twisted the bandanna and tied it around her hair, then hurriedly applied a green, minty-smelling facial mask. If she was turning over a new leaf, she might as well do it properly. She would give herself a full beauty treatment, even a pedicure. Kicking off her slippers, she jammed wads of cotton between her toes and headed toward the kitchen, nail polish in hand.

The sound of an approaching engine brought her to an abrupt halt. She breathed a heavy sigh of relief, then hurried through the parlor.

"Bless you, Beth! Bless you for having such perfect timing!" She smiled broadly, ignoring the sudden blast of winter air as she yanked open the kitchen window to greet her.

Why would Beth be driving a Jeep? she wondered as she watched the vehicle winding up the narrow caliche road. And pulling a small boat behind it? With the possible exception of swimming pools—complete with lemonade, sunglasses and floppy-brimmed hats—she'd never known her friend to have much interest in outdoor activities.

The vehicle slowed to a stop. Jerri leaned forward, squinting as she tried to see through the Jeep's cover of canvas and murky plastic.

Dear Lord! Her hand flew up to cover the gasp that rushed past her lips as the driver got out of the Jeep.

Beth Ferguson wasn't six foot four in boot heels. What's more, she didn't have the ability to take Jerri's breath away and send her pulse racing out of control at the same time.

And Beth Ferguson certainly didn't wear a black Stetson, she told herself as she spun out of Tyler's sight, her back against the wall. She took her hand away from her mouth, her eyes suddenly focusing on the green goop smeared across her palm.

Without thinking any further, Jerri took off for the bathroom. Ducking her head into the sink, she slapped handfuls of water onto her face and groped for a towel to rub away the remaining streaks of mask.

A knock sounded at the kitchen door as she rushed for the bedroom, tossing her robe aside and throwing her largest suitcase across the bed.

"Jerri?"

"Just a minute," she called out. Why hadn't she unpacked last night? she asked herself, her hands shaking as she rummaged through the once-neat stacks of clothing.

Finding a bra, she fumbled with the hooks and tugged on first one strap and then the other.

"It's me—Tyler."

She whirled around, startled by the nearness of his deep baritone voice, and then let out her breath as she realized he must be calling to her from the open window in the kitchen.

"Come on, Smoky. Let me in."

"I'll be right there," she yelled, pulling a sweater over her head, then jamming her legs into her slacks. The knock on the kitchen door changed to an insistent pounding, and she heard him jiggle the knob.

"I said, I'll be right there," she screamed, fighting back the panicky feeling rising from the pit of her stomach. She hadn't seen Tyler for almost a year—since right after Chad was born. Why couldn't he show up after she'd had a couple of hours to fix herself up?

She yanked off the red-and-white makeshift headband, using her fingers to fluff her hair. Straightening her sweater, Jerri turned and took several calming gulps of air on her way back to the kitchen. She reached for the knob, only to spot the wads of cotton sprouting from between her toes.

"Open the door, Jerri. Come on."

"I will, I will," she mumbled impatiently. "Just give me a minute!" Watching his broad, towering silhouette against the door's filmy curtain, she hopped on one foot and then the other while yanking at the cotton. Finally she reached for the knob again, opening the door and transforming her facial expression to a light smile in an attempt to hide her nervousness with an air of casual friendliness.

"Hi, Tyler," she said, her voice sounding far too low and raspy to be her own. She cleared her throat, her fingers squeezing the ball of cotton in her hand. "What a surprise."

"I'm sure it is." He stepped into the kitchen, his curious, dark blue gaze darting around the room and finally settling on her.

"What are you doing here?" she asked, avoiding his eyes
by pivoting to shut the door after him. When she looked his
way again, he had moved to the doorway that led to the
parlor. He stopped there, at the far end of the kitchen.

She watched as he glanced around the doorway and into
the parlor. His eyes moved back to hers then, holding them
with an intensity that was positively unnerving. His smile
was soft, she decided, and beautiful. She had never seen him
smile quite that way before. As she waited for him to answer, she realized how dry her throat felt—as if she had
swallowed the wad of cotton that was growing damp in her
hand. She ran her tongue across her bottom lip, then swallowed hard.

"Beth asked me to come by." Still studying her intently,
he crossed his arms in front of his broad chest and leaned
against the door frame. He shifted after a moment, taking
off his hat and hooking it on the back of a kitchen chair.

"Oh?" Jerri asked, her spine touching the curtain on the
kitchen door. Her gaze moved to his scar, and she tried to
sound pleasantly surprised as her heart took a quick plunge
at the mere mention of Beth's name. "She did?"

"Yeah." He ran his fingers through his dark hair, then
propped his shoulder on the door frame again. And again,
he eyed her closely. "She told me all about . . . your problem."

"You're kidding!" Jerri's mouth dropped open, and she
felt her cheeks grow hot as she turned away from him. He
must think her an idiot, carrying a torch for him all these
years. "No," she moaned, her fingers grasping the curtain.
She lowered her head and stared at her bare feet, feeling as
though her heart had just fallen that far down in her body.

How could Beth betray a confidence like this? she wondered, her mind ablaze with a mixture of alarm and anger.

"Look, Smoky," he said from behind her, his voice low
and infinitely gentle. "There's no need to be embarrassed.
I know just what you're feeling."

"You—you do?" Her head came up, her eyes wide open as she focused on the sheer fabric of the curtain. Was it too much to hope for? That he could have had the same feelings all these years?

"Why?" she asked hesitantly. "I mean, how can you know what—"

"Because I've felt the same way myself."

"You have?" Jerri whispered, a soft, curious smile forming on her lips as she turned to face him. How could that be? she wondered. She had never thought he knew she was alive, much less—

"Yes. I know exactly what it's like."

"Well." She swallowed the lump in her throat as she watched him advance slowly toward her. "What do you...think we should do about it?"

"That's easy," he said, his voice a deep, tender caress as he reached toward her. "First things first."

Jerri held her breath, wondering for a fleeting moment if she was going to die right here, right now, waiting for him to touch her.

His hand came up, spanning the entire side of her face, and an eternity passed before she felt his palm brush lightly against her cheek. His fingers raked through her hair, his thumb grazing the sensitive skin along the edge of her mouth. Her lips parted, but she still couldn't speak. Still couldn't breathe.

Jerri closed her eyes, praying she would be able to catch her breath. If she really was going to die, she decided in that split second, she wanted to do it in his arms.

But not yet, she thought, not until after his lips touched hers. She had waited far too long for this moment....

Chapter Two

Tyler continued to watch her, wondering when she was going to open her eyes.

He had to admit he'd never seen Jerri Davenport looking so approachable. She'd always had that wall around her, that cool, solid wall of perfect manners and poise that seemed to protect her from the world at large, and especially from him.

But right now, he decided, she looked warm. Incredibly, deliciously warm. And inviting.

For a split second—and not for the first time—he thought about kissing her. And then what would she do? he wondered, still studying her regal, uptilted face. It was a question he'd asked himself a number of times.

He leaned closer to her, taking in the sweet scent of gardenias that always seemed to drift in the air around her, the scent that was now being overpowered by the strong, cool smell of mint. Reminding himself of the reason he was here, he stopped hesitating and stepped back. At the moment, she might appear approachable, but he knew she wasn't. Not to him, anyway. He had decided a long time ago that this one was holding out for a prince—and he sure as hell didn't fit the category.

"Look at me, Jerri." He watched as she opened her eyes. "Now listen," he said, choosing his words carefully. "I know you're going through a rough time right now, but I can help you. So hand them over."

Her lips moved, only a fraction of an inch, but it was her beautiful, mysterious gray eyes that were questioning him.

"Give them to me now, honey," he reasoned with her, "and I'll take care of them." He was speaking to her slowly and distinctly, the way he would talk to a child who was totally out of control. But he knew from his own experience with kicking the habit that it might be the best method.

"Give you...?"

"Come on, Jerri, let's stop playing games. I told you, I've been through this myself." Tyler held his left thumb in front of her eyes. Then, to prove his point, he wiped the green smudge down the leg of his Levi's. "I know all the tricks, so a little toothpaste isn't going to fool me." He held out his palm. "Now give me the cigarettes."

"You mean you were talking about— You thought I was..."

He watched her eyes widen as she groped for the words she was searching for, and it dawned on him that he had never seen her looking so angry. Hell, he had never seen her looking angry, period.

There was more to it than anger, though. She looked almost desperate.

"I know you were smoking," he said quietly. "So where did you hide them? Just tell me and I'll get rid of them for you."

He watched as her mouth dropped open. When her hands flew to her hips, he patted the air in a calming gesture. "I know you hate me right now, Smoky. But believe me— someday you'll thank me for this."

The statement wasn't exactly original, Tyler realized, but maybe it would work. He took a step closer to her. And as he made the move, he could almost see that damned wall of hers shooting back up again.

"I don't have any cigarettes!"

"Then what were you doing for the ten minutes that you couldn't let me in the door?"

"It wasn't ten minutes. It couldn't have been." She lifted her chin. "I was getting dressed!"

"Oh, yeah? And why is this window open?" He crossed the room and closed the window in question. "It's forty degrees in here. Do you expect me to believe you wanted a little breath of fresh air?"

"I thought you were Beth, for heaven's sake! I was just going to..." She squared her shoulders, looking both furious and defensive. "Is there some reason why I should have to answer to you? I told you I wasn't smoking. That's pretty simple, isn't it?" Her gray eyes sparked fire as she tilted her head. "You do understand English, don't you?"

The question made his spine stiffen, but Tyler ignored it. "What about the toothpaste then? And why were you holding your breath just now if you didn't think I was trying to check it?"

"That wasn't toothpaste, it was a facial mask. And for your information, I was holding my breath because..." She gave him a look of stubborn indignation. "Well, because that's the way I exercise my lungs. Does that meet with your approval?"

His gaze roamed downward, taking in the soft, plum-colored sweater that, though oversized, did nothing to play down her womanly curves. Her lungs, he decided, didn't need any exercising. On the contrary. They were just perfect the way they were.

He glanced back up. "An interesting story, to say the least. But I'm not buying it." He blinked once as she flung something at him—something white and fluffy that ended up on the floor between them. Suddenly he wondered what it was that was bringing out all the pink in her high cheek-bones. Was it the plum sweater or her fury? Or both?

"I'll tell you something," she said, her voice almost a hiss. "If the state police could see you interrogating me, they'd give you a sixty-watt bulb and put you to work!"

"Look, Jerri, quit trying to change the subject. I smoked for almost twenty years before I quit nearly a year ago. I know all the tricks."

"Call me a liar all you want, mister," she yelled at him, "but believe me, there's not one blasted cigarette in this whole place! I know that for a fact, because if there were one, I would've found it myself. If the state police *had* been here this morning, they would have hired *me*—and gotten rid of three of their best bloodhounds!" Her index finger shot out, pointing toward the other rooms. "Go ahead. Look for yourself. And if you find one, I'll pay you a hundred dollars for it." She sucked in a big gulp of air. "No. Make it a thousand!"

He watched in awe as she spun to the counter and grabbed her handbag, then pitched it aside and frantically started going through the contents of her wallet.

"I forgot," she said, her voice suddenly quivering as a single, huge tear rolled down each of her cheeks. "I don't have any money." Her elbows sank to the countertop, and she leaned over and buried her face in her hands. She stopped fighting the tears then, and her voice was a pathetic moan. "I can't even write you a check."

"There, there," he murmured, turning her around and taking her into his arms.

"I swear, Tyler," she said through her sobs. Her hands came around his waist, inside his coat, and she clutched the fabric at the back of his shirt. "I wasn't smoking. I wasn't!"

"It's okay, honey," he whispered. "Everything will be okay. You'll see."

He held her close. "Shh." His hand circled her neck, his fingers combing through the silky hair at the nape as he kissed her temple.

And as her crying finally began to subside, he realized how good she felt in his arms, how much he enjoyed the rise and fall of her breasts. They were warm and full and just soft enough to feel right against the hardness of his chest.

He was beginning to enjoy her too much, he realized all of a sudden. It was impossible to ignore the way she moved her hands up and down his back, holding on to his shirt and the muscles beneath it. He could feel the occasional stroke of her fingernails—and that, along with everything else she was doing, was suddenly beginning to drive him crazy.

She was trying to regain control, he knew, but she was still holding on to him for dear life. Considering her frenzied state, she might not notice how she had affected him. But if he didn't peel her off him pretty quick, there wouldn't be any secrets left between them.

"Smoky?" Glancing up, searching for any kind of a diversion, he spotted the shining red light on an elaborate-looking coffee machine. "I don't know about you, but I could use a cup of coffee."

And several cold showers, he added mentally.

"I...I can't drink it," she said, still sniffing back her tears as she looked up at him, her eyes pleading. "Not without a cigarette to go with it. The very thought of it is—" She had stopped crying, but her body jerked as she tried to talk. "That's what made me start ripping this place apart."

"Come on now. You can do it." Reaching to wipe away her tears, he quickly decided against it. Instead he stepped back, holding her at arm's length, and removed a clean white handkerchief from the back pocket of his jeans. He dabbed at her eyes before unfolding the square and pressing it into her hand. "Let's sit down," he said, his palm at the small of her back as he led her toward the table. "The first cup's not easy, but I assure you it can be done."

He pulled out a chair, seating her before he went back to find two mugs. Making an effort to steady his hands, he poured the blistering-hot coffee into the mugs, then carried them across the kitchen and placed them on the table.

"Here," he said, prying the handkerchief away from her before lifting one of the thick mugs. He wrapped her long, slender fingers around it, holding her hands under his own for a few seconds longer than necessary. "It's too hot to drink, but you can warm your hands on it for now."

Tyler smiled, lifting his brows. He watched her as he raised his own cup to his lips and blew on the hot coffee.

She had always acted so damned prim and proper; he wondered if she had any idea how vulnerable, how basic and real and touchable she looked right now. Still grasping the coffee cup, she was staring at his mouth, running her tongue across her upper lip with excruciating slowness. . . .

He had always pictured her with some Ivy League type, some aristocrat who didn't know the first thing about pleasing a woman. But maybe with some other kind of man, he decided, she might look exactly the way she did right now. Wide-eyed and sexy—innocently sexy. Maybe even like a warm, real woman instead of a cold and perfect lady.

And what would her voice sound like, he wondered, if she were underneath him, moaning his name? Would it be low and throaty and—

In a sudden movement, as if to answer his silent questions, she shook her head and placed her cup on the table. She lifted her shoulders, and he couldn't help noticing the proper little smile on her face as she stood.

"Excuse me for just a moment, Tyler," she said on her way out of the room. "I'll be right back."

Peering over the top of his coffee mug, he watched her head toward the bathroom as he took a long swallow of the steaming liquid.

"Dammit!" he muttered, then rushed to the kitchen sink to splash cold water into his mouth.

Maybe he *should* kiss her, he decided as he leaned over the sink. Now that he'd burned the hell out of his tongue, she could probably supply him with the perfect remedy.

Yeah. A little ice was just what he needed.

* * *

Jerri stood in front of the bathroom sink, pressing her hands to her hot cheeks.

"Oh, no," she groaned. She'd probably been drooling as she'd sat there ogling Tyler from across the table. Thank goodness she'd come out of her trance and gotten away from him when she did. If she had stayed another five seconds, she might have...

Might have what? she wondered. Ripped off his clothes and begged him to take her right there on the kitchen table?

Good grief, she thought, her face taking on an even more vivid shade of pink as she dropped her hands and stared into the bathroom mirror. How could such thoughts even flicker through her mind?

Quickly grabbing a washcloth, Jerri held it under the cool water from the tap, then wrung it out and lifted it to cover her cheeks and eyes. "Bless you, Beth," she said, her voice muffled by the damp fabric. "Bless you for not telling him the whole truth."

And darn you, Tyler Reynolds, she fumed inwardly. Darn you for *not* knowing I'm alive.

No, she corrected herself. He did know she was alive; he simply disregarded her. And now what must he think? She'd never let go of her emotions in front of anyone like that. Not even in solitude had she ever ranted and raved and sobbed uncontrollably the way she had when he'd held her in his arms.

Jerri took the already warm washcloth away from her face. Letting Tyler hold her had felt so good. So right. Pressing against his body, feeling his strength against her softness, reveling in the touch of his fingers through her hair...

And what had she done in return? Instead of acting like a grown woman, she had wasted her first real encounter with him by clinging to him and crying like a baby.

Well, she decided, at least he no longer thought of her as an immature coed. No, indeed. Instead he had treated her as if she were a helpless child who took his reprimands and then yearned for his comfort.

She folded the washcloth and hung it up neatly, then sat down on the side of the old claw-footed bathtub and wrung her hands. How was she going to go back to the kitchen and face him after acting like a raving psychotic?

The sounds coming from the parlor shook her out of her dazed state, and she squared her shoulders. Unless she chose to continue acting like a child, she had no alternative but to quit hiding and go out there and face him. At least now she could exhibit some of her usual control over her emotions.

Entering the parlor, she noticed Tyler's coat on the arm of the sofa and welcomed the warmth coming from the fire he had just built in the wood-burning stove. After pausing a moment in front of the stove, as though she could gather courage from its heat, she joined Tyler at the kitchen table and thanked him as she took the cup he offered. Again, he was staring at her, and Jerri wondered briefly if those intense blue eyes might actually have the ability to burn a hole straight through her. She had to do something, had to think of something to say.

"How's your daughter?" she asked.

"Samantha's fine."

She glanced out the window, peering toward the Jeep. "Is she with you?"

"No."

"Oh, that's right. Today's Monday—she must be in school."

"No, the Christmas holidays aren't over till tomorrow."

"Oh." Even though she was genuinely curious about Samantha, this polite exchange of words was beginning to gnaw at Jerri's already-frazzled nerve endings. It had suddenly dawned on her that she was asking all the questions, and that Tyler's answers were definitely of the no-frills variety. He seemed to be too busy studying her to take an active part in the conversation. "Uh, Sam must be getting pretty big."

"Yes," he said with a mocking smile. "Growing like the proverbial weed."

"How old is she now?"

"Twelve. Almost thirteen." He put down his cup, then leaned forward and propped his chin on his fist as he lifted his dark brows. "Pardon me if I'm wrong. But I was under the impression you were having coffee at the kitchen table—not serving tea in the drawing room."

Jerri repositioned herself on the chair. He certainly had a way of calling things exactly as he saw them. "Yes," she replied sheepishly, averting his glance, "you're right. I guess I was just trying to... postpone the inevitable." She looked up at him then. "Tyler, I must apologize for my irrational behav—"

"You don't have to apologize," he said, an edge to his tone.

"Oh, but I must."

"Oh, but you mustn't."

Why was he mimicking her like that? she wondered. And why did he look so angry?

"But Tyler, I just want to say I'm sorry for putting you through—"

"For God's sake, Jerri, you don't have to apologize for being human."

"I wasn't trying to—" Seeing the fierce look in his eyes, she clamped her mouth shut. He was obviously furious with her now—no doubt because of her horrible behavior—and yet he refused to let her apologize.

Unnerved by his piercing gaze, she struggled for a change of topic. "The...the fire feels marvelous," she said, glancing toward the parlor. "I hadn't realized how cold it was in here."

Jerri rubbed her arms, waiting for some kind of reply. When he said nothing, she filled the nerve-chilling silence that loomed over them like a shroud. "I was waiting for Beth to show me how it works." She gestured toward the wood-burning stove. "I'm not exactly—"

"Pioneer stock?" he finished for her, his expression almost cynical.

Her hand moved to the tabletop, nervously searching for her gold lighter and her—"Well, I have to admit I don't know much about survival out in the country. I guess I'm accustomed to things that work automatically. Thermostats and such."

"I'll show you how it's done," he said, leaning back in his chair, "before I leave."

"Is...is Beth going to be here soon?" she asked, noticing that the look in his eyes had finally softened.

"Well, yes and no."

"Meaning?" she asked, trying to keep the fresh sense of panic from creeping into her voice. She needed her best friend, more now than ever.

"Meaning Chad's coming down with a cold, and Beth doesn't want to leave him with anyone but her husband." He took a swallow of coffee. "Doug's business trip is taking longer than he thought. She'll be here, but not for a few more days."

"Great."

Tyler smiled. "Did I detect a note of sarcasm there?"

"No, no." She glanced away from him, her hands moving back and forth in front of her as if she were polishing the old table. "I'll be down to conjugating *verbs* by that time, but that's fine. No problem."

"Look, Smoky." He trapped her hands under his, stopping their frantic movement, and looked directly into her eyes. "A friend of mine has a private lake a couple of miles down the road, so when Beth asked me to come out here and give you her message, I made arrangements to get away for a while—do some fishing and camping out. But it's not anything that can't wait a few more minutes."

"What are you trying to say?" she asked softly, then watched the look of fury rekindle in his dark blue eyes.

"I'm trying to say that if you'll just ask me, I'll stay for a while." He leaned forward, his eyes pinning her to the back of her chair. "If you'll just come out and admit that you're human—that you need some help every now and then, just like the rest of us—then I'll be glad to stay for a couple of hours and help you. Try to get you on the right track."

"Help me?" she asked, her voice rising. "Get me on the right *track*?"

"Yes."

It was true, she thought as she glared at him. He did think of her as a child. The realization hit her like a cold, hard slap across the face. At the moment, she didn't know whether it left her feeling angry or sad. Or both.

"Let's get something straight, Tyler. You may be Samantha's daddy, but you're not mine."

"Meaning?"

"Meaning, thank you, but I don't need your help. In case you haven't noticed—and I'm sure you haven't—I'm a grown woman. I can take care of myself."

"Fine. Whatever suits your fancy." With a frown, he picked up the heavy mug, saluting her. "I'll just finish my coffee and leave—providing, of course, that that's soon enough to please you."

"That's fine," she said, glowering right back at him. "Have a second cup if you like. It doesn't matter to me, one way or the other."

She sipped her own coffee, feigning nonchalance as she wondered about his uncanny ability to make her lose the composure she'd been so well trained to hold on to. He was managing to find emotions and sensations that she had never known were inside her. And not only was he bringing them to the surface, he was sending them toppling over the edge.

She glanced his way again, not knowing whether she wanted to scream or wring his neck or...or throw herself onto his lap and cover him with kisses, trying to erase the scowl she was responsible for putting on his face.

Never, she thought all of a sudden, never had she wanted a cigarette as badly as she wanted one at this very moment. And that, she realized just as quickly, was exactly what was causing her to act this way. Breaking a bad habit apparently brought out a person's latent hostilities, and the realization of that fact carried with it an overwhelming surge of shame.

No wonder he looked so angry, she decided as she drank her coffee and watched him over the rim of the mug. He had shown up at a time when she needed him the most, and she had repaid his kindness by being rude.

But how could she make it up to him? If her previous attempt was any indication, another apology might do nothing but set him off again.

Jerri took a deep, steadying breath. "I have an idea, Tyler," she said abruptly, looking at her wristwatch as she placed her cup on the table. "It's a little early for lunch, but brunch would be appropriate. Why don't I make you a decent meal before you go off into the wilderness?"

"I don't eat quiche and I don't do brunch." He set down his coffee. "Beyond that, I don't need a decent meal. You're a grown woman, I'm a grown man. I can take care of myself, too, you know."

"Of course," she answered quickly, wishing she had thought for a moment before speaking in the first place. "I didn't mean to intimate that you couldn't. I just thought, well, since you were kind enough to drive out here and give me Beth's message, it's the least I can do."

"No thanks." Again, he lifted the mug. "I'll just finish this cup of coffee and then make myself scarce."

"All right. If you're sure." She glanced down at her hands and then back up at him again, as if her gaze were being pulled back to his against her will. "Before you leave, though—whether you want me to or not—I'm going to apologize for my rude outbursts. I had no right to talk to you the way I did. I've been an absolute bear, and there's no excuse for the way I've been treating you, except that this quit-smoking campaign has me on edge." She raised one shoulder. "Well, you said you know how it is, right?"

It was his eyes, she decided, that had done her in. Those eyes could make any female lose her composure. If Emily Post had been sitting across the kitchen table from him, the poor, unsuspecting woman probably would have found herself stirring her coffee with her butter knife!

Never had Jerri seen such brilliant, serious, intense blue eyes. They seemed almost indigo now, and she wondered about the various passions, beyond anger, that might cause them to darken. If he were making love to her, for instance, would his eyes be that same breathtaking shade of—

"Yes," he was saying. "I know exactly how difficult it is to quit. That's why I was trying to give you some advice on how to lick your problem."

"Thank you, Tyler, but I think I have everything under control now." As she watched his jaw clench, Jerri wondered why he kept insisting on giving her his darned advice on how to quit smoking. Advice was the last thing she wanted from him.

His eyes seemed to catch fire. "For once in your life, lady, I don't think you do."

"Do what?" she asked, thoroughly exasperated with him.

"Have everything under control!"

"Well, I beg to differ with you. All I need is a little time to get over this feeling of . . . restlessness. And then I'll be fine."

"Leave it to you," he said with a bitter laugh, "to put such a polite label on it. I hate to break it to you, but what you're going through is a lot closer to insanity."

"Well, whatever." She waved her fingers in an offhand gesture. "Let's talk about something else, shall we?"

"I think we'd better talk about smoking."

"Why?" Jerri asked. Realizing her hands were once again groping for nonexistent cigarettes on the tabletop, she

quickly stopped their movement and shoved her fingertips
between her body and the chair.

Tyler leaned forward, making an obvious display of
watching her sit on her hands. "Because judging by the way
you're acting, I think you've got a real problem. And I think
you need to go at it from a different angle."

"Oh?" she asked, feeling her anger rise as she watched
the all-knowing look on his face. "Well, go ahead, Tyler—
since you're obviously not going to be satisfied until you
give me your fatherly advice."

Maybe he was right to treat her like a child, she decided
as she stared at him, waiting for his easy, unsolicited answers. She had been childish all these many years, dwelling
on what she'd thought were his virtues and refusing to see
any of his faults. Maybe she ought to kiss Beth's feet for
giving her the opportunity to open her eyes.

"Please, Tyler. I'm waiting with bated breath!"

"All I wanted to do was tell you what worked for me," he
said. "But never mind. It's obvious you don't want to hear
it."

"No, go ahead. Tell me!"

"All right." He laced his fingers behind his neck, then
leaned back against them. "It's mind over matter, that's all.
First you have to admit to yourself that it's the toughest
thing you'll ever have to do. And then you have to convince
yourself it'll be easy, once you put your mind to it. It's all
attitudinal."

Was there anything he didn't know? she wondered, a
syrupy smile masking the rage building inside her.

"Well, thank you, Tyler. It's nice to know that you have
it all figured out—and that you're so willing to share your
pearls of wisdom with poor little weak-willed, needy me."

"Meaning?"

"Meaning, I don't appreciate your coming in here sniffing around—literally—and treating me like a helpless child,
bombarding me with your nasty, unfounded accusations

and then . . . and then verbally attacking me for some reason I'm still trying to figure out." Involuntarily her hands moved to her hips. "Believe it or not, I came here to quit smoking, and that's precisely what I'm going to do. I know exactly what my problem is, and I'll approach it from whatever angle I choose!"

"Fine. And while you're at it, why don't you work on your other problem?"

"Meaning?"

"Meaning, why don't you climb down off that high horse of yours, lady?"

"Why, you . . ." She gritted her teeth, trying to gain control over the volume and tone of her voice. "I don't know what you're talking about, but—"

"I'm talking about your attitude."

"Fine! You want to talk about attitudes? Let's talk about yours!"

"What about it?"

"It's . . . it's substandard, that's what!"

"Here we go again," he mumbled, a disgusted look on his face as he rolled his eyes.

"Meaning?"

"Meaning, those fancy words you're always slinging around. Why the hell do you always come up with some ten-dollar sentence when a two-bit phrase would say it just as well if not better? And with a lot more honesty." He leaned back, crossing his arms in front of his chest. "Why don't we just call 'em like we see 'em, Smoky? My attitude might be substandard, but yours stinks." He lifted his eyebrows. "Now. How's that for a two-bit phrase?"

"I don't know where you come off—"

"Whoa." He held up his hands. "Be careful now, Smoky. You're beginning to sound like one of the human race."

"You want human?" she asked, her temper reaching a full boil. "You want *honesty*? Well, here goes—" The chair legs scraped against the worn wooden floor, and she jerked to her feet. "Just remember, mister. You asked for it!" She glared at him, her fists positioned firmly at her sides as she paced the kitchen. "Beth sent you out here on purpose, you know, and I'm beginning to think I should be eternally grateful to her."

"I told you, Beth called because she—"

"Just sit there and shut up for one minute, will you?" she demanded, crossing the room to stand over him. Her index finger pushed against his chest. "You're going to hear me out, whether you like it or not." She stalked back across the kitchen, reaching the counter and then whirling to face him again. "This was obviously a setup. Beth sent you out here because I made a confession to her yesterday. I told her that ever since I first laid eyes on you, I've had this ridiculous... Well, I've been sort of..."

Jerri crossed her arms in front of her. "All right, Tyler. To put it bluntly, I've had the *hots* for you!" She tilted her head, a self-satisfied frown on her face. "Now, how's that for a two-bit phrase?"

"You've—?"

"Oh, hush!" she yelled. "Believe me, I'm just as stupefied by it as you are. I know it sounds crazy. I know it doesn't make any sense." Her hands lifted into the air. "For the life of me, I can't figure out why I've always thought I *liked* you!"

Her mind raced, and she started wearing out the kitchen floor again. In the same instant, another brutally honest thought came to her: she was furious with Tyler Reynolds, yet she was even more furious with herself... because regardless of the way he'd been acting, she did like him. Or at least she thought she liked him, although she could come up with no earthly reason why, especially considering the way he'd been pushing her into corners ever since he'd arrived. But more than anything, she needed a chance to figure it out.

Turning, she faced him squarely. "I'd like to take you up on your offer, Tyler. Because now I know how I can get over this little bout of insanity, this ridiculous...thing I've had for you all these years." She stood perfectly still, glaring at him. "Do me a gigantic favor, will you? Stay here with me for a while, just long enough to drive me completely over the edge with your smug, self-righteous, Mister-Know-It-All ways. If you'll just give me—oh, I'd say twenty-four hours would be more than enough time—I'm sure I can get you out of my system once and for all!"

Judging by the look on Tyler's face, hearing her confession had shocked him almost as much as it had shocked her to hear herself admitting it. But she had already made a complete fool of herself, and there was nothing she could do to erase it.

Why doesn't he say something? her mind screamed as she began pacing again, lifting her palms. "Just think of yourself as Tarpley's answer to *The Exorcist.*"

A sudden idea flashed through her mind, bringing her to a stop, and she smiled angelically as she pointed toward the bedroom. "To show you what a good sport I can be, I'll even let you have the bed. I'll take the couch."

Jerri clamped her mouth shut, wondering why she had used that particular statement as a point of persuasion. There were only two options that came to mind: either nicotine withdrawal was actually capable of bringing out every ounce of meanness inside her to the point where she wanted him to suffer a fitful, sleepless night on that horrible mattress, or she had simply conjured it up as an enticement, a final, desperate fling at convincing him to stay. Whichever it was, she decided as she straightened her shoulders and mustered what little courage she had left, now wasn't the proper time to question her motivation.

"Well?" she asked, her chin in the air, her arms folded in front of her breasts.

Jerri watched in horror as Tyler stood up and calmly pushed his chair under the table. Without a word, he picked up his hat. And then he walked out the door.

Chapter Three

Intriguing little package, Tyler told himself as he sauntered toward the Jeep.

Jerri was going through a rough time right now; he could certainly sympathize with that. But if this was how kicking the habit affected her, he was all for it—for more than the usual health reasons. This was a side of her he'd never seen, never even known existed. All he knew for sure was that he liked it...and wanted to find out more about it.

Yeah, he admitted to himself. At the moment, he was feeling every bit as grateful as he was sympathetic.

He reached into the back of the Jeep, then walked back to the cabin and opened the kitchen door. She was standing in the same spot.

"You're..." Her jaw dropped. "You're staying?"

"Sure," he answered, stashing his gear beside the door. "I told you, all you had to do was ask."

Beyond that, he added mentally, what normal, red-blooded man could resist a challenge like the one she'd just issued?

She turned away from him and started rummaging through the cardboard boxes that were lined up on the countertop. Tyler smiled as he realized how jittery she looked.

"I think I need to keep my hands busy," she said, her cheeks taking on that enticing shade of pink again. "You know, instead of thinking about . . . a cigarette. I'll just finish unpacking, and then I can start lunch."

Yeah, he decided as he propped himself against the kitchen counter. Nervous as a virgin at a prison rodeo. Or maybe, to be more accurate, nervous as a grown woman who'd just asked a grown man to spend the rest of the day and night with her.

"While I'm getting things organized," she said, "why don't you decide what you'd like for lunch?"

"Okay," he answered, still distracted. "I'll give it some thought."

As he watched her, it suddenly dawned on him that she was more than nervous. She had blurted out her confession in a momentary fit of desperation for a cigarette. She'd been honest with him, and now she was downright embarrassed about it. There was a heavy cloud of tension hanging over them, and he definitely needed to do something about it.

Glancing into one of the three boxes, he picked up an unidentifiable object and held it in front of him, turning it first one way and then the other.

"An orange-peeler," she said, answering his unspoken question.

"I've seen expeditions leave for Africa with less than this." He handed over the odd-looking plastic gadget. "You brought all this stuff with you?"

"Yes. I like to be comfortable, that's all." Judging by the tone of her voice, she was still on the defensive. "I like to have...my things about me, so to speak. Is that all right with you?''

"I guess so. It sure seems like a lot of trouble, though. Give me a bedroll and a camp fire any day.''

"Men!" she said, giving him a wry smile that was the first halfway-natural one he'd seen since he walked in. "How can you stand sleeping out there on the cold, hard ground? Sharing your sleeping bag with bugs and snakes and—''

"It's great. Have you ever tried it?''

"Tried what? Sharing a sleeping bag with bugs and snakes?''

"Roughing it. You know—no orange-peeler, no room service? Eating off unmatched china?''

"No, but only because...well, I don't know much about the outdoors. I don't imagine I'd be very good at it.''

"Ahh," he said, leaning against the counter again. "That's what we macho men do best, you know.''

"No, I don't know." She gazed up at him, those mysterious gray eyes searching his as she laughed. "What?" she asked. "What is it you macho men do best?''

"Survive," he stated, putting a husky growl on the last syllable. "Provide.''

"Well, I know you'd rather be out there roughing it, Tyler. But why don't you just look at the next twenty-four hours as the perfect way to test your manhood?''

"How's that?" he asked, quirking one eyebrow.

"I'll *provide* you with a few meals, and you stick around to see if you can *survive* them.''

Tyler laughed, realizing he could think of far better ways to test his manhood while he was here.

Jerri's eyes widened, as if she had just realized what alternative might have crossed his mind. She turned away quickly and went back to her chore, looking tense as she waved her hand in a gesture of dismissal. "Why don't you sit down? Take off your hat and relax, have another cup of coffee. You're making me...'' She took a long, deep breath. "I'm not used to someone standing over me in the kitchen.''

"Whatever you say." Tyler refilled both mugs, then handed her one and took his to the kitchen table, depositing his hat on the way.

He propped his boots on the seat of the empty chair, crossing one ankle over the other as he leaned back against his hands. Maybe he should take a different tack, he thought as he studied her movements. Maybe silence was what she needed.

She looked incredibly busy, but after four or five minutes had passed, he noticed the boxes were still brimming over with utensils and appliances.

She finally stopped short and turned to face him. "I really wish you'd stop watching me like that," she said. "In fact—" she swallowed hard and then lifted her shoulders "—why don't you just go ahead and say it?"

"Say what?"

"I have no idea, but I can see your mind churning over there." She rolled her eyes, then pushed out a long sigh. "So why don't you just spit it out? Whatever it is, I'd like to get it over with."

"All right," he answered. "I was just thinking..." Still watching her closely, he settled farther back against his hands. "If you had the 'hots' for me, you sure—"

"For heaven's sake, Tyler, I didn't really mean..." She lifted her palm. "Well, you might as well know. I have this...this tendency to overstate things sometimes."

He continued to study her. She might be embarrassed, but he wasn't about to drop the subject. "Whatever happened to being honest? Is that a problem for you? Do you find that impossible to do, or what?"

"No!" she said, her spine straightening.

"Prove it, then. Let me finish what I was trying to say, and then give me an honest reply."

"Fine," she said bluntly, her chin in the air. "Go ahead, since we're being so darned honest around here."

He could almost see the stubborn determination building inside her. "I was just thinking," he repeated, "that if you had the 'hots' for me, you sure had one hell of a way of hiding it.''

"Oh, I wasn't hiding it," she stated flatly. "You just weren't noticing it.''

Her gray eyes, he decided, reminded him of clouds on a rainy summer afternoon. Stormy, menacing. And at the same time, soft and appealing. "Like when, for instance?''

"Like the night you took me and Beth to that dance in Bandera, for instance.''

"Hmm," he said, pretending to think about it. He fully expected her to plant her hands on her gorgeous hips, and when she did just that, he realized that every time she'd moved her hands toward her body, his eyes had followed. Since she did that *a lot*, he had become increasingly aware of her... assets. If she looked this good in a big, heavy sweater, he wondered, what would she—? He stopped the thought, shaking his head as he moved his eyes back up to her face. When hadn't he been noticing her? Right now, he couldn't imagine. "A dance? When was that?''

"It was Christmas Eve," she went on, looking more determined than ever. "And as I recall, I'd spent about three hours' worth of time—and nine dollars' worth of eyeliner—getting dolled up to impress you, and what'd you do? You took one look at me and said, 'What happened to you? You walk into a wall or somethin'?' "

Watching her standing in the middle of the kitchen giving him what for, listening to her singsongy imitation of his voice, he couldn't help laughing. "I never said that.''

"You certainly did.''

"Well even if I did, I can guarantee you I never said it that way." He lifted his shoulders. "Could I help it if you didn't have a sense of humor?''

"Oh, I had a sense of humor, all right. Could I help it if I was a tad more dignified—a tad more discreet, shall we say—than those floozies you were always keeping company with?''

"Since I still have no idea what you're talking about, why don't you fill me in?" He knew what night she was talking about, but he wasn't about to pass up this sort of opportunity. He had a feeling her version would be a lot more interesting than the one he remembered.

"Come on," he coaxed her, smiling. "I realize I'm probably walking into a mine field, but go ahead. What particular floozy are we talking about here?"

"I'm referring to that blatantly obvious floozy who was pawing you all night at that Christmas dance." Her tongue clicked against the roof of her mouth. "Surely you remember!"

"No," he said, shaking his head. "I don't think I do." He remembered Jerri being there, all right, but for the life of him, he couldn't picture the "floozy" she was talking about. "Why don't you tell me about her?"

Striking an overly dramatic pose, Jerri fluffed her hair. "Flaming red tresses, straight out of a bottle?" She turned to the side then and threw back her shoulders. "Pink sweater a good three sizes too small? And those jeans! They were so tight, she couldn't possibly have zipped them up without using pliers or a tire tool or something!" She was really on a roll now, Tyler decided as she went on. "I guess I can't blame you for not noticing me that night. She was pretty unforgettable!"

"You must be talking about..."

"Marty," she finished for him. "Marty Cunningham."

"God," he said, shaking his head. "I haven't thought about her in years." The woman had been some last-minute date arranged by a friend of a friend, and Jerri was pretty accurate in her characterization—but he wasn't about to admit it. "And she wasn't pawing me," he lied. "Marty was the affectionate type, that's all."

"Excuse me, Tyler. I was trying to use the proper two-bit phrase, but I guess 'pawing' wasn't quite on target."

"But something tells me you've got a ten-dollar sentence that'll do the trick. Am I right?" Watching that sarcastic, knowing smile on her face, he realized that she was enjoying this every bit as much as he was.

"Let's just put it this way: if demure little Marty had stripped off all her clothes and writhed on the floor in front of you, it would've added a refreshing note of subtlety to the evening!"

"That's a bit of an exaggeration, don't you think?"

"No, I certainly don't. And if you'll remember, Marty was having an especially difficult time trying to contain herself in the car after the dance was over. Beth and I couldn't see everything from the back seat, of course, but as I recall, Marty was just itching to give you a full dose of that 'affectionate nature' of hers." She rolled her eyes toward the ceiling. "When I heard all her bracelets jangling, I thought for a minute she wasn't going to have the decency to wait until you two were by yourselves!"

Lord, she was right, he thought. Marty Cunningham had been wearing enough jewelry for a Mr. T Starter Kit. But the night Jerri was talking about was so many years ago. How the hell, he wondered, did she remember it in such vivid detail?

And he could tell by looking at her that there was more. He lifted his eyebrows. "This 'total recall' of yours is fascinating, Smoky. A bit warped, perhaps, but fascinating."

"And as I recall," she continued, ignoring his statement, "you weren't exactly fighting off her affections that night, either. When it came to dropping off Beth and me so that you and Marty could be alone, you seemed pretty anxious yourself. In fact, when you pulled up in front of Beth's house, I don't believe you even brought the car to a complete stop."

"Did anyone ever tell you—" he bit the insides of his cheeks, trying to keep from laughing "—that you're the queen of the overstatement?"

"Quit trying to change the subject, Tyler." Jerri crossed her arms in front of her breasts, then tilted her head and gave him a smug smile. "And while we're still on the subject, I've often been curious. After you threw Beth and me out of the car that night, after you left us lying there on the side of the road in a cloud of dust, just how far *did* you two go?''

Tyler lifted his gaze to the ceiling, drumming his fingers against the table, and finally shrugged his shoulders. ''About twenty, thirty miles, I guess. As I'm sure you recall, Marty lived in Hondo.''

Jerri slapped the countertop. ''You are an infuriating man, you know that?''

''Funny,'' he said. ''That's just what Marty told me that night.''

''When, dare I ask, might that have been?''

''When I dropped her off at her place and refused to take what she so generously wanted to give me.''

''And just what's that supposed to mean?''

''Think about it for a minute.'' He brought his hands around in front of him, his fingers forming a steeple, and tilted his head as he studied her. ''Don't you think it's possible that Marty's 'blatantly obvious behavior,' as you so politely called it, might've been a bit embarrassing for everyone that night? Including me?''

''Oh,'' she said, looking sheepish all of a sudden as she glanced away. ''I guess I never thought of it that way. I thought you men enjoyed that sort of thing.''

''Not always, Smoky. It depends on the circumstances, and where you happen to be at the time.'' He stopped, waiting for her to look at him again. ''And more than that,'' he added, his eyes capturing hers, ''for at least some of us men, it depends on who the woman happens to be.''

She simply stood there, watching him. For the first time since their conversation had started, she seemed to be totally speechless.

''Now,'' he said. ''Does that satisfy your curiosity? Does it make you feel any better?''

''Maybe,'' she said, then raised her chin. ''All right, yes.''

Tyler watched as Jerri reached up and slid her fingers through her light, shining, ash-brown hair. The short style was usually smooth with a few soft, natural waves. At the moment, though, it looked fluffy and uncombed and almost...inviting. As if she'd just crawled out of bed. As if she wouldn't mind at all if he took her right back.

She cleared her throat, her voice low and velvety as she asked, "Have you thought about what you want, Tyler?"

"Yes," he answered, surprised by her direct question. "What's there to think about?"

A sudden blush colored her cheeks. "I mean, for lunch? What do you want for lunch?" She turned away from him, opening and closing cupboards, and finally stopped to stand beside the stove. "Whatever you want, just name it. I can make other things besides quiche. I can make..."

Lunch wasn't what Tyler wanted. In fact, if he had to spell out his priorities at the moment, lunch would come in somewhere around ninety-seventh on the list.

But then again, he decided as he watched her, maybe she knew that. She was standing there looking all wide-eyed and innocent, acting as if she didn't know a damned thing about the opposite sex, and he wondered if she was just being coy. Was this her idea of teasing him, or was it simply her way of trying to shut him out again?

Whichever it was, he didn't care for it. He'd played both games before—more than thirteen years ago, with someone just like her—and it didn't sit any better with him now than it had way back then.

The muscles in his jaw started working, flexing, as old anger boiled up from somewhere deep down inside him. "Look, Jerri," he said, glaring at her. "You can cut the eyelash-batting. It's wasted on me."

"Eyelash-batting?" she asked, her tone suddenly incredulous. She waved an eggbeater at him. "Do me another favor, Tyler. I realize I'm asking a lot here, but try to speak English, will you? Because I don't have the slightest idea what you're getting at."

"Oh, I think you do." He crossed his arms in front of him. "I'll admit that Marty Cunningham was a bit flashy, and she wasn't the most intelligent woman I've ever met—"

"Ha!" she interrupted. "An understatement if I've ever heard one."

He ignored her sarcasm and continued. "But there was one thing you could say for Marty. At least she was down to earth."

"Down to earth?" Jerri asked, her tone even more incredulous. "Well, that's a polite way of putting it. I'd say it was a lot closer to 'groveling at your feet'!"

"All right, maybe she was obvious about what she wanted that night, but at least she didn't come across as the precious little debutante out slumming with the country bumpkin."

"Why, of all the nerve!" Her gray eyes glinted. "I never acted like that. You're just saying that because... because I didn't gush over you, because I didn't drape myself all over you like Marty did. Well, pardon me, Tyler, but that's just not my style!"

"Oh?" he asked, trying to keep his voice level. "What is your style, then?"

Jerri opened her mouth, seemingly at a loss for an answer. "I—I have a little pride, that's all. I have too much self-respect to act like... some kind of an animal in heat!" She opened a drawer, slung the eggbeater inside and slammed it shut. "And I certainly couldn't help it if you were too thick-skulled to pick up on the fact that I was interested in you!"

Her final statement sent his jawbone clenching again, and he watched as she lifted her hands in a gesture of surrender. "But go ahead and blame it on me, Tyler. Young and foolish as I was back then, I still should've known I wasn't your type."

"And what have you decided is my type?"

"Girls who play fast and loose, like Marty Cunningham." She glared at him. "Girls with hard bodies and marshmallow minds!"

"Wrong!" he said, his fist hitting the tabletop, his voice booming. "I don't like girls of any type. I like *women*."

Jerri stormed out of the kitchen, then reappeared just as quickly and went back to work unpacking. Tyler's pulse kept right on pounding as he stared at her.

Her frenzied activity came to an abrupt halt, and she stood motionless, her back to him as she took several deep breaths. "Look, Tyler," she said, her back still to him. "That was a ridiculous display of—" She turned to face him. "Of stupidity. That Christmas dance was a hundred years ago, back when I *was* nothing but a silly girl. I was young and impressionable and... And whatever happened between you and Marty that night was none of my business, anyway. I never would have brought it up in the first place, if it hadn't been for..."

Her breathing was still uneven, but she struggled to control it as she continued. "I don't understand what's gotten into me, except that—to be perfectly honest with you—I'm feeling mean right now. Just plain mean and ugly and spiteful. Every nerve in my body seems to be screaming at me, and I guess that's why I'm screaming at you. But I am sorry, Tyler. I apologize."

"Apology accepted," he said quietly, realizing that he never should have encouraged the conversation in the first place. Considering the state she was in, he needed to be more sensitive.

"Good," she replied. "Then we'll start all over again." She stood up straight and made an attempt at smiling. "Now. What would you like for lunch?"

"Go put some shoes on," he suggested. "We'll go out to eat."

"But I don't mind—"

"Maybe not, but I do." He stood up and crossed the room, closing the distance between them.

"I don't want to go anywhere, Tyler. I want to stay here."

"Well, I don't. It'll do us both good to get out of here for a while." He took Jerri's arm and pointed her in the direction of the bedroom. "The General Store's right down the road. They serve steaks, catfish, hamburgers, whatever you want."

"No, Tyler." She turned and looked up at him, meeting his gaze. "I can't!"

"Why not?" The desperation he saw in her eyes made her look warm. And real. Until today, he realized, he had never thought of her as feeling helpless, even momentarily. Still holding her arm, he pulled her closer to him. "What is it? Are you afraid you'll be tempted to smoke?"

"No," she said, her answer coming too quickly to sound convincing.

"It'll be okay," he murmured, bringing her another step closer to him. The smell of mint was gone now, he realized. There was nothing but the smell of her, along with the faint scent of gardenias that reminded him of fragrant southern nights...heated whispers...the quiet sound of creaking, gently swaying porch gliders.

He cleared his throat. "You have to face temptation sooner or later. It might as well be sooner, and don't worry. I'll be there to look out for you."

Before she pulled away from him, he felt her body stiffen.

"Fine," Jerri said as she glared at him again. She turned on her heel, mumbling under her breath as she made for the bedroom. "By all means, let's do it your way."

Thoroughly perplexed, Tyler watched her flounce through the parlor, her arms swinging at her sides. As she slammed the bedroom door, his eyes blinked once, hard, in a sudden reflex action.

The wall was back up, the scent of gardenias gone.

Jerri pressed her spine against the closed bedroom door, taking a series of deep, ragged breaths while she made a conscious effort to unclench her balled-up fists. She didn't know whether it was giving up smoking or the general effects of Tyler Reynolds, or both. But whatever it was, she felt like one gigantic, exposed raw nerve.

And no wonder, she told herself. There was no arguing with that man. He thought he knew everything!

And to top it off, she was furious with herself. Not five seconds ago, she was out there in his arms again, aching for him to kiss her, reveling in the scent of after-shave and clean, virile male. And what was *clean, virile male* doing all that time? she asked herself, making a face as she turned and glared into the full-length mirror. He was busy thinking about "looking out" for her.

"Great," she muttered out loud. "Just great."

Turning away from the mirror, Jerri forced herself to concentrate on the task at hand: getting her black suede boots from the bottom of her suitcase without mutilating the stack of clothing on top.

She still couldn't believe what she'd told him about having the "hots" for him—not to mention that tacky little tirade about Marty Cunningham. But why should it shock her? she wondered, grabbing the boots and pushing the clothes back into place. If he had gazed at her and asked, she no doubt would have told him anything else he wanted to know: her measurements, her age, her weight. And she probably would have confessed to her true weight, instead of what she'd been claiming on her driver's license all these years.

Sinking onto the mattress, she admitted to herself that she had known exactly what she was doing. She had blurted out her ridiculous confession and challenge for one reason: she had wanted him to stay.

For the first time in her life, she had thrown caution to the wind and bared her soul. She knew she ought to be embarrassed. But for some odd reason, she wasn't. If anything, it had actually felt good to tell him the truth. Perhaps it was part of the cleansing process, she decided, part of the steps she knew she had to take in order to start being practical.

Yes, she reminded herself, she had to start being practical. She had to pry her eyes open and face reality, or she would end up alone and lonely, just like her mother.

That fact had come crashing down on her only a couple of days ago. Jerri had flown to Miami to spend part of a day with her mother. It had been the few hours between docking and sailing, the only time they could manage together during the holidays. They had gone to a nice restaurant with several members of the ship's crew, and Jerri had noticed that the man sitting across the table from them, Howard Bentley, one of the ship's officers, seemed particularly interested in Kathryn Davenport.

Jerri had brought it up later, when she and her mother were alone, but Kathryn simply brushed it off and gave her stock reply: "Your father was the only man in the world I could ever love." Jerri had come back with something like "For heaven's sake, Mother! Twenty years is long enough, don't you think? You've got to stop romanticizing about the past. You've got to start being practical."

Her advice hadn't done any good. But for some reason, after their confrontation, it had suddenly dawned on Jerri that she had been just as guilty of "romanticizing" as her mother had. In fact, it had dawned on her that perhaps she had actually been lashing out at herself.

And that, Jerri reminded herself, was the precise reason she was stuck in this godforsaken cabin. She had made this trip in order to do more than quit smoking. She was here to give herself a strong lecture about the foolishness of hanging on to a silly schoolgirl's crush. She wasn't going to end up alone and lonely like her mother, a widow of more than twenty years who was still clinging to memories.

Jerri remembered little about her father, except that she had adored him. But the sheer process of maturing had eventually caused her to cull more than adoration from her childhood recollections. Lately, she had begun to realize that beyond being wonderful, Jerry Dean Davenport had also been human—a unique mixture of strengths and weaknesses, just as all people are.

After the lecture she'd given her mother, Jerri finally realized that she had been doing the same thing: putting Tyler Reynolds on a pedestal of her own making. How could she have preached to her mother about the very practice she herself had been following for eight long years? It was time for both women to get on with their lives and stop romanticizing about the past. All Jerri needed to do was reason with herself and exorcise her ridiculous "if only" fixation with the almighty Tyler Reynolds....

And that, Jerri admitted to herself, was the reason she had asked him to stay. She wanted her eyes to be open, even if they had to be pried open. She wanted to get to know Tyler Reynolds for what he really was, instead of idolizing what he might be.

Yes, she told herself, it was high time she discovered his faults and concentrated on them. And considering the way he'd been acting, that shouldn't be too difficult.

With renewed purpose, she pulled on her boots and stood, vowing to go out there and be nice. For a short period of time she could be nice to anyone, even Mister Know-It-All out there. He could be as rude as he wanted to be, but she would show him she was a lady. She might end up detesting him, but she darned sure wouldn't give him a reason to despise her.

Glancing at her wristwatch, Jerri lifted her shoulders and smiled brightly on her way to the bedroom door. Some of their time together had already passed, and it probably wouldn't even take the full twenty-four hours, anyway.

It was really kind of humorous, too, she decided. He thought he knew everything, yet there was one thing he didn't know. What he didn't know was just how big a favor he was doing for her by agreeing to stay.

Feeling a newfound sense of confidence, she opened the bedroom door and breezed through the parlor. She stood in the kitchen for a moment, watching him through the window. He had already unhitched the boat from the vehicle, and now he was making room for her by tossing a rolled-up sleeping bag from the passenger seat into the back seat. Her pulse, she realized, was racing just from watching him.

But that wouldn't be the case much longer, she told herself, grinning pleasantly as she squared her shoulders and opened the kitchen door.

Yes, Jerri repeated inwardly. In twenty-four measly hours she would have Tyler Reynolds completely out of her system. Once and for all.

That was all it would take, and then she could get on with her life!

Chapter Four

As it turned out, The General Store was a quaint old establishment with everything rolled into one: a restaurant and gasoline station, a convenience store with the basic necessities of life, and a local meeting place where neighbors could gossip or shoot pool and drink a beer.

As Tyler and Jerri made their way toward the cash register after polishing off huge, delicious steaks, Jerri stopped midway down the narrow aisle. She picked up a cake mix from the shelf, then realized she was penniless.

"Could we get one of these, Tyler?"

"After all you just laid away," he asked, shaking his head and grinning, "you still want a chocolate cake?"

"Yes," she answered, not knowing what to say next. If he knew her reason for wanting it, he would simply make fun of her. Beyond that, she wasn't accustomed to having to ask anyone for money. "I'll be glad to pay you back when I get my cash from Beth."

His smile faded just as quickly as it had come across his face, and a muscle in his jaw flexed once before he spoke. "For God's sake, Jerri. I can afford to spring for lunch and a damned cake mix."

"I didn't mean to intimate that you couldn't. I just thought it was the right thing to do."

His jawbone, she noticed, finally began to relax again. "Get whatever you want. Whatever you need."

"All right," she said, reminding herself of her vow to be nice, no matter what. She was beginning to suspect it would be a monumental task.

Jerri reached for a can of prepared frosting to go with the cake. She headed for the front counter with Tyler behind her, his voice low and playful as he said, "I know you've just stopped smoking, but if you keep eating like this, you're liable to ruin your girlish figure."

Even though she knew he was teasing, it irritated her that he would refer to her figure as girlish. "Who knows?" she said over her shoulder, keeping her voice even. "Maybe I'll surprise you and fill out in all the right places."

Before he had a chance to respond, an elderly man called out to him from the pool-hall section of the store. Tyler excused himself for a moment, and she watched the two men approach each other, smiling as they shook hands. She held the cake ingredients in one arm, nestling them against her chest, and turned toward the checkout area.

Jerri's breath caught in her throat, and she swallowed hard. Wide-eyed and unblinking, she stared at the neat rows and vibrant colors of the display directly in front of her.

One more pack, she thought as she continued to gape at the enticing cellophane-wrapped packages. If she could just have one more pack of cigarettes before quitting for good— maybe even half a pack—it might make it possible to get through the next twenty-plus hours without going completely crazy. She had barely made it through lunch, having to sit across the table from him, shuttling back and forth between chewing her food and making polite conversation while he studied her endlessly. He had watched her from one angle, then another, until she had wanted to scream.

Involuntarily her fingers reached out to fondle the end of a pack with familiar green letters, a pack that seemed to be calling her name. She wouldn't be abandoning her resolve, she reasoned with herself. She would simply be postponing it for a few hours. Not even one full day...

Jerri slid the single package toward her, then tucked it behind her left arm, between the cake mix and the can of frosting.

No! she told herself all of a sudden, squeezing her eyelids shut. Quitting this terrible habit, she had promised herself, would be the first important step in changing her life. She turned her head and glanced at Tyler, remembering the Christmas Eve dance they had just "discussed." Having a cigarette in her hand, she had thought erroneously that night, made her appear sure of herself at a time when she certainly wasn't.

But now, Jerri reminded herself, forcing her gaze away from him and back to the display, she wasn't that insecure girl anymore. She no longer needed a cigarette as a crutch. And even though she had become physically hooked on them, she was determined to change her whole—

"Ready?" Tyler asked from behind her.

"Oh!" Startled, she pulled the purchases snug against her breasts. "I didn't know you were there. You scared me to death."

He had walked around to stand at her side. With her arms still folded in front of her, she attempted to wave him away with the fingers of her right hand. "Why don't you go look for a cowbell to put around your neck?"

"Not necessary." He reached for the items she held in her clutches. "I'll just pay for these things and we'll—"

She looked straight up into his dark blue gaze, not daring to glance down as he reached between her breasts. Her heartbeat seemed to stop and race, stop and race, and she couldn't form a single thought.

"And what have we here?" he asked, holding the pack in front of her face.

"That's . . . that's the brand I used to smoke. Before I quit."

"Ahh," he said, drawing out the word. "Interesting." He put the cigarettes back where they belonged on the display, then pointed to a row of red-and-white packs alongside. "And that's the brand I used to smoke—before I quit."

"Yes," she said, nodding her head, trying to appear nonchalant, trying to ignore the knowing smile on his face. "Yes, I remember." Her pulse lurched again as he took the remaining purchases from her arms and set them on the counter, and she wondered briefly what he would think if he knew exactly how big a fool she'd been all these years. She had never seen an ad for that particular brand of cigarettes without visualizing him instead of the men who were always pictured in them. Tyler Reynolds, she had decided a long time ago, made the ads' infamous, rugged-looking cowboys look like guys who sipped tea with their pinkies stuck out.

"Uh, look," she murmured, licking her lips. "Despite what you think, I was getting ready to put those back myself."

"Uh-huh. Sure."

"I was!" she said, irate at his obvious disbelief. "Just before you walked up to me, I decided I didn't really want them. So stop looking at me like that."

"Okay, okay," he said, holding up his hands in an attempt to placate her. "But I'll warn you right now: checkout stands are going to be your worst enemy for a while. Impulse-buying will get you every time. So instead of looking at the cigarettes, look for something else to buy." He glanced up, grabbing a deck of playing cards from a peg and handing them, along with the bill for their lunch, to the clerk who had just appeared. "These, for instance," he said, his gaze moving back to hers. "We can get these and play poker tonight. That'll keep you occupied."

The clerk rang up the total, then sacked the items as Tyler reached into his back pocket for his billfold.

Poker? her mind screamed as she watched him thank the clerk. She didn't want his advice about impulse-buying, and she certainly didn't want to be "occupied" by a brisk round of poker. Not tonight of all nights!

"I don't play poker, Tyler."

"Why doesn't that surprise me?" he asked wryly. He lifted the paper bag from the counter, then shot her a sidelong glance. "You do play bridge, I suppose?"

"Yes, but with only two of us, I don't think—"

"I don't play bridge, Jerri."

She turned, mumbling on her way to the door, "Why doesn't that surprise me?"

Once they were in the Jeep and heading back to the cabin, Jerri convinced herself that what felt like awkward silence was probably for the best. Instead of trying to make conversation with him, which always seemed to backfire on her, she kept her gaze glued to the breathtaking scenery. Her eyes scanned the tops of the rocky-edged, rolling hills, searching for the various types of animals on the exotic game ranches that abounded in the area. In less than a few minutes, she spotted both an Axis deer and a swift, graceful gazelle.

"Beth mentioned you were on vacation," Tyler finally said. "How much time do you have?"

"All I want," she answered, adding an emu to her mental list of exotics.

"Where do you work?"

"I'm a curator at an art museum in Houston."

"It must be nice, being able to take off and be gone as long as you want."

"That would be nice—if it were the case." Wondering what he was getting at, she couldn't help glancing his way. "I haven't had a vacation in several years. Therefore, I'm due a long one."

The answer seemed to satisfy him, and Jerri went back to her visual hunt. *A black buck antelope. And a—*

"Which museum?"

"The modern art museum, downtown."

"There's only one?"

"No, but I work at the biggest one, the Reis—" She kept her eyes on the scenery. "I'd really rather not talk about my job, Tyler, if you don't mind."

"Why not?" he asked. "Because you're on vacation?"

"No."

"Why not, then?" He turned off the main highway, steering the Jeep along the caliche road that led to the cabin.

Jerri shifted her position, then lowered her arms to brace her palms flat against the seat. "Well, if you must know, and I gather you must, I'm not very happy with it."

"Then why don't you quit?"

She settled back against the seat, crossing her arms in front of her as she stared at him in disbelief. "You do have answers for everything, don't you, Tyler? And you make them all sound so very simple."

For the first time, he glanced away from the road—to give her what could only be termed a dirty look. "I repeat. Why don't you quit? Do something different?"

She let out a labored sigh. "Because good jobs are hard to find. You know—steady income, health insurance, inconsequential things like that."

As they approached the cabin, he finally looked her way again. "They sound like inconsequential excuses to me."

"Whatever you say, Tyler," she commented under her breath as he pulled the vehicle to a stop. She snatched the paper bag from between them, jumped out of the passenger side and made for the cabin.

"Why don't you rest for a while?" he asked after he followed her inside and closed the door. "Take a nap?"

"Because I'm not tired."

"You may not be tired, but you sure are cranky."

Ignore him, Jerri repeated inwardly, turning away. She took a deep breath, then removed the cake ingredients from the paper bag.

For some reason, she found herself envisioning him with his daughter—leaning over her, smoothing her hair. Jerri had always wondered what he had whispered to Samantha that Easter afternoon while he was putting her down for a nap. She had always imagined it was something sweet and sensitive and loving. Instead, he'd probably been saying, "You may not be tired, but you sure are cranky!"

And as she thought about him using the same techniques and dialogue on her as he did on his daughter, Jerri felt herself becoming furious all over again. Gathering what little calm she had left, she turned to face him. "It's been ages since I've been put down for an afternoon nap, Tyler. Besides that, I have too much to do to be sleeping."

"Like what?" he asked, hooking his Stetson on the chair.

She grabbed two items from the boxes still cluttering the kitchen counters, hurrying across the room and putting them away as she argued with him. "Like unpacking, for instance. And baking this cake and starting dinner, and—"

"And inconsequential things like that."

"Oh!"

Just as she spun around, he caught her by the arms and pulled her backward. With steady hands he held her spine against the wide, hard wall of his chest, and she fought the temptation to lean back, to relax and let him—

"All of that can wait," he said, his voice a husky murmur against her hair. "After watching what you did just now, I don't think you'd get much accomplished, anyway."

"What . . . what did I do?"

"You shoved an electric coffee grinder in the fridge and then tossed a spatula in the garbage." His teasing laughter was so quiet that she felt it rather than actually hearing it, along with the warm whisper of his breath against her ear.

"If you try to do any cooking while you're in this condition, you're liable to poison us both."

"Okay," she said, laughing softly. "Maybe you're right."

"I am." His big hands moved to her shoulders, his fingers circling, pressing, rubbing the back of her neck. "You're wound up tighter than a spring. Take it from me. You have to get your rest or you'll be . . . susceptible."

Susceptible? she wondered, basking in the pressure of his strong, sure fingers as they moved slowly, languorously, washing away the tension in her neck and shoulders. She had a feeling no amount of sleep could erase the susceptibility she felt when she was with him, when he held her captive—willingly—against the muscular length of his body, when he whispered to her and surrounded her senses with his clean, distinctively male scent.

Her head drifted to the side. A soft, guttural sound escaped her throat, and she felt herself burning with desire, aching with curiosity. What would it feel like if he leaned even closer, giving fully of his warmth and his strength? If his lips were touching her skin, brushing her nape? If his hands were—

"There," he murmured. "That's it. Just let yourself relax."

Realizing she dare not let herself relax any further, Jerri cleared her throat. "What will you do," she asked, "while I'm asleep?"

"There's a good fishing spot on the property," he answered quickly. "I'll get in some fishing."

"All right," she whispered. "If you're sure."

"I'm sure." His hands slid down, enveloping her arms, and he gave her a tender shove. "Go on now. Get some rest."

As Jerri walked toward the bedroom, Tyler watched the gentle sway of her hips and decided his reasoning had sounded halfway sensible, anyway. Considering the way he was feeling at the moment, if they stuck around here together much longer, he was afraid he'd tell her exactly what he felt like doing. And it sure wasn't napping. Or fishing. Or baking chocolate cakes and unpacking boxes.

Jerri reached the bedroom doorway, then pivoted suddenly and asked, "It is temporary, isn't it, Tyler?"

"What?"

"This...this insanity. Or whatever it is." She stood there, her eyes pleading with him as she wrung her hands. "Please tell me it's temporary."

"Yeah," he answered, smiling. "It'll pass. Just give it time."

As soon as she closed the bedroom door, he realized he didn't know for sure what she'd meant by that last question. She had used the same word to describe both of her "afflictions," so which one was she talking about? Her desire for nicotine—or her desire for him?

And that brought up another question: which one did he hope she was talking about?

"Insanity," Tyler mumbled. And in the same breath, he muttered a two-bit expletive to go with it. If he had any fool notions about something developing between the two of them, he reminded himself, her choice of words would be right on target.

What was he even thinking about? he wondered all of a sudden. He couldn't stand spoiled society-types. He'd had dealings with one woman—one girl—who was just like Jerri Davenport. And that was one too many to suit him.

Frowning, he retrieved the misplaced items from the fridge and the garbage, chucking them back into one of the boxes. She'd brought all the comforts of home with her, and she acted as if she couldn't exist a minute without them. But, he reminded himself, what more should he expect from a pampered little blue blood who had been an art major, no less? One who was wasting her time as a curator at some stuffy museum?

She'd had a fine, fancy, private education handed to her on a silver platter—something he would've given his eye-teeth for—and she was frittering it away by working at a job she hated.

So, he lectured himself, he needed to stop dwelling on the attraction he felt for her. He needed to concentrate on the fact that they were worlds apart.

And even though Jerri didn't know a damned thing about him, she had sensed it too, judging by her remarks. Things like, "Try to speak English, Tyler!" and "You were just too dumb to pick up on it."

He rubbed his tight jaw, then shook his head and laughed. Even though he hated some of those wisecracks, there was something intriguing about that sarcasm of hers, something especially intriguing about the way she propped those hands on her hips before she started working that beautiful, smart-alecky mouth.

Every time she started in on him with her facetious remarks, he found himself torn between two courses of action. One was to lean back and give her full rein—it was one hell of an enjoyable and amusing sight to behold. The other was to walk over, yank her up in his arms and shut her up by covering her mouth with his, giving that sharp, sassy tongue of hers something better to do.

All right, he admitted to himself, maybe he was putting those two choices in the wrong order. His gaze moved toward the bedroom, and he wondered what she was wearing right now. He had always loved the way she looked in blue or blue-gray, but he liked that plum color, too. He liked the way it highlighted her cheeks every time she blushed, the way it made her look so innocently sexy. Was that the way she'd look, he wondered, curled up on that bed?

He stopped the thought and tried to stop his body's response as he dragged his gaze away from the bedroom.

Yeah, he decided, shaking his head again as he grabbed his hat and made for the kitchen door. Insanity was a great word for it. Jerri Davenport and Tyler Reynolds would mix almost as well as oil and water. Almost.

Chapter Five

This, Jerri told herself as she drummed her fingers against the card table, *is what insanity is all about.*

After washing the dinner dishes, they had moved to the parlor and decided to compromise by playing gin rummy. And now she was going crazy waiting for Tyler to draw a card.

How long, she wondered, had he been sitting across from her, staring at the cards in his hand? Better yet, how long had she been staring at them? Fanned easily behind his wide, long fingers, the standard-size cards looked like the miniature ones kids sometimes receive as party favors.

Jerri sorted her own cards for the umpteenth time and glanced back up at him. He was undoubtedly planning some unbelievably shrewd strategy for his next play—but what?

"Are you going to play, Tyler?" When he looked at her with an odd stare, she waved her fingers in front of him and amended her question. "While we're still young?"

"Oh. Is it my draw?"

"Yes, Tyler," she said, trying to keep at least a shred of patience in her tone. "It has been your turn—" she glanced at her wristwatch "—for the last six minutes and forty seconds. That's a fairly rough estimate, of course."

He studied his cards for another moment or two, then announced "gin" as he started laying them out in groups.

"But you didn't even draw!" She leaned across the table, her fingers rifling the sets of cards. "You mean you've been sitting there with a 'gin' all this time?"

"Yeah," he answered, as if it were perfectly normal to play the game in that fashion.

"Great," she said, tossing her cards on the table. "I hope I brought a calculator with me. We'll need it to count up all the mismatched face cards in my hand!"

Tyler lifted his eyebrows, then smiled. "I think I can handle it," he said, reaching for the pad and pencil he had used to keep track of the three hands she'd already lost to him. This was infuriating, she decided. He was infuriating.

Despite the saggy bed she'd slept on, Jerri had had a refreshing two-hour nap. After waking up she had baked the cake and prepared an elaborate dinner. But then Tyler had come back from fishing, and he'd been moody ever since he'd walked through the door—probably because he hadn't caught a single scaly thing. Masculine pride, she told herself, could be downright disgusting. A lot of good it had done her to bathe and primp and put on something nice. Steel blue was her best color, but for all Tyler had noticed, she could have worn her ugly old chenille bathrobe instead of her favorite silk-and-wool sweater and matching slacks.

She, on the other hand, had certainly noticed how wonderful he looked after he showered and shaved and came to the dinner table. He was wearing nothing special—just old button-fly jeans, the denim slightly faded and worn-out in what seemed the most provocative of places, and a light blue Western-cut shirt. Its icy color provided a marvelous contrast to his dark hair and blue eyes, and when he unsnapped the cuffs and rolled up the sleeves to just below his elbows, she hadn't been able to resist staring at the wealth of dark, springy hair on his forearms. Between that and the growth on his chest—what she could see at the top of his shirt as well as the shadowing of crisp hair under the fabric—he'd had her so damned nervous and distracted she hadn't been able to keep track of her own cards, much less his.

She watched Tyler as he made a dramatic display of tabulating the cards, one by one. Then he touched the sharpened end of the pencil to the tip of his tongue. Why, she wondered, did that gesture seem...suggestive? He was gloating, lording it over her by writing down the score with great care, and here she was gaping at his mouth and practically salivating over him.

"For heaven's sake, Tyler! I don't even have any money with me." She yanked the pad from his hand, glaring at the numbers and then at him. "So why are you making such a big deal of adding up all these points?"

When he simply shrugged his shoulders, as if it were a ridiculous question, she jumped up from the straight-backed chair. "I think I'm ready for dessert. Would you like coffee with yours?"

"What? No espresso?"

"Sure," she answered. "My machine makes all three. Would you rather have espresso or cappuccin—?"

"I was kidding, Jerri." He gave her the most absurd look. "It was just a joke. Coffee will be fine."

"Oh." What else could she say? she wondered as she turned toward the kitchen. Just then, she realized he was following her. "If you'd like some brandy in it, I think I packed a bottle."

"I'm sure you did," he answered as she poured water into the coffee machine. "But no thanks." He braced his hand against the counter, glancing down into one of the boxes she still hadn't finished unpacking, and then watched her as he added, "No brandy, no amaretto, no nothing. Just plain coffee would be great."

"Regular," she asked pointedly, "or decaf?"

"Plain, regular coffee," he answered, settling back and crossing one boot over the other. "Nothing fancy. Is that a problem?"

"No," she said, measuring coffee into the cone-shaped basket and then switching on the machine. "I just don't want any more of your complaints coming back to me later." One hand at her waist, she pushed her hip against the edge of the counter. "I don't want to hear the same complaints about coffee that I heard about dinner, that's all."

"I didn't complain about dinner," he stated flatly. "In fact, I complimented you on it."

"You did not!"

"I did too." His hand shot out, pointing at the table. "After dinner I leaned back in that chair and said, 'Thanks, Smoky. That was a fantastic meal.' As I *recall*, I even patted my bulging stomach. So what's that, if it's not a compliment?"

His hand returned to his side, his fingers spanning the snug, faded denim riding low on his trim waist. *Liar!* she wanted to scream. *Bulging stomach, my foot.*

"What else did you want me to do?" he asked. "Unfasten the top button of my jeans?"

"Of course not." Forcing her gaze up from the front of his Levi's, Jerri lifted her chin. "I'm not talking about what you said after dinner. Everyone knows that's a mere formality. I'm talking about what you said during dinner."

"All right," he muttered in exasperation. "I give. I'd have to be crazy to pit my memory against yours, so go ahead and tell me. Just exactly what did I say during dinner?"

"You took two bites and told me you'd rather have meat loaf."

"Wrong. I said you didn't have to go to all that trouble, and then I said meat loaf would've suited me fine."

"To which I replied, 'It was no trouble. It was easy.' To which you replied, 'It doesn't taste easy.'" She lifted her hand, then slapped it down on the countertop for effect. "Obviously we went to different schools, Tyler, but is that your idea of a compliment? 'It doesn't taste easy'?"

"To hell with what schools we went to," he said, the muscles in his jaw stretched tight. "What I meant was, it was delicious. It tasted too good to be easy."

She turned away from him so that he couldn't see the satisfied smile on her face, and cut two slices of the rich chocolate cake. She had spent over two hours on that meal, and it had really disappointed her when she'd thought he wasn't enjoying it.

"Now," he said from behind her. "Is that cleared up?"

"Yes," she answered simply, handing him the plates to carry to the other room. "And thank you. I'll take that as a compliment." She followed him to the parlor, setting his coffee in front of him before sitting down and taking a bite of her cake.

"You know," he said as he watched her closely, "it's really not a good idea to replace one bad habit with another one."

"I assume you're referring to smoking," she said. "But what other bad habit are we talking about here?"

He used his fork to gesture toward her slice of cake. "Judging by your figure, I don't imagine you usually eat—" His gaze slid down from her eyes to her sweater, then quickly up to her eyes again. "Something tells me you don't usually lay away the groceries like you have been today. Don't you think it might be a good idea to slack off a bit?"

"Thank you for sharing that thought with me, Tyler," Jerri said, her voice and expression mockingly serious. "I must say, I've never felt closer to you than I do at this very moment. And I'll certainly keep your advice in mind." She stood up, walked to the kitchen and came back with a second slice of cake on her plate.

"Nice move," he said, sarcasm oozing from his tone. "I guess you really showed *me*."

"I'm not eating this cake because I'm hungry, Tyler. I'm eating it strictly for medicinal purposes. It's therapeutic."

"That's one I've never heard," he stated wryly.

"It's a well-known theory," she remarked, picking up her fork. "In case you don't know, chocolate is supposed to be soothing. Almost like a tranquilizer." *And if ever I needed a tranquilizer,* she added mentally, *tonight's the night.*

"That's not the theory I've heard."

"And what, pray tell, is the theory you've heard?"

"Are you sure you want to know?"

"Of course, Tyler. I'm waiting with bated breath."

"I've heard that it leaves you feeling euphoric." He leaned forward, propping his chin against his fist as he smiled and raised his eyebrows. "Sated," he said, his gaze still holding hers. "Almost like the feeling you're left with after making love."

"Oh." Jerri's fork clanked against the plate, and she waved her fingertips as she glanced away, then back at him. "Well, that's not what I've heard."

Good grief, she thought, picking up her fork once again as she frantically searched her mind for a change of topic. "What does Samantha do when you go off on these fishing trips of yours?"

Tyler leaned back, still looking happy with himself. "Sometimes she goes with me, sometimes she doesn't. It just depends on the circumstances. Her schedule, my schedule, things like that." He tilted his head. "Why?"

"I was just curious, that's all." She lifted another morsel of cake toward her mouth, trying to act nonchalant. Seeing the renewed smile on his face as he eyed the chocolaty sliver, she decided not to eat it. "You said you were planning to be gone several days. Does she stay at a friend's house or—"

"She's at home."

"Alone?"

"No," he answered. "I have someone who's there in case she needs anything. Someone who lives in."

"Oh?" she asked casually, her mind suddenly conjuring up a vision of a woman who bore a striking resemblance in both looks and dress to Marty Cunningham. Except that this floozy had *platinum* hair that was straight out of a bottle.

Tyler said nothing. He simply laced his fingers behind his head and lounged back against them.

She squirmed against the chair, then smiled and asked, "What's she like?"

"She's a he. And he's a great old guy."

Jerri cleared her throat, not wanting to sound as foolishly relieved as she felt. "Oh, that's wonderful. How did you find this person?"

"Cotton and my dad were childhood friends."

As she noticed the flickering look of sadness in his eyes, Jerri realized how little she knew about Tyler. All she knew about his dad was that "Big Sam" Reynolds had passed away about fifteen years ago and that up until the time of his death, the two men had had an extremely close relationship. Why they'd called Tyler's father "Big Sam," she had no idea, since he had passed away before Samantha was born. Possibly it was because of his stature—if he'd looked anything like Tyler.

Jerri swallowed hard, then asked, "Do Samantha and Cotton get along well with each other?"

"Oh, yeah." A melancholy smile touched his lips as he leaned forward and placed one hand over the top of the coffee mug. "He's sort of taken over, become the grandpa Sam never had."

"That's really wonderful." A tightness filled her chest cavity, squeezing at her heart, and Jerri fought the urge to reach out and cover his hand with hers. Or to put her arms around him, to hold him and ask him why he'd looked so sad only a moment before.

"I—I'll be right back," she said abruptly, standing up and heading for the kitchen.

Once there, safely out of his view, she buried her face in her hands. Her mind was reeling, flitting, lost in a mixed-up jumble of sensations and emotions.

It was pathetic, she told herself as she shook her head, pressing her fingers against her closed eyes. *She* was pathetic. One minute she'd been eaten up with senseless, petty jealousy over a woman she'd thought was living with him— a nonexistent woman, as it turned out. And then, not ten seconds later, she had ached to put her arms around him and take away his sadness.

"Oh, Lord," she whispered against her palms, fighting back the tears of desperation and confusion welling up behind her eyes. What was she going to do now? This simply wasn't going the way she had planned. She wasn't getting Tyler out of her system at all. And how could she, when she was feeling this way? How could she expect to get over him and start changing her life, when any time she even pictured him with another woman she felt this disgusting, distressing need for a scratching post and a saucer of milk?

"Surely you're not getting a third slice of—" Somewhere behind her, Tyler stopped dead in his tracks. "Smoky?" he asked quietly. "What's wrong?"

"Nothing," she said, bringing her hands down but refusing to face him as she swallowed the lump in her throat. "Nothing at all. I was just checking on the coffee. I'll be right there."

She heard his footsteps advancing across the floor, then saw him from the corner of her eye as he stopped by her side. She looked the opposite way, trying to keep her voice light as she said, "You're always sneaking up on me. I should've bought you that cowbell."

"There is something wrong," he stated.

"No, there isn't. Please, Tyler, just—"

He took her chin in his hand, gently turning her face toward his. "You're crying," he said, his tone reflecting his puzzlement.

"No, I'm not," she insisted, realizing that her voice was cracking as she spoke.

Slowly he swung her around, cradling her in the hard, comforting warmth of his arms. "It's okay, honey. Go ahead and cry."

"I don't cry, Tyler!" Her body jerked, and he pulled her closer as she choked out the words. "I'm not the kind of person who cries." Her hands went around his waist, raking his back. "I don't—I don't know what's wrong with me."

"Cry all you want, sweetheart. It's okay." His breath was hot as he whispered against her hair. "Women cry." The reference registered immediately, despite her distress. "Men cry sometimes, too." His jaw stroked her hair, and she felt the rumble of concerned laughter as it pulsed through his throat. "When I quit smoking, I felt like crying a few times myself."

"But I don't want you to see me like this, Tyler. I don't—"

"Shh. It's okay." His words were gentle, tender, as he encompassed her in his arms, rubbing her back, soothing her as if she were a little—

Her body stiffened at the thought. This wasn't the kind of attention she wanted from him, and she had no one to blame but herself! She dropped her hands, pulling away from him as she swiped at the tears still running down her cheeks. "You don't have any idea why I'm upset," she said quietly, her words still coming out in gasps as she fought to control her racing heartbeat. "I'm not crying because of wanting a—I'm crying because I'm angry with myself."

"For what?" he asked, confusion apparent in his eyes.

"I—I never should've asked you to stay." She stood back from him, her fists balled up at her sides but her voice oddly calm. "This simply isn't working out, Tyler. I should've known it wouldn't."

She drew in a deep, steadying breath while his blue eyes continued to question her. "I'm sorry," she murmured. "I don't know what else to say, except that if it's any consolation to you—'' her voice dropped even lower, her eyes still held by his beautiful, searching gaze ''—I'm just as perplexed by my behavior as you seem to be.''

Before he had a chance to ask for answers that she didn't have, Jerri headed through the parlor. ''I'll change into my nightclothes, and then you can have the bedroom.''

She closed the bedroom door, her forehead leaning against its solid coolness as she told herself that, for her own good, she had to make her plan work. She wanted love, a home, a husband and children...all the things a woman had a right to want. And even though he had finally referred to her as a woman, he was never going to see her as one, not when she kept falling apart every time he turned around.

The sooner she accepted that fact and stopped feeling sorry for herself, the better off she would be. She wasn't going to spend the rest of her life aching for a man who didn't want her...the way she wanted him.

Hearing the sound of wood being added to the stove in the parlor, Jerri brought her forehead away from the door. She moved across the room, quickly doffing her outfit and dressing in an oversized man's undershirt that she sometimes wore to bed because it was so roomy and soft, and ''Old Blue,'' her chenille bathrobe that had seen better days. She wanted to show him that she wasn't trying to be alluring, that she meant what she'd just said.

''All right,'' she mumbled, sinking onto the edge of the bed. She wanted to show *herself* that she meant what she'd said. This was a mistake, she repeated inwardly, a ridiculous plan that wasn't working. They didn't get along. So they would simply go to sleep, and before she knew it, it would be morning and he would be on his merry way.

Tugging on a pair of warm, glittery-looking ski socks, since she refused to go so far as to let him see her in those horrible fluffy slippers, Jerri stood up resolutely. She glanced toward the nightstand, looking for her lighter and cig—

Well. It was only natural that she should be reacting this way, she assured herself as she unwrapped a piece of bubble gum from the supply she'd brought with her just in case she felt the need. And right now, she most certainly felt the need. Yes, she decided. It was nicotine withdrawal combined with the sense of oral deprivation that went hand in hand with quitting smoking that was making her feel as if her nerve endings were raw and exposed. She hated to admit it even to herself, but Tyler had been right about why she'd been stuffing herself with food all day.

Working the gum between her teeth, she grabbed linens and a pillow before opening the door and entering the parlor. The lamp had been switched off, but she saw Tyler lounging on the room's one easy chair, his long legs stretched out in front of him. The only light was the glow of the wood-burning stove he had readied for the night; nevertheless, she didn't miss the shocked expression on his face as he watched her chewing her gum for a second, then looked her up and down as he studied her nighttime garb.

"The bedroom's all yours." She blew a bubble and started fitting a sheet to the sofa cushions, but he didn't move a muscle.

"I've figured out what's wrong with you," he said, shifting positions but still leaning his head back against the chair's upholstery. He propped one boot against the opposite knee and folded his hands over his lean stomach. "And if you'll stop chomping on that gum for a minute, I'll tell you what it is."

She abandoned her bed-making chore and spoke with renewed determination. "I know exactly what's 'wrong' with me, Tyler—and I'm not chomping. I've simply got oral urges to satisfy."

He stood up and walked toward her in the darkened room. "I know. So why don't you give me the gum—" he held out his palm "—and start satisfying them."

"What's that supposed to mean?" she asked, her eyes combing his body then settling on his face to give him a look that clearly said "you're crazy." At the same time, she decided that no mortal man should be allowed to smell so intoxicatingly good.

"That means, why don't you just let me kiss you?"

She forced a tiny laugh from her throat—where her heart suddenly seemed to have lodged. "Why, of all the—" she began weakly.

"Quit acting like the outraged female, Smoky." His words were incredibly slow, incredibly quiet. "We've been skirting around this all day, so let's just go ahead and do it." He lifted one muscular shoulder. "It's only natural. I'm a man, you're a woman. So why don't you just spit out the gum and admit you want me to kiss you?"

"I don't know where you dreamed up this latest theory of yours, Tyler." Jerri managed to roll her eyes, although his face was so close to hers that she couldn't seem to breathe anymore. "But you're way off base."

"Am I?" he asked, smiling. "You mean I'm wrong? You mean this isn't what you've been wanting me to do ever since you asked me to stay?"

"Yes. I mean no. I mean—" Her voice was so low, she wondered if he'd heard her over the whispery crackle of the fire. "That's . . . that's ludicrous."

"No, it's not," he said, lifting his dark eyebrows. "If you've had the 'hots' for me, you must have thought about kissing me. You must have wondered about it."

"Well. Once or twice, maybe," she lied. "But I'm getting over you now. I'm getting you out of my system." Her brain said move, but her body didn't want to listen.

"All right," he agreed. "But even so, don't you think you owe it to yourself?"

"Owe what to myself?"

"Letting me kiss you—just once, anyway."

"That sounds rather pompous, don't you think?"

"No, not really." One corner of his mouth curved up into a half grin. "Oh, I have been told I'm pretty good at it, but that's not what I mean."

"I may be sorry for asking this, but just what do you mean, then?"

"Even after the twenty-four hours are up, even after you've gotten me out of your system—" his voice was low and husky "—if you don't let me kiss you, you're liable to always wonder how it might have been. Right?"

"Well..." As she continued to stare directly into his beautiful, darkening blue eyes, she realized there was no air left in her lungs. "I guess you could be right. It does sound reasonable, that I might always wonder." Her voice sounded breathless against the quiet room. "One never knows...how one might feel about things like that. In the future, of course."

"That's so true. And there's another way of looking at it."

"What's that?"

"If you can make it through this one kiss and still get me completely out of your system, then you'll accomplish what you set out to do." His hand slid around her neck, his fingers reaching the sensitive flesh along the column of her throat. "Just think of it as...the ultimate test."

"You really are sure of yourself, aren't you, Tyler?"

"Umm-hmm." He nodded, then slowly grazed his thumb across her lower lip. "Now give me the gum."

"I think I need to do this," she murmured, her heartbeat pulsing in her neck, throbbing against his strong fingers as she stared up through the glow of the firelight to the burning heat of his unflinching gaze. "I think I need to do it to prove something to *you*."

"Mmm." He lifted his eyebrows, as if in the slightest gesture of agreement. "Maybe so."

She pushed the bubble gum to the front of her mouth, her tongue moving it to his waiting fingers, and watched him drop it onto the end table. His fingers had never moved from their firm hold around the back of her neck, and his other hand slid behind her to bring her body against him.

His head lowered, descending toward hers in what seemed like a suspension of time. She was eager for the taste of him, painfully eager for his mouth to take hers, and as soon as their lips touched she felt herself melting against the warmth of his hard body. Blood pounded in her ears, her pulse still drumming against his hand, and she moaned....

Her mouth opened to his tongue, welcoming it, wanting it, begging for its tender, loving assault on hers. He whispered her name, his mouth caressing hers, making slow, sweet love to her, and she knew she had never felt anything like this before. She had never known such gentle strength existed, such excruciatingly tender passion, and she realized that involuntarily her hips had moved against him. Every inch of her body yearned for his touch, his mouth. His heat and desire.

He brought his head up momentarily, taking a long, deep, ragged breath as his gaze fixed on her eyes. And when his lips again took hers, the tempo suddenly changed. His strong hands moved around her, gliding downward from her back, to her waist, then lower. Her breathing stopped and then quickened as he held her against his hardness, as she felt the strong, hard evidence of his need for her. Her hands circled his neck, her fingers twining in the soft, thick hair at his nape as her tongue made love to his.

Fire seemed to be flowing through her veins, and she felt an emptiness—a heavy, burning, pulsating emptiness deep down inside her. She pushed her body harder against him, wanting to give all of herself, wanting all that he had to give.

Abruptly his mouth left hers, his hands reaching for the sash at her waist as she fought for breath. He brought her robe down from her shoulders, not letting it fall from her body. Instead he kept the fabric around her back and used it to pull her heaving, aching breasts against him. He held her to the hard wall of his chest—so tightly that she could feel the soft, crisp growth of dark hair beneath his shirt.

His hands gripped the chenille at the sides of her breasts, the rough pressure making her yearn for more. And when his mouth captured hers, she suddenly realized he was no longer sharing himself with her. Instead he was taking what he chose, ignoring what she wanted to give. It felt like bitterness—like open disdain—and she struggled against his grip, fought against the sick churning that quickly rose from the pit of her stomach.

Why would he feel that way toward her? she wondered, a sense of alarm building as his strength intensified, as she twisted away from his hold. Her breath came in gasps as she stood back from him, her eyes focusing again in the near-darkness of the room.

He was smiling softly, and for a moment Jerri wondered if she had imagined feelings that weren't actually there.

He reached out and slid the robe back up to cover her shoulders, leaving it to hang free over her T-shirt. His hand moved then to the thin white fabric, and she felt his fingertips under her arm as his hand gently but surely enveloped the entire side of her breast—as if he were checking, making sure her nipple was sufficiently aroused and hard. As if he had been proving something, to himself or to her, and was simply confirming the fact that he'd accomplished it.

"Well?" he said at last, his voice low, almost teasing.

"Well what?" she asked, the words barely more than a whisper as she watched him, searching his face, praying for some indication that she was wrong—a sign that her imagination had conjured up something that wasn't really there. But there was no sign. Just the heat of his hand through her T-shirt as the heel of his palm rubbed slowly against her, keeping her nipple taut.

"Well?" he repeated, his tone light. "How was it?"

"It was...okay, I guess."

"It was okay?" His voice had changed, roughened, and his hands moved to the sides of her robe.

When he found the loose strip of fabric, tying the sash with a yank, she knew it wasn't her imagination. It hadn't been desire. It had been some kind of hostility, and the finality of knowing without a doubt brought with it a sharp, twisting stab of regret, of heart-wrenching grief. He had wanted something, but that something wasn't her at all. The realization hurt her with the fierceness of physical pain.

"With that ten-dollar vocabulary of yours," he said angrily, "that's all you can come up with? It was *okay*?"

Her self-defense mechanism came to the front, shoving aside the confusion racing through her mind and the pain ripping at her heart. Whatever it was he'd been trying to prove, whatever its purpose, she wouldn't allow him to do it at her expense. Never.

"It was a kiss. It was okay. What did you want me to say, Tyler?" Her voice continued to rise as she lifted her hands into the air. "That it was wonderful? That you took me to new heights of... of uninhibited, animalistic passion or something?"

"No! All I wanted was the truth."

"All right, fine. Here's the truth." She made a conscious effort to lower her voice, to control the trembling inside her body. "It was a kiss. It was okay. I passed the ultimate test."

He stared at her, almost sneering. "You're going on a bit too much, don't you think? Just exactly who are you trying to convince, you or me?"

"You! But as usual, you're just too slow to pick up on it."

"I may be slow, Jerri, but I'm not stupid. I know something about the way women respond to men—so whose body was that, anyway?"

"It was mine! I am a woman, so yes, I responded. I got caught up in the heat of the moment. But it was a moment, a brief moment, and I'll be damned if I'll let you back me into a corner and make me—"

"Make you what? Make you drop that sarcastic front of yours long enough to admit you enjoyed it?"

The question hit her like a brutal slap across the face, forcing her to retaliate.

"Let me put it in two-bit terms you'll understand, Tyler! Just who do you think you are, anyway? The finest stud in these parts?"

"That's what I'm talking about. You just can't do it, can you? You can't stop slinging around that sarcastic crap!"

"Thank you, Tyler," she said through clenched teeth, her inner rage threatening to explode as she whirled away from him and started yanking on the corners of the sheet. "Thank you for everything." Fighting to keep her voice even, she was grateful he couldn't see the sudden tears running down her face. "The twenty-four hours aren't even up yet, and I think I've already gotten you out of my system."

"Great! That suits me just fine." He turned, heading straight for the bedroom.

"My sentiments exactly!" she screamed, addressing his broad, retreating back as she threw herself down on the sofa and plumped her pillow with fury. "Good night!"

Tyler frowned into the pitch-dark room. He pushed against the sagging mattress, again rolling away from its sunken middle.

How many rodeo riders had trained on this bed before going on to the easy stuff, he wondered, like bucking broncos and ill-tempered Brahma bulls?

He groaned, then turned toward the nightstand to grope for his— Good God! he thought, flopping his head back against the one lousy excuse for a pillow and squeezing his eyelids closed. He hadn't had the desire to smoke for over six months. But right now he wanted a cigarette, and he wanted it bad. Jerri'd had him so damned frustrated he hadn't known what he was doing all day. All evening!

She had really thrown him by flouncing out in that ridiculous getup. For some reason, it had made him realize just how much his mind had fantasized about her over the past eight years. Hell, what had he thought she slept in on a nightly basis? A diamond tiara and a ball gown?

That frock had gotten another reaction from him, too, a physical reaction that had both surprised and shocked him. It had made him want her even more than he'd always thought he did. In fact, she could've pranced out there and stood in front of the flickering light wearing a roll of plastic wrap and it wouldn't have aroused him as much as seeing her snapping that gum, popping bubbles, flitting around in that god-awful robe and socks and man's undershirt. For some strange reason, in that getup she had looked so...touchable. Unbearably, unbelievably soft and feminine.

He'd dreamed up his brilliant strategy while adding logs to the fire and waiting for her to come out of the bedroom. He'd been trying to figure out what, besides quitting smoking, had been making her act so erratic all day—but he hadn't given one thought to what his own reaction might be when he kissed her. He had simply decided it was what she wanted, what she needed.

Then, in the middle of kissing her, he had realized just how much he was enjoying it. As soon as he'd felt himself drowning in the sweet scent of her, the warm, delicious feel of her softness, the sudden, tempestuous press of her body against his, he'd realized he hadn't wanted to enjoy it. What he had wanted to do was to prove to her that he was a man, that she was a warm, real, responsive woman. That she could let her hair down once in a while instead of always acting like some cool, prissy little debutante.

And he'd proven just that, he decided, judging by her response to him and then that little performance she'd staged afterward. Even though she wasn't about to admit it, she'd enjoyed the hell out of it, too. So why wasn't he feeling overwhelmingly satisfied with himself for a job well done? For "putting her in her place" by proving his point?

Instead, he was feeling more confused and irritable than ever. And now he was doomed to eight hours on a lumpy mattress complete with linens that surrounded him with her light, gardenia scent and kept reminding him of the way she'd felt in his arms, the way she responded so easily, then pulled away from him just as quickly and mysteriously.

But then again, he reasoned, why shouldn't she pull away from him? Her highfalutin private education had taught her

something, anyway. After only a few hours with him, she'd
been smart enough to figure out that *he* wasn't *her* type,
either. That was more than he could say for Pauline, who
hadn't figured it out until after she was pregnant with Samantha.

Tyler wadded up the pillow, propping his arm behind his
head as he pushed out a lengthy sigh. His memories of
Pauline had faded at some point way, way back—he wasn't
sure exactly when. But it didn't take much to recall his first
impression of Jerri so many years ago. There she'd been one
Easter Sunday, this perfectly dressed, perfectly mannered
girl Beth had acquired as a roommate when she started college. And he could still remember staring at Jerri when she
wasn't watching. He could still remember studying her
mouth as his mind drifted to the thought that those beautiful, enticing lips that had obviously been made for kissing
had probably never been kissed by anything but a Harvard
man. And what a waste, he'd concluded. What a terrible
waste that was. . . .

Yeah, he could still remember his initial reaction to her,
something he'd discounted as purely physical, something
he'd told himself was forbidden, too, because of her tender
age. He'd already had one kid to raise—Sam had been only
four or five at the time—and he hadn't needed another.

But Jerri sure wasn't a kid anymore. If he hadn't realized
that before, she had certainly convinced him of it tonight.

She'd shown him something else, too: that there was more
behind her facade, something a lot more basic than the
proper, ladylike image she had always projected. And that
was what had surprised him—okay, pleased him—the most.

That, too, was exactly what he'd been trying to prove to
her. It was what had caused him to get rough with her.
When he'd realized he was kissing her like she was some
damned porcelain doll, he'd been angry with himself. . . angry with her.

But regardless of the way she had responded to him tonight, and the way he'd responded to her, none of it can-

celed the fact that they might as well be from two different planets. She was gourmet dinners and cappuccino, he was meat and potatoes. She was fancy private schools, he was just now—

"Dammit," he muttered into the darkness. That's what really made him mad. He should be here trying to concentrate on one goal, one project—his real reason for being on this sham of a "fishing trip" in the first place. And instead of concentrating all his energies on that, his mind was getting screwed up trying to figure out Jerri Davenport and his own reactions to her.

She was doing nothing more than whiling away a few days in the country, and here he was letting her tie him up in knots!

A short, bitter laugh escaped his throat. Jerri Davenport didn't have the slightest idea what she wanted. And even if she did know what she wanted, much less what she *needed*, she was certainly too prim and proper to let herself admit it. So why the hell was he wasting his time trying to figure it out for her? Especially when he was so damned confused that he couldn't figure out his own thinking?

Tyler rolled over and punched the pillow yet again. He would give her the twenty-four hours she asked for, and then he would gladly hit the road.

Yeah, if she wanted anything else from him, he'd say thanks but no thanks. Whatever it was she needed in order to amuse herself, he wasn't about to let her do it at his expense. He'd had enough of her type to last him *more* than a lifetime.

Tyler smiled and closed his eyes. When 10:00 a.m. rolled around, and it couldn't roll around soon enough for him, he would kiss her goodbye and get on with his life.

Stretching out his legs, he let his feet hang over the end of the bed and then brought them back under the covers. He thrashed around for a few seconds, trying to get into a more comfortable position, and finally frowned as he stopped struggling and let the mattress roll him back to its sagging middle.

Correction! he thought, turning his face to the side and instructing himself to ignore the floating cloud of gardenia scent. Come ten o'clock in the morning, he would *shake her hand* goodbye. There was no way—no way on God's green earth—that he was going to let himself fall into that trap again!

Chapter Six

As early-morning light began to seep into the parlor Jerri sorted the papers spread out on the card table. Then she reached into the portable file on the floor beside her feet and brought out another stack.

Seven o'clock, she noted, a gloomy frown on her face as she checked her wristwatch again. She had been up since five, resigning herself to the fact that she might as well get started on her project. She had made a mess of everything the night before, and in a matter of hours Tyler would be up and gone.

Somewhere in the middle of a virtually sleepless night, she had realized it was entirely possible that she'd made a drastic mistake in judgment. For some reason it had dawned on her that Tyler had been trying to tease her all day; she'd just been too nervous to let herself relax and enjoy it.

Perhaps he really had wanted her, she'd decided then, while she continued to toss and turn on the sofa. She knew precious little about the man; perhaps as far as he was concerned, teasing was simply an enjoyable preliminary to lovemaking.

And once she'd realized she might have made the wrong interpretation of his behavior, it had dawned on her that she could hardly come right out and discuss the possibility with him. No, she reminded herself, a small sigh escaping her lips. She could never—

The bedroom door opened, and Tyler walked out. He looked deliciously warm and sexy, running his fingers through his dark, tousled hair as he headed for the bathroom and shut the door behind him.

Jerri couldn't help thinking there was a certain air of intimacy to the scene: he in a pair of jeans and what had appeared to be the top from a pair of long johns, she still dressed in her robe and socks. His shadow of a beard, her unstyled hair. It was as if they'd lived together for years, as if they'd seen each other this exact way at least a thousand times before.

She smiled at the thought of it. To her, he had never looked more wonderful—but as soon as he caught a glimpse of her dressed like this in the full light of day, he no doubt would decide she looked even more frightful than she had the night before. Once he pried his eyes open and took a good look at her, he would probably make a run for it.

The door opened and again Jerri looked up from her papers. She watched him lift his arms and grasp the door frame, stretching and yawning. The parlor was cool and crisp, and he moved to the wood-burning stove, stooping long enough to add logs and rebuild the fire.

"Boy, this feels great," he said, standing and reaching out his arms for another languorous stretch.

"I should think you'd be used to waking up in this marvelous hill-country air."

"I wasn't talking about the air." He put his hand behind him, a pained look on his face as he rubbed the small of his back and groaned. "I was talking about getting out of that bed."

Jerri glanced down and brought her hand to her forehead, using her fingers as a visor to hide her smile as she pretended to study her work. Serves you right, she thought playfully, for talking me into kissing you last night and blowing the last shreds of my theory to hell and back. Father figure! What a laugh that was.

"Didn't sleep too well?" she asked, her tone both innocent and concerned as Tyler fell back against the sofa and slammed his eyes shut. She stood up and moved to the kitchen. After sentencing him to a night on that bed, the least she could do was pour him a cup of coffee.

"No, I didn't." He opened one eye, peeking at her when she came back with the mug. He thanked her as she handed it to him, then asked, "How about you?"

Jerri watched as he raised his head and propped himself on one elbow. And suddenly she knew she couldn't let him leave without at least an explanation. She knelt in front of the sofa, within inches of him, and let his gaze hold hers as she sat back against her feet and decided what to say.

"I didn't sleep very well, either. I had a lot to think about, I guess, after all the yelling I did." When his lips parted, she held up her hand. "Please, Tyler. Let me finish. I'm not apologizing, I'm just trying to explain why I screamed at you and raved like—" she glanced down, nervously folding her robe over her knees before looking back up into his eyes "—like a bitch. I can't explain it, except to say that I let my imagination run away with me. I think I must've read something in the way you kissed me, something that wasn't there. I know that must sound odd, but—"

"No," he said quietly. "It wasn't your imagination."

Moments passed as Jerri's eyes studied his. She tried to form a question but found that she couldn't. Instead, she concentrated on the movement of his throat as he swallowed and slowly began to speak.

"I've always thought of you as—" He placed the mug on the coffee table, then looked back into her eyes as he smiled faintly, self-consciously. "I know this must sound pretty

odd, too, but I think I wanted you to assure me you were a
real woman. Instead of some perfect little lady."

"No," she whispered. "It doesn't sound odd at all, Tyler, not considering the way I am—or at least the way I was
until yesterday, it seems. I'm not trying to be perfect, really,
it's just that I've always tended to keep my emotions to myself."

"Ah," he said, the lightest teasing smile curving his lips.
"At last, an understatement."

"Yes," she murmured, clearing her throat. "But there's
nothing normal about the way I've been acting since you
arrived yesterday, and I think that's why I've been so on
edge. It's giving up smoking, for one thing. I'd still pay a
thousand dollars for a cigarette." She smiled softly in resignation. "But there's more to it than that. Somehow you've
been forcing me to feel things that I've never... Well, since
you've been here, I've been experiencing some emotions I
never knew I had. Or maybe I knew they were there all along
but I was afraid to let them out. Some of them felt
good—" she took a deep, steadying breath "—and some of
them were really painful, like anger and—"

Jerri stopped the sentence, realizing she couldn't admit to
jealousy. "But for some reason, no matter which kind they
were, afterward I realized that it felt good just to allow myself to experience them, just to let them out and see what
they felt like. Maybe you've helped me discover that I am
real."

Judging by the expression on his face, he seemed to understand what she'd been trying to say, even though she
didn't fully understand it herself.

"I am real, Tyler," she whispered, still watching him as
he looked deeply into her eyes. "And about the kiss—" Her
fingers toyed with the fabric covering her thighs. "It was
one of those feelings that was good. Really, really good."
Glancing away, she felt his gaze drawing her back. "I did
enjoy it."

He reached out, his big hand spanning and caressing her cheek, his fingers brushing into her hair. "So did I."

Jerri covered his hand with hers, basking in the warmth and pressure of it against her face, her hair. She turned her cheek and kissed his palm.

"Thank you," she murmured, "I'm glad you did."

Realizing what she had done, Jerri released his hand. It had seemed such a natural movement, almost like reflex action. "I just wanted you to know that before you leave."

She stood then, feeling awkward as she moved back to the card table.

"What are you working on?" he asked, as if they had just finished talking about the weather or the stock market or the current status of soybean commodities. As if there hadn't been a word said about his leaving.

"Something I brought with me. A long-term project to keep my mind occupied."

"What is it?" he asked.

"An outline I'm working on, trying to refine."

He picked up his coffee cup and moved to her side. "An outline for what?"

"A book—a proposed book, I guess I should say—on art therapy for children. We do some work with kids at the museum. Field trips, things like that." He moved closer, looking over her shoulder, and she tried to concentrate on her file folder instead of on the hand he'd propped next to it ... instead of on the sprinkling of dark hair on the backs of his knuckles. "That's what got me interested in the subject in the first place." As she felt his warm breath touching her, Jerri wondered for a fleeting moment if any of her words were making sense. "About three years ago I started taking evening classes, extra courses in psychology, and I think I've come up with a different approach of sorts."

"Hmm. Sounds like heavy stuff."

"No, not really," she said, her voice reflecting the excitement she felt about her idea. Until now, she'd kept it to herself. "That's what makes it different, in fact. It's a layman's approach for ordinary parents to use with their children, something to help normal, healthy kids channel some of their tendencies in more constructive ways."

"That does sound different. Marketable, too." He seemed to be genuinely interested and, at the same time, momentarily puzzled. "But are you doing this in conjunction with your job?"

"No. I'm doing it on my own, which is why it's a long-term project. I don't have much free time to devote to it." Still unnerved by his nearness, she closed the file he appeared to be busy reading, the one with her list of chapter headings, and waved her fingers. "It's probably just a pipe dream, anyway."

"From what I saw it looks great, and parents love that sort of thing. Why don't you take steps to make it a reality?" He walked back across the room, taking a seat on the sofa. "You said you're not happy with your job. Why don't you quit? Give your full attention to the book?"

She let out a short, incredulous laugh. "We're not talking about a hot best-selling novel here, Tyler. People wouldn't exactly be stampeding to their bookstores and trampling one another to get a copy. Even if I could finish it—even if I were lucky enough to find someone who wanted to publish it—the advance probably wouldn't cover the cost of typewriter ribbons and postage!"

"So that's it," he said, smiling. "You're afraid you'll have to lower your standard of living for a while."

"No, of course not! I can't just quit my job, though. I have obligations. Expenses."

"Afraid you can't make it without your manicurist? Your maid and your doorman?"

"That's ludicrous, Tyler." Thoroughly perplexed by his remark, she stared at him as he shook his head.

"Poor little rich girl."

"You . . . you think I'm rich?"

"Let's just put it this way," he said as he leaned back and continued to study her. "I think you've been pampered a bit too much—to the point where you don't know the difference between reasons and excuses.''

She tilted her head and pushed out a loud, weary sigh. "This is what truly amazes me about you, Tyler. You make all these quick, easy judgments without knowing anything about me!"

"I know enough."

"Like what, for instance?" When he didn't answer immediately she stood up, still smiling in disbelief as she grabbed the side of her old blue robe. "In case you haven't noticed, I'm not exactly dripping in diamonds and furs." She held up her other hand, her eyes searching the room. "Do you see any personal servants flocking around here, falling at my feet, ready to do my bidding?"

"Cut the sarcasm, Jerri. I'm talking about your fancy private schools and that cushy job you won't leave even though you hate it."

"You're kidding!"

"No, I'm not kidding."

"Let me set you straight on a couple of things, Tyler." How could he appear to be so darned calm, she wondered, when she wanted to wring his gorgeous neck? "I work hard at what you seem to think is a 'cushy' job. It doesn't pay a fortune, but I have valid reasons for not leaving it just to pursue something as insecure as a dream. And just because I attended private schools doesn't mean I'm some . . . some shallow little debutante who's been mollycoddled all her life. If you think for one minute that I chose to live in boarding schools and dorms all those years, then you're mistaken."

Fighting against the sudden pang of sadness she felt, Jerri managed to keep her tone even and cool. "My mother worked like a demon to send me to the best private schools, but she had her reasons, too—although I've never agreed with them. She wanted to make sure I met 'the right man,' so I wouldn't end up marrying someone who'd leave me struggling all my life the way she's had to do ever since my daddy died. She has this absurd theory that's based on where she's convinced she went wrong. She was madly in love with my father, but he wasn't worth a dime, so she's spent a lifetime trying to drum it into me that it's just as easy to fall in love with a rich man as it is a poor one. But that's my mother's theory, not mine.''

The way he was sitting there watching her, letting her go on and on without so much as a word of argument, was making her even more upset with him. But how could he argue with her when she was doing nothing more than stating the truth?

''In fact,'' she added, her voice rising as she crossed the room, ''if you'll recall, my ridiculous fascination with you started when you had nothing more than a few acres, some loose change in your pockets and a toddler to rear all by yourself!'' She stood over him, her hands at her waist as her voice continued to rise. ''I have no idea what your financial situation is now, Tyler, and I really don't care. But back then I don't think you had enough money to furnish the inside of an outhouse!''

He reached up then and grabbed her wrist, pulling her down to his lap. Before she could protest he had his arm around her back, holding her body against him while his other hand slid behind her neck.

With infinite ease and provocative tenderness, he lifted her face and brushed his lips against hers. Every muscle in Jerri's body seemed to relax as he held her, as he kissed first one corner of her mouth and then the other. Her arms went around him, one palm cradling the back of his head as he supported her weight, the fingers of her other hand slipping inside the neck of his soft shirt to share the heat of his body. He felt so good, she thought, so right.

Her lips parted under his, inviting the moist warmth of his tongue, encouraging its sure, swift search for hers. The room...the world...seemed to be spinning, tilting at an angle, and when his mouth finally left hers to skim along her cheek, to travel in slow motion to her neck and then down to the sensitive spot he'd discovered at the base of her throat, she fought to control her heavy, ragged breathing.

"What . . . what was that all about?" she managed to ask when he held her back from him momentarily, his gaze locked with hers.

"That was my way of saying I'm sorry," he murmured, his own breathing raw and uneven, his lips still only inches from hers. "Apology accepted?"

"Yes," she whispered, a soft smile on her face as he let her fall back gently and, in the same smooth movement, positioned himself next to her on the narrow sofa. He bent his knee, one long, powerful leg covering her thighs as he stretched out on his side. "Yes, of course," she answered, her eyes searching his as he propped himself on his elbow and gazed down at her. "But why did it bother you so much, Tyler, when you thought I was—"

"It didn't bother me," he said quietly, his free hand reaching to stroke her flushed cheek, to comb through her hair. "It was just an assumption, that's all."

There was more to it than that, she decided as she relaxed further, her breathing more controlled as she took in the sedative of his purely male scent. But possibly he wasn't ready to share his reasons with her. She reached up, her fingers tracing the faint scar at the edge of his eye as she realized how very much she didn't know, how very much she wanted to know about Tyler Reynolds.

"I've always been intrigued by this scar," she said, her voice barely audible over the hissing fire, the movement of her hand almost as still as the room itself. "How did you get it?"

"Just a fight I was in," he answered, his head dipping so that he could wash a stream of tender kisses along her temple. "When I was a kid."

His breath was hot and gentle against her ear, sending electric shock waves up and down the length of her body. Jerri smiled, reveling in the feel of his hard warmth pressing against her softness. "Why were you fighting?"

"It was nothing important," he whispered, then lifted his head and smiled down at her. "Look, Smoky, what I really want to do is kiss you again. So for the time being, can we skip the small talk?"

"Small talk?" she asked, swallowing against the air that was suddenly trapped in her throat. "You mean the kind of talk people engage in when they're getting to know each other?"

"Yeah," he murmured, "but there's a time and place for it."

"And when might that be?"

"Any time but now," he answered dryly, still smiling as his mouth began lowering toward hers.

Jerri rolled off the sofa and stood up, looking at her wristwatch and then at him. "It's almost time for you to leave, Tyler. But you're welcome to stay for breakfast if you like."

"That's it?" he asked, scrambling to his feet and following her to the kitchen. "Just like that? I've done my duty? I'm dismissed?"

"Yes." She turned to face him, making a conscious effort to keep her words calm and her expression blasé. "As far as I'm concerned, you've fulfilled your obligation, so you can leave any time you like. The twenty-four hours is almost up."

"Not yet, it isn't! I promised you twenty-four hours and that's what you're going to get. If nothing else, I'm a man of my word!"

"That's not necessary, Tyler." Proud of herself for keeping her composure for a change, Jerri noticed that Tyler's jawbone was flexing, while a vein in his neck looked as if it might burst. And he'd actually been yelling.

"The purpose of your staying," she continued, "wasn't just for you to get to know about me. I realize this probably sounds outlandish to you, but I wanted to get to know you, too. You're obviously not willing to give me that, so why don't you just leave?"

His jaw was stretched tight as he paced the floor, then stopped and gave her an odd, suspicious look. "If I leave now, you're liable to backslide and start smoking again." He poked himself in the chest. "You think I want that on my head?"

"That's why you're here?" she yelled back at him, her temper coming quickly to a full, rolling boil. "You think I can't be trusted?" Her hand shot up from her side, gesturing toward the landscape beyond the kitchen window. "You think I have a pack of cigarettes stashed in a hollow tree trunk or something?"

He crossed his arms in front of him, looking disgustingly smug. "A whole carton, for all I know."

"That's a prime example, Tyler! If knowledge about each other were leather, collectively we couldn't saddle a flea!"

"The inside of an outhouse," he muttered irritably. "Saddle a flea! Where do you come up with these good-ol' country expressions of yours?"

"My mother was raised on a dirt farm in Oklahoma, but of course you wouldn't know that!"

"There's one thing I do know." He ran his fingers across his scalp, breathing deeply in an obvious effort to control his anger and keep his voice level. "You're the damnedest woman I've ever met."

"And you, mister, beat anything I've ever stepped in!" Her fists were clenched, and she propped them on her hips. "Now! How's that for a two-bit country expression?"

"Perfect. I just wish I'd used it first—when it crossed my mind last night!"

She straightened, her chin held high as she pointed toward the kitchen door. "I'm going for a walk, to get that carton of cigarettes I've had hidden away all this time. And when I get back, I expect you to be gone so that I can enjoy every last one of them."

"Fine!" Tyler yelled at her as she flounced out of the kitchen. "No problem."

Not even bothering to close the door behind her, Jerri pulled her robe close to her body as she stepped gingerly across the caliche drive, trying to ignore the biting cold, the rocky surface poking up through her socks, and Tyler's final declaration resounding behind her.

"Give me three minutes—four, tops," she heard unmistakably, "and I'll be out of your hair once and for all!"

Four hours later, Tyler flung open the kitchen door and slammed it shut before throwing his gear on the table.

"Not one word from you until I'm through," he demanded, his eyes threatening Jerri as he tossed his hat aside and headed for the parlor.

Hell, he decided as he glared at her, she was just as bad as he was. There she was curled up on the sofa, looking all sweetness and light—holding a book that was upside down, for God's sake—and pretending she hadn't given one thought to what had been going on between them the whole time they'd been together.

"Just what I need," he said, grabbing the book and turning it right-side-up before shoving it back into her hands. "Some smart-mouthed woman giving me a bunch of lip and thinking she has to call all the shots. Well, I don't mind telling you, I've had enough!"

"But, Tyler—"

"For once in your life, Smoky, just shut up and listen to me." He paced the floor, his fingertips propped low on his hips. "I've got something to say, and whether you like it or not, you're going to keep your mouth shut long enough to hear me out!"

Her gray eyes widened, her spine stiffening against the cushion that was propped haphazardly behind her.

"Before I say it, though," he went on, pointing emphatically toward the bedroom, "you can just march yourself in there and change into something decent. I'm tired of looking at you in that robe."

With a defiant look on her face she raised her chin and said, "I was just getting ready to change, anyway."

"You always have to have the last word, don't you?" he muttered, then watched as she got up and calmly headed for the bedroom.

She closed the door, leaving him standing in the middle of the parlor shaking his head. That idiotic getup she had on wasn't fit for a scarecrow, yet every time he saw her in it he wanted to peel it off her and drag her into the nearest bed. And that was exactly what had had him questioning his sanity for the past four hours. He kept picturing the way the tightly tied sash showed off her full, perfectly shaped breasts, her narrow waist, the gorgeous curve of her hips. The soft undershirt she'd worn beneath it was long, but not too long, and he was certain that she was completely nude underneath it. He kept remembering the flash of smooth, firm thigh he'd started watching for every time she walked... and the warm, just-right pressure of her breasts when he'd held her against him.

Tyler shook his head again, trying to clear the visions from his brain. If he'd been having erotic fantasies about Jerri Davenport wearing a slinky dress with slits clear up to there—or even a garter belt and spike heels—he could have felt halfway sure about his sanity. But an old blue bathrobe and glittery ski socks? It didn't make one lick of sense!

Then again, he told himself as he pulled off his coat and threw a couple of logs into the stove, nothing that had been happening since yesterday had made a lick of sense. From the moment he'd arrived they'd been fighting constantly about everything and nothing—when what he wanted was to make love, not war.

Jerri flounced back into the room then, dressed in dark jeans and a baby-blue sweater and, thankfully, what appeared to be a bra underneath it. Without a word she took her place on the sofa again, bringing up her shapely, long legs and clasping them in front of her.

"You've screwed up my fishing trip, but I'll be damned if I'll let you screw up my life," Tyler declared. He crossed the room once more, rubbing his jawline. "I hate to admit it," he said as he turned to her, "but I've just been struck by this crazy notion that I might be attracted to you—that, God forbid, I might even *like* you."

"Really?" she asked, her voice quiet, her expression one of surprise—or was it satisfaction?

"Yes, really!" He resumed his pacing. "Don't worry, though. There's a solution." He halted and glared at her. "Do me a favor and let me stay awhile—just long enough to drive me completely over the edge with your fancy words and your sarcastic, pushy, never-risk-anything ways." He raised his hand, his index finger slicing out in the direction of the kitchen. "Not to mention your six hundred pounds of creature comforts in there!"

"But I don't understand, Tyler. What was it?"

"What was what?" he asked, his patience running out.

"What was it that made you think you like me?"

"There! There's another thing I forgot to mention—that damned curiosity of yours. Hell, if you had an audience with the Queen of England, the first thing you'd probably ask her is what she's got in that purse she always carries around with her. And you know what she'd tell you?"

"No," she answered, her eyes getting big and round. "I've always wondered about that! What *does* she have in—"

"Geez, Jerri! I don't know. I was just using that as an example. To make a point." He stared at her, breathing a little unevenly, and finally remembered the point he had intended to make. "The Queen would tell you the same thing I'm fixing to tell you: there are a few things in this world you don't have to know. Some things are none of your business. Now shut up and let me finish."

"Fine." She crossed her arms in front of her breasts, then lifted her proud chin again. "Go right ahead."

"As I was saying, just let me stay for a while. I can guarantee you it won't take long. If you'll give me—oh, I'd say twenty-four hours would *easily* do the trick—I'm sure I can get you out of my system once and for all!"

"I don't know, Tyler," she answered, looking wary all of a sudden. "Maybe that's not such a good idea."

"Well," he stated disgustedly, "if that doesn't beat all. Who was it, just yesterday, who was bragging about being such a 'good sport'? After I gave you the time you asked for, this is the least you can do for me, wouldn't you say?" He flashed her a phony smile, something like the one she'd given him the day before, and added, "I'll even take the couch—to show you what a good sport I can be."

"Hmm," she pondered, glancing off into the air and finally shrugging her shoulders. "Well, maybe you're right... about owing it to you, I mean. And what could it hurt, now that I'm—" she flipped her wrist "—now that I'm positive I'm over my silly crush on you." Her back straightened then, and she gave him a stern look. "But only on one condition."

"What's that?" Tyler asked, then watched her grin smugly before she reached down and smoothed the cushion beside her shapely legs.

"I get the couch."

He stared at her in disbelief. There she was, trying to call the shots again. He didn't know whether he wanted to laugh or pull his hair out.

Dammit! He had a project going, a dream of his own, and there was no way he could start making it a reality until he took care of this unfinished business with Jerri. His concentration was down to zero thanks to those erotic daydreams he'd been having about her.

His eye caught the movement of her hand as she patted the sofa again. In those daydreams, he reminded himself, neither one of them was doing any sleeping, and her palm sure wasn't stroking a damned couch cushion!

He glanced at his watch and set a new time limit for himself. To hell with twenty-four hours. If this was the way she wanted to play it, he'd let her think she had the upper hand. If that's all she thought it would take to make her happy, fine. Because he had news for her. During the past few hours, he'd made up his mind about what would do them both a world of good. He had a plan, and whether she knew it or not, sometime in the next couple of hours, by two o'clock this afternoon, she was going to be taking a very active part in it.

Yeah, he reminded himself, he had to get this unfinished business out of the way so that he could get on with his life. It was definitely what he needed. Let her sit there looking smug, he thought, because he knew he was right about what she needed, too. Maybe she didn't know it for sure, just yet, but she'd find out soon enough.

"Okay," he said, smiling right back at her. "No problem. That lumpy old bed will do just fine."

Chapter Seven

Jerri took another bite of her lunch, a simple meal of Western omelets that Tyler had prepared quickly, easily and beautifully. Considering the speed with which he'd finished eating, he must have been famished, but Jerri still hadn't savored the last portion of hers.

Tyler put his plate in the sink, then refilled their coffee cups and once again took a seat across the table from her.

"Thanks," she said, grasping the warm mug between her hands and trying to concentrate on the steam billowing up from it. Still elated that Tyler had come back less than an hour before, demanding his own day, Jerri hadn't been able to keep herself from gaping at his ruggedly handsome face throughout lunch. "I've done my share of gourmet cooking, but I can't make an omelet like this. It's absolutely delicious."

"Nothing to it," he said, ignoring his coffee long enough to reach down and unzip the bag that held his gear. He handed her a yellow legal pad and a pencil. "Here. Feel free to take notes."

"Notes on what?" she asked, setting aside her coffee as she automatically took the two items he gave her.

"Notes on the questions you're getting ready to ask. You've been sitting there dying to ask me Lord-knows-what, so go ahead and ask."

"No! I don't need this." She held the writing implements in the air, a nervous laugh escaping her throat as she tried to hand them back. True, she was eager for details about Tyler's life, but the last thing she wanted was to get caught up in another argument with him. She still couldn't figure out how all the others had started, or how her plan had gone haywire from the very beginning.

"Oh, yeah," he commented, a teasing smile on his face as he took the pad and pencil from her outstretched hand. "I forgot about that memory of yours."

"That's not what I meant, Tyler. If I wanted to grill you, I would've started an hour ago, when you walked back through that door." Beyond that, Jerri told herself, she darned sure wasn't going to mess up this new opportunity. She was feeling rather sure of herself after hearing Tyler's confession about liking her, about being attracted to her, but she wasn't feeling *that* confident. No. This time around, she was going to be subtle.

She picked up her fork again. "This really is the best omelet I've ever eaten. Who taught you to cook like this?"

He leaned forward, grinning as he propped his chin against his big hand. "My dad."

"Oh. I thought it might've been your mother."

With his expressive, dark blue eyes he gestured toward the pad of paper beside his elbow. "Are you sure you don't want this?"

"Of course not, Tyler." She waved her fork and glanced down at her food. "I'm simply making polite conversation."

"Ahh," he said, drawing out the word. "And here I was, thinking it was 'small talk.' I guess I was confused there for a minute."

She decided it would be best to ignore the comment. Slowly she chewed another bite, then asked, "Was your mother a good cook, too?"

"I don't think so. From what I've been able to gather, she wasn't very good at anything." He stopped then, raising his index finger alongside his cheek. "I'll take that back. There was one very basic activity she must've been pretty good at."

Jerri clamped her mouth shut, not knowing what to say.

He sighed deeply and settled back against the chair as if he had finally decided to relax for a few minutes and join in the conversation. "I never really knew my mother, Smoky. She ran off with the propane salesman before I was three years old."

"I...I'm sorry, Tyler," she murmured. "That must have been terrible. The propane—"

"Come on, Jerri!" Evidently the look on her face was one he found amusing. "I thought you knew all these old country expressions. I didn't mean that literally."

"Oh," she said quietly. "I'm sorry. I didn't—"

"You don't have to be sorry. It's okay. I'm okay." He smiled and lifted a shoulder. "It's not even a very interesting story. But you seem to want to know, so I'll tell you." He propped one boot heel on the extra kitchen chair, then leaned back against his laced fingers.

"When my dad and Cotton were just kids, they took off and went out to Colorado—breaking horses, trapping, doing whatever they could do to scrape by while they were having a wild and woolly time, deciding whether they wanted to be men or boys."

Jerri smiled as she watched him glance upward and laugh, a sincere, touching laugh that must have been set off by remembrances of old stories his dad had told him as a child.

"Anyway, he met her in Denver. Her name was Elise Tyler, and she was nothing but a kid herself—impressionable enough, I guess, to be captivated by a rugged daredevil of a cowboy. When she got pregnant with me, Dad tried to do 'the right thing by her' and brought her back home with him. He started raising cattle on the little piece of family land that's mine now. He wanted to marry her, but she kept putting him off. Evidently she was never happy here.''

How very sad, Jerri thought, that Tyler's mother had cared so little that she'd left her lover and her child, her namesake, only a few years after giving birth to him. Jerri wanted to know all there was to know about Elise Tyler, but she managed to sound casual as she touched her fork to the omelet. ''Why wasn't she happy, I wonder?''

''Who knows for sure?'' He lifted his shoulders again and went on. ''They were too different, I guess. So maybe he just couldn't hold her interest.'' He seemed so far away, she realized. He could have been telling the story of total strangers instead of his own parents. ''Whatever the reason, after I was born she started looking for greener pastures—someone with more land, more money. My dad's brother had never gone through a 'wild and woolly' stage, so he'd accumulated quite a lot by that time. He'd buckled down and by then his ranch was thriving, so apparently she found him a lot more interesting.''

Beth's dad? Jerri wondered, pushing back her shock as she tried to remember whether there were more than two brothers in the family. Surely there was another one, she decided. Elise Tyler couldn't have run off with Charlie Reynolds: he and Beth's mother had been happily married for years. In fact, they'd had a big thirtieth anniversary party the previous summer. And Tyler was only, what? Thirty-four? ''But you said Elise ran off.''

''She did. A couple of years later, I guess—when things didn't pan out for her here.''

Thinking about Tyler as a young boy, forced to share his father's bitterness, was enough to break her heart. ''Your dad told you all of this?''

"Heavens, no," he answered, his tone matter-of-fact as he picked up his coffee. "He only told me the good things about her, the things he seemed to want to remember. I think he always blamed himself, at least partially, for not being able to make her happy. Keep her down on the farm, as they say."

"Then how do you know everything that happened, Tyler?" She put down her fork. "Surely your dad's brother wouldn't have told you."

"No, of course not. When I was about fourteen I found a handful of letters my dad thought he'd hidden real well. They were written to my mother, signed with nothing but a very distinctive capital C." As soon as he said it, her eyes widened with renewed curiosity. "I never knew if she left them behind intentionally, to hurt my dad, or because she was in a big hurry when she took off, but it really doesn't matter. In fact, I was glad I found them, because I finally knew why there had been such a falling-out between my dad and his brother. They'd been real close ever since they were kids, but all that had changed around the time I was five or six, which must have been when Dad ran across the letters himself. I guess it was easier for him to hate his own brother than it was to hate her."

"Then besides the brothers—and your mother, of course—you're the only one who knows what caused the rift between them?"

"Yeah, as far as I know. I burned the letters right after Dad died, and I've never told anyone what was in . . ." His expression suddenly changed to one of suspicion. "And now I'm trying to figure out what made me tell you about them." He pointed at her, his eyes intense. "Charlie made a mistake, but he's not such a bad guy, and I don't ever want any of this to get back to him or his family. I swear to you, if you breathe one word of this to Beth, I'll—"

"Oh, Tyler, of course not! You can trust me. Beth's the dearest friend I have in the whole world. Telling her would only hurt her. All this must have happened before her parents ever even met, and they seem to love each other deeply." She reached out, her hand grazing the top of his. "I would never want to hurt Beth. You have to believe that." As he drew his hand back she looked directly into his eyes. "And I would never want to hurt you, Tyler."

"It wouldn't hurt me," he said quickly. "It happened. It probably sounds pretty sordid to you, but it's nothing more than a fact of life. This sort of thing happens to all kinds of people, all the time, so you can quit looking at me like that."

"Like what?"

"Like you want to jump up and come over here. Like you want to hold me to your breasts and—"

"I'm not pitying you, Tyler, if that's what you think. You were telling me; I was listening." And learning, she added mentally, waving her fingertips in an offhand gesture.

Just hearing what he'd said about his mother, she felt she'd learned volumes. Why should he automatically trust Jerri Davenport, when he'd conditioned himself to distrust women in general? In fact, she decided suddenly, she knew exactly what she needed to know. All this time he'd been fighting with himself, not with her. He was beginning to trust her—otherwise, he wouldn't have told her a story he had never shared with anyone else. But he didn't *want* to trust her.

"Look, Smoky, you asked about this scar." He pointed to the faint outline along the edge of his eye. "I'll tell you about it, and then we'll move on to something else. In junior high, some kid called me a bastard and I didn't like it. I lit into him with my fists, and he lit into me with a rock. It's as simple as that." He leaned back and went on, his tone reflecting his healthy acceptance of the situation. "It used to bother me when I was a kid, but I'm a big boy now. I've had plenty of time to figure out that people are fallible, and that I have my own life to lead. I wasn't the first person to be born out of wedlock, and I certainly won't be the last."

"For heaven's sake, Tyler!" Jerri said, her tone both sincere and incredulous. "You think I'm feeling sorry for you because of that?" She frowned a mild reprimand. "That sort of thing happens in every family, doesn't it? And even if it didn't, why would I want to waste my time feeling sorry for you, when you obviously have it all worked out in your own mind?" She fluttered her eyelashes. "I'm not some fragile little flower whose sensibilities are easily shocked, you know. In fact, if it'll make you feel any better, I'll be the one to change the subject."

She lifted her index finger. "But first, there's one last question I just have to ask." She gave him a playful leer. "What'd the other kid look like? After the fight, I mean."

He laughed, shaking his head. "You're somethin' else, you know that?"

"Well?" she asked, prompting him with her hand. "Tell me. What did he look like?"

"Trust me, Jerri," he said, his teasing tone assuring her he was again at ease. "You don't want to know."

"Okay, then," she grumbled. "I'll leave that one alone for now—but we may get back to it later." She glanced at the ceiling, as if she were plucking a topic from somewhere in the air. "Your ranch is close to here, isn't it?"

With his thumb he pointed over his shoulder, toward the hill that loomed behind him. "Just a few miles over."

"What do you have? Cattle?"

"No. I quit trying to raise cattle several years ago."

"Why?"

"I got tired of fighting a losing battle. I never had too much land to work with, so it wasn't exactly lucrative. Or even fulfilling."

"What, then? Horses?"

"Water, mostly."

"You raise water?"

"I guess you could say that, although it's actually been there all along. Crystal-clear spring water, great for drinking."

He seemed much more comfortable, Jerri realized, now that he was talking business instead of emotions. She questioned him with her eyes, urging him to explain.

"After the stock show auction in San Antonio a few years ago, I went to dinner with a couple of big, burly cattlemen from Corpus Christi, and they both ordered bottled water." He chuckled, then shook his head. "I thought they were crazy, but then I looked around and noticed how many other people were drinking the same stuff. It amazed me. It didn't taste as good as my own, from the springs, and that's when I got the notion to do something with it besides watering cattle."

"You mean, you have your own bottling company?"

"Yeah. I started out with the bare necessities, doing most of the work myself, but I've got several employees now. And oddly enough, Corpus Christi's ended up being my biggest market."

"Why Corpus? Are people there more health-conscious?"

"No more so than anyplace else," he stated, quirking his eyebrows. "But during dry weather, they buy a lot of bottled water to help conserve the municipal supply. And during wet weather, the heavy rains wash all kinds of unsavory things into the lake that feeds their system and the tap water starts tasting and smelling pretty potent."

"Is it sold everywhere?" she asked, fascinated by the way that, with a little ingenuity, Tyler had turned a struggling cattle ranch into what sounded like a success. "In restaurants, too?"

"Anything from The General Store—" he pointed in its direction "—to high-class eateries in New York City and Los Angeles. Not exactly everywhere, but quite a few places." He stood up and crossed to the refrigerator, then came back with two small bottles clasped between his knuckles. "Right here, in fact."

"You mean, Nirvana is your brand?" He nodded, as if it were nothing, and she flattened one palm against her breastbone. "I can't believe it! I drink this all the time, Tyler." She laughed then. "I guess you must know that already, though, since I brought it with me. They sell your water in every grocery store in Houston. Every restaurant!" She turned the bottle around, reading the back label. "All it says is Nirvana Bottling Company, in the Texas Hill Country. I had no idea this was you." She set the bottle down with a thump. "I've always thought the claim on the label, that it tests out purer than the imported brand, was why Nirvana is so popular. But for some reason I thought it was only sold in Texas. You must be some kind of a marketing genius."

"No," he stated simply. "I just worked hard, I guess. Developed the right contacts along the way."

"You said you had 'several employees.' How many?"

"Over thirty."

"And... and when I asked what you raised, you said 'water, mostly.' Just exactly what else do you do on that modest little ranch of yours?"

"That's all. That and a few TV commercials."

"A few *national* TV commercials, I suppose?" she said, laughing as she rolled her eyes.

"Uh-huh." Again, he seemed totally blasé about the whole thing. "The jeans commercials—the ones with the cowboy riding a horse, with the hills in the background and—"

"And the gorgeous, glistening, bubbling springs, with the sunlight bouncing off the water?" she asked, still dumbfounded. "Right? The ones they show about fourteen times during every prime-time show?"

"You really are the queen of the overstatement," he said, then shrugged his shoulders. "I do all right for myself."

"I guess you do!"

"Yes, and if you'll pick your teeth up off the floor, Jerri, you can probably finish eating." When she looked at him questioningly, he went on. "Does it shock you that much that I'm able to make a decent living for myself? That the local yokel made good?''

"No," she assured him with an amused sigh, letting him know she was amazed with herself, not with him. "I've just had this completely different picture of you all these years. The struggling cattle rancher, eking a living out of the land, raising his daughter all by himself. That sort of thing."

"Well, I hate to mess up your image of me, Smoky. But I guess I'm what might be called a fairly successful businessman."

"Speaking of which...am I keeping you from something, Tyler? Do you have some important meeting to attend?"

"No," he answered, looking perplexed. "Why do you ask?"

"Well, it's just that in the last few minutes you've glanced at your watch several times, and—"

"I was just checking the time." He leaned forward, then cleared his throat. "The sun was bouncing off the crystal, so I had to look several times before I could read the hands, that's all."

"Oh. All right." She watched as he put his fingers to the watch, illustrating his point by moving the face back and forth. "Well," she continued, "I don't mind telling you I'm fascinated by your success story. More than that, I'm actually inspired by it."

"That's going a bit far, don't you think?"

"No, I don't! In fact, it's amazing what you've made me realize about myself in just one day. I think I should take a lesson from you."

"A lesson?" he asked warily, glancing at his watch once more then covering the face of it with his palm. "A lesson about what?"

"About my book, and what you said about reasons versus excuses. You helped me realize that, regardless of my job with the museum, I've been afraid to actually write it, afraid to take the big risk instead of simply dreaming about it." In the four hours Tyler had been gone, Jerri had replayed every minute they had spent together, reexamined every word they had exchanged. "I think I've always felt safe doing what I thought the world expected of me, being the good little girl, the dutiful daughter." She lifted her shoulders, tilting her head as she gave him a tiny smile of admission. "The perfect lady, as you so astutely called it. If I wanted something badly enough, I always managed to get it by following the safe, secure, socially acceptable channels of hard work and perseverance. I've never rebelled or taken any chances in life, and maybe it's time I did. Even if it means I might fail."

Tyler smiled knowingly, raising his eyebrows. "Or you might succeed."

"Yes! And that's exactly what I mean about inspiration, Tyler. Starting your businesses undoubtedly involved a lot of risks, financial and otherwise. And just look at you now. I think it's wonderful that you've made such a success of your life. While I've been floundering, petrified of doing something that might bring failure, you've been busy doing it—turning all your dreams into reality."

"Come on, Jerri!" He seemed irritated all of a sudden. "What makes you think I've got all the answers? Done everything I set out to do with my life?"

"I don't, really, but I do think you have a right to be proud of all you've accomplished so far, of all the chances you've taken to get where you are." She smiled, hoping her explanation would make him less edgy. "That's what I've always admired about you, you know—your maverick spirit." She lifted her hand, ready to own up to all her possible motives. "Maybe there was some envy in there, too. But nevertheless, I've always admired the way you seem to do exactly what you want to do, the way you say to hell with what the world thinks."

"I think you're glamorizing it, Jerri. That's not how it always goes. It's true, sometimes I do what instinct tells me is right. But sometimes I do what I plain old have to."

"Regardless of what you say, I admire you. For some unknown, unfounded reason, I've always admired you. Hearing what you've done with your ranch simply affirms what I've thought about you all along."

His jaw flexed as he frowned. "I didn't tell you about my businesses to get your admiration. You asked; I told you."

"Oh, I know that. I just—"

"Then why don't you quit going on and on about it? Admiration is not what I want from you, so why don't you just save it?"

"Is that so bad? That I think you're—"

"Look, Jerri, there's a lot you don't know about me." He leaned forward, jabbing himself in the chest. "I'm just a man, an ordinary man with an ordinary man's needs, and my life isn't the perfect little picture you seem to want to paint in that head of yours."

"All right," she said quietly, vowing to stay calm as she picked up her plate and walked to the sink. "I never said I thought you were perfect. But I do admire you, and if for some reason that upsets you, Tyler, then I'm sorry I ever brought it up."

"And quit apologizing to me!" Glaring at her as she moved around the kitchen, he bounded out of his chair. "What the hell are you looking for?"

"Rubber gloves." Still confused about what had set him off, she kept her eyes and hands busy. "To wash the dishes."

He started pawing through one of the cardboard boxes she still hadn't unpacked. "Are you sure you've looked everywhere? Behind the pasta machine? The fondue set?"

"Well," she stated. "Look who's getting sarcastic now."

Ignoring her, he moved to the second box and rummaged through it. "Maybe they're under the encyclopedias or the VCR!"

Taking several deep breaths, Jerri leaned back and pressed the heels of her palms against the counter's edge. "I don't know why my possessions bother you so much, Tyler, but I'll be glad to explain them. For too many years I never had a real home, and I've been trying to capture that feeling with 'things.' Granted, I'm finally beginning to realize it hasn't been too effective, but that's my problem, not yours." Lifting her chin, she crossed her arms in front of her. "And while we're talking about excess baggage, why don't we discuss what you seem to be carrying around with you?"

"Meaning?"

"Meaning, you seem to have some kind of giant chip on your shoulder, and I don't think it has anything to do with me. Whatever your problem is, maybe you should think about working it out on your own time instead of taking it out on me."

"Great," he mumbled under his breath. "Go ahead." He threw his hands into the air and started pacing the kitchen floor. "That's just what I need! Some woman with a few courses in psychology under her belt, ready to analyze my every word and move."

Frowning at him, Jerri slapped her hand against the countertop. "You know, Tyler, I'm sorry now that I didn't bring a VCR with me. Because right about now I wouldn't mind watching something a little more soothing—a tad more pleasant, shall we say—than some of the conversations we've been having."

"Like what, for instance?"

"Oh, I don't know," she answered, flipping her wrist. "*Nightmare on Elm Street*, maybe."

"And maybe I could stand to watch *The Taming of the Shrew*!" He stopped pacing, his fingertips propped on his lean hips. "Maybe that'd give me a few pointers on how to deal with you!"

Refusing to let tears come to her eyes, Jerri spun to the sink and begin filling it with water and dishes. She heard his boots as he started toward her, then stopped.

"I . . . I'm sorry, Smoky," he said from behind her, his voice suddenly quiet and under control. "That remark was stupid and uncalled for."

"You don't have to apologize to me, either," she said, shutting off the tap water.

"Yes, I do. You're going through a rough time right now, and I certainly haven't been making it any easier."

Jerri bowed her head, smiling as she closed her eyes. Even though he didn't think so, he actually had been making it easier for her. How could she worry about cigarettes, when she was going crazy trying to figure out Tyler Reynolds? When she was realizing how she still felt about him, how she was afraid she would always feel about him?

Again she heard his footsteps. And again she heard them stop, as if he wanted to touch her but was afraid of what might happen if he let himself do it. As if he were fighting an internal battle about walking across the room and simply putting his arms...

Her eyes opened, her smile taking on a new light as she raised her head. It was exactly the way he'd acted about trusting her! she realized all of a sudden. He had started to trust her, but he refused to let himself allow it, for fear of the same thing happening to him that had happened to his dad.

She straightened and glanced at her watch. He was going to fight it tooth and nail; she knew that. But maybe, given a little time, she could calm his fears.

No, she decided, she wasn't going to waste time feeling sorry for Tyler Reynolds; she had other things to do. He didn't seem to be wasting any time feeling sorry for himself, and she wouldn't, either. He seemed to have accepted what had happened so many years ago with no hard feelings toward Beth's family. What had happened truly seemed to be water under the bridge as far as he was concerned. It had simply left him with a sour taste in his mouth when it came to women who wanted to get close to him.

Well, Jerri told herself, she would take care of that soon enough!

"I'm fine, Tyler. Really I am." She turned, smiling brightly at him. "I can take sarcasm almost as well as I can dish it out." Especially, she added mentally, when I know the reason behind it.

She watched as he started pacing again, looking like a caged animal. His jaw was working a mile a minute, and it suddenly dawned on her that anger wasn't the only emotion that made his jawbone flex that way. He was stewing over something, and the knowledge of it gave her an extreme sense of satisfaction, an overwhelming sense of calm. He was fretting over how he was beginning to feel about her. He had used sarcasm for the same reason she'd been using it—to fight her own feelings about him, to keep herself from being hurt if he didn't return those feelings. Now the tables had been turned.

The sensations that flooded her at that very moment were nothing less than exhilarating. She had never felt more feminine, more powerful.

And why hadn't she realized this before now? she wondered. She wanted Tyler, he wanted her—it was as simple as that. Earlier in the day, on the sofa, she had sensed how she affected him.

Jerri bit the insides of her cheeks, trying to keep her smile from looking smug. Who was she kidding? When he'd had his leg over her, pinning her to the sofa, she had plain old felt how she affected him. The evidence had been pressing against her hip.

And at this very moment he was trying his best not to look at her for more than a few seconds at a time—raking his fingers across his scalp, pacing, then stopping and then starting again. Poor helpless man, she thought, realizing she had no choice but to give him some time to himself. Considering the state he was in right now, her conscience wouldn't allow her to just . . . back him up to the refrigerator and take advantage of him.

"Tyler," she said, trying to sound nonchalant, "the way you were looking at your watch, I can't help believing you have some business matter on your mind."

"Well," he said hesitantly. "Actually, there is this project I'm supposed to be getting a start on, but—"

"Then why don't you go on and get it started? I'm sure that would make you feel better, and I can always use the time to work on my book." It sounded reasonable, she decided, then panicked when she realized her wording had also sounded vague. He might think she was suggesting he leave for good! She thought fast, then held up her hands in a gesture of surrender. "You realize, of course, that I'm only suggesting a few hours' postponement—a break between rounds, so to speak. I know you're not about to let me cheat you out of the twenty-four hours you asked for."

"That's right," he answered emphatically, his spine straightening as he squared his broad shoulders. "There's no way I'm going to let you squirm out of our deal. You still owe me. But as long as we're clear on that fact, I guess it wouldn't hurt for me to take off for a while." He checked the time, looking thoroughly satisfied with the new plan. "After all, we've already gotten a good start here. By noon tomorrow, I'm sure I'll have you out of my system once and for all."

No way, mister. Not if I can help it. Again Jerri chewed the insides of her mouth, then smiled cheerfully as she replied out loud.

"Good. It's settled, then." She checked her own wristwatch, making a mental list of all the preparations she needed to make—and all the primping she wanted to do while he was out. "I can have dinner ready by seven. Will that give you enough time?"

"Sounds perfect," he said, heading for the door. "Seven o'clock, it is."

"Seven o'clock," she repeated firmly, giving him a goodbye smile as he reached for the knob. "I'll be ready for you."

Jerri stood at the sink, watching him saunter unsuspectingly toward the Jeep. As he got behind the wheel, she wondered if he realized he hadn't thought to take his hat and coat.

"I love you, Tyler," she whispered, her lips barely moving, her smile softening.

There. She had said it. She had admitted it, and it felt fantastically, unbelievably good—as if a tremendous worry had been lifted from her shoulders.

There was one sure way to prove to Tyler how much she loved him. And she knew beyond a shadow of a doubt that once she had shared herself with him, he would feel differently about trusting her.

"Go ahead, darling," she murmured, smiling confidently as she watched him turn the Jeep around and peel out of the drive. "Spin your wheels all you want, because that's all you're doing. Spinning your wheels."

Still smiling excitedly, she pivoted toward the bedroom. She had things to do before he returned.

Jerri smothered a sudden giggle as she realized the irony of the situation. He was taking off from here thinking he was simply preparing himself for the next battle—but that was fine. Because she knew better. He could fight her till the cows came home, but she wasn't going to back down. She knew exactly what he needed, and as soon as dinner was out of the way, she was going to make absolutely sure he got it!

Chapter Eight

Tyler slammed the book shut and sighed as he pitched it across the desk top. He pushed back, leaving the leather swivel chair and moving toward the far wall of his study. It was a sad day, he decided as he folded his arms over the window frame, when a man didn't feel at ease in his own home.

For the past three hours he'd been trying to keep his mind occupied, attempting to start on his project. But it was a hopeless cause. What he needed right now, he decided with resignation, was to back up and regroup, to shore up his defenses before he went back for the next "round" as Jerri had called it.

There was one thing he could be thankful for, he thought as he stared out at the hilly terrain. He had the house to himself. As soon as he'd left the cabin he'd stopped at a pay phone just to check in and see how things were going on the home front. Cotton had been ready to leave the house to run errands, and Sam was scheduled to stay after school for basketball practice. As soon as Tyler heard they'd be eating in town afterward and wouldn't be back till seven or eight, he had hotfooted it home—fully intending to spend a few peaceful hours on what he'd been meaning to do on this damned fishing trip in the first place.

But for the umpteenth time he had realized he couldn't concentrate on the task at hand.

He breathed deeply, getting past the smell of fine old leather before he decided his study still held the faint odor of tobacco. Lord! he thought, how good it smelled. If he were smoking a cigarette right now, maybe his mind wouldn't be dwelling on the sweet smell of flowers. The scent of gardenias mixed with the scent of . . .

Tyler shook his head and frowned. It was driving him nuts, this unfinished business with Jerri. And what could he do about it now? At noon he'd stormed back in there, ready to have his way with her and then simply get on with his life. But then she'd started being all the things she was: curious as all get-out and gorgeous and clever and funny—and downright caring and understanding. And then she'd started admiring him, for God's sake.

Sure, he'd wanted to rip her clothes off her and give her what he'd decided she needed—what he knew *he* needed. Once he'd gotten a taste of her, he'd been like a starving man who couldn't get enough. He wanted to taste all of her; he wanted her to taste all of him. . . .

But he wasn't a complete heel, either. Only a cad could think about being casual about making love with a woman like Jerri Davenport. And that was exactly what'd started clawing at his gut. There was nothing casual about the way he felt when he was with her.

No, he hadn't been able to go through with it. If nothing else, he had a sense of honor. Over and over again Jerri had pushed him, and that comment about "excess baggage" had done the trick. She had finally made him realize he'd been judging her unfairly from the minute he first laid eyes on her, and that's when he'd been forced to engage that sense of honor. All this time, all these years, he'd been intent on trying to convince himself that Jerri was just like Pauline. But she wasn't—in the exact same way that Samantha wasn't.

He moved to the bookshelves across the study, his eyes settling on the photo of his daughter. He picked it up, a laugh escaping his throat as he studied it. Physically, Sam was the spitting image of her mother, but that's where the resemblance stopped. And rightly so, since when it came to Pauline, that's all there had ever been—a physical surface. A haughty, classically beautiful surface, draped with beautiful clothes, surrounded by beautiful things, and not one lick of substance underneath. No character, no goodness, no nothing.

Outer surface, he thought. That was what he'd been concentrating on all this time. That was where he'd gone wrong. From the minute he'd laid eyes on Jerri so many years ago, he'd zeroed in on the physical similarities: the way she carried herself, the way she spoke so perfectly, so formally. He had wanted Jerri Davenport from the minute he first saw her, but he'd told himself there was no way on God's green earth that he was going to let himself want another woman who was just like Pauline.

Tyler moved back to his desk, laughing out loud as he visualized Jerri flouncing around in that old blue robe. No, Pauline wouldn't have been caught dead in that getup. Beyond that, she couldn't have carried it off. Jerri, on the other hand, could probably throw on a feed sack and still look like a queen at her coronation. God, how he admired her.

"Dammit," he muttered. That was the problem right there. That admiration crap, and all that stuff about what he'd made her realize about herself, all that stuff about her book and reasons versus excuses. For some reason, when she'd started in on that, he'd thought about what she'd said about her mother wanting to make damned sure she ended up with the right man. And he couldn't help wondering what her mother would think of her at that exact moment, locked away in a secluded cabin with a man who, at age thirty-four, had only received his high-school diploma a few months before. When it came to reasons versus excuses, somehow he didn't think Jerri *or* her mom would buy his reasons for dropping out of school way back then. To someone who had graduated from college with honors— something he knew didn't come easy—an ailing ranch and an ailing parent would no doubt sound like the flimsiest of excuses.

And maybe they were, he decided all of a sudden. Maybe he'd put other things first for too many years. Or maybe he could've worked harder. If he'd worked harder, he would already have all this behind him.

Tyler opened the file folder on the desk, his fingers tracing the logo from Trinity University in San Antonio as his gaze moved to the body of the letter: the conditional letter of acceptance for the spring term that would begin in only a few weeks. And everything hinged on getting through the college entrance exams he was supposed to be cramming for now, since they would be taking place next Saturday.

He reached up then, counting the pages of his desk calendar as he flipped through them. After the twenty-four hours he'd asked for were up, he would have ten days to study intensively—so that he could accomplish what he'd been wanting to do for ten years. Whether due to reasons or excuses, it had taken him a full ten years to get his life to the point where he could start turning this particular dream, his ultimate dream, into a reality. Until he did turn it into a reality, he and Jerri would still be worlds apart.

She had sat right there across the table, going on and on about how much she admired him. And that's what had done him in. He had suddenly realized that that *was* what he wanted. As much as he wanted her, he wanted her admiration. She was admiring him without knowing everything she needed to know about him. But what was he supposed to do? Burst her bubble?

She was too inquisitive for her own good; she just *had* to know everything. But dammit, there were things he didn't want her to know, and whether she was aware of it or not, she didn't want to know them, either. She was intent on admiring him—intent on clinging to her illusions about the way he had turned his dreams into reality. She needed to be inspired, to finish her book, and if that was the one decent thing he could do for her before his twenty-four hours were up, then that was what he would do.

Beyond that, he reminded himself, Jerri was no Marty Cunningham. She wasn't the kind of woman who'd just casually fall into bed with a man and then kiss him good-bye when he up and left her the next day. She deserved more than that, and now that he'd resigned himself to that fact, everything was going to be okay. He'd march himself back there and get it over with. No true confessions. No bursting of Jerri Davenport's bubble.

"Yeah," he said out loud, confirming his decision. He would just go back there and act like the perfect gentleman, and if there were things she didn't know about him, fine. At least he'd leave there at noon the next day with his pride intact, knowing she still admired him. That was what was important to him. And considering the way Jerri had gushed about it, that was what was important to her, too.

Tyler glanced at his watch. He just had time to study for an hour or so and then clean up before going back for dinner. He'd get his mind on scholarly things, he decided, instead of the tightening in his groin every time he thought about Jerri Davenport.

He leaned forward and opened the book, thumbing through a couple of pages and then slamming it shut again.

"Dear Lord," he mumbled aloud. "Let her be wearing anything tonight—" he covered his eyes, trying to erase the vision "—anything but that damned blue robe with nothing underneath."

Tyler pushed back from his desk, realizing that studying wasn't going to cut it. He'd just have to switch tactics, move on to Plan B. He headed down the hallway and into his bedroom, checking his watch again.

Yeah, he decided, nodding confidently as he rubbed his aching jaw. No problem. Tomorrow would arrive soon enough, and he could get back to his studying then. For now, he had enough time to take three, maybe four cold showers.

Five to seven.

Jerri stood in front of the full-length mirror in the bedroom, her hand at her waist as she casually rolled her hips to one side and then the other. The outfit she had chosen—and altered—was a long lounging dress made of a jersey fabric that was just clingy enough to be interesting. And just clingy enough to rule out undergarments, even if she had wanted to wear any.

She filled her lungs to capacity, her breasts lifting as she tied the sash a fraction tighter. Leaning forward from the waist and taking in the view of her cleavage, she decided she could afford to unbutton one more button.

After doing just that, she turned and reached for the manicure scissors, making the slits she had already fashioned in the seams an inch deeper on first one side of the dress and then the other. Midthigh was good, she decided, her hands smoothing the fabric as she studied her reflection once more.

A little brazen, perhaps, Jerri told herself, the corner of her mouth slanting upward as she lifted one shoulder. But that was the point, wasn't it? After all, Tyler was off somewhere preparing for battle—girding his loins. And she was here, ungirding virtually everything she had while she waited for him to return.

"Okay, kid," she said into the mirror. "This is it." She slowed the words, practicing, trying to make them sound deep and throaty. "Just keep telling yourself you've done this a thousand times before."

All right, she admitted inwardly, making a face at her own image. So she hadn't done it a thousand times before. So what? The way she felt right now—after thinking about Tyler all day, anticipating his lovemaking—she had herself almost convinced that she was relaxed about the whole thing. And the way she looked right now, Tyler didn't have to know she was…a little nervous inside. He didn't have to know most of her private schools had been girls' schools. And he certainly didn't have to know that in the years since she'd graduated from college, she hadn't spent her Saturday nights seducing droves of men.

True, she told herself as she pivoted and left the bedroom, she was a little inexperienced at playing the vamp. But he was a man and she was a woman. And the mere thought of it was enough to make her feel warm. Inside and out.

The parlor was dark except for the dim flicker cast by the wood-burning stove, and Jerri moved quickly to the kitchen. Opening the oven, she smiled as she took in the aroma of dinner, then flipped on the small fluorescent strip over the sink and turned off the overhead light.

"There," she said aloud, assuring herself there was nothing she hadn't thought of, nothing that could possibly spoil the mood she'd worked so hard to set.

She heard the Jeep, then smiled anew as she noted that it was seven on the dot—just as she had known it would be. Determined as Tyler was, she thought with a laugh, he'd probably been parked at the foot of the hill until thirty seconds ago.

Jerri glanced down to check her appearance one last time as she heard the engine stop. Spotting a tiny thread hanging from the latest alteration along her left thigh, she grabbed a paring knife, snipped the thread and tossed the knife back into the drawer, striking a seductive pose just as she watched the turn of the doorknob.

"You really should keep this door locked, Jer—"

Tyler stopped dead in his tracks, his hand still on the knob, his eyes wide as he gaped at her. Jerri ignored her inclination to follow his gaze and scan the length of blue-gray jersey that alternately hugged and skimmed her body. Instead, she held her stance and smiled innocently—as if she didn't realize the quick gust of cold air had caused her nipples to harden.

He blinked twice and cleared his throat, then let go of the door to continue speaking in a nonchalant tone she knew was feigned. "I had no idea we were dressing for dinner. I would've worn a suit and tie."

"Heavens, no," she said lightly, ignoring the sarcasm she knew would cease soon enough. "You look wonderful just the way you are. Have you been home?"

"Yeah. Why do you ask?"

"You've changed clothes." She walked over to him, her hand reaching up to stroke his smooth cheek as she breathed deeply of his marvelous, masculine scent. "And it's obvious you've just showered and shaved."

Tyler took one step backward, as though her touch had blistered his cheek. "I do try to clean myself up on a fairly regular basis."

"And you do a fine job of it. You look wonderful." Smiling, Jerri took one step forward. "You should wear suede all the time." She lifted her hand, and he eyed her suspiciously as her fingers slid down the lapel of the sport coat he wore over a crisp white shirt and dark blue Levi's. "There's something sensual about the feel of suede, don't you think?"

"I never really thought about it."

"Well," she said airily. "I'm sure you're hungry, Tyler. Dinner's ready."

"Great!" he said, his tone far too enthusiastic. "I'll…I'll set the table."

"Oh, no. There's no need for that." She touched his arm, guiding him to the darkened parlor and watching as his eyes adjusted to the flickering light before he focused on the card table she'd prepared for dinner. Luckily, she'd been able to find an old white sheet—now folded into a makeshift table-cloth—and two storm candles that were waiting to be lit.

"Someone's birthday?" he asked wryly.

"No," she said, leaving his side to pick up the box of kitchen matches and lean provocatively, just as she'd practiced earlier in the day, to light the candles. "No, I just thought I'd try to make dinner festive. After all, by tomorrow night, you'll be out there in the wilderness." She glanced up and smiled softly. "Surviving. Providing."

"That's right," he answered happily, as if he couldn't wait. "Eating beans out of a can, the whole bit."

"Yes, so I thought I'd give you something nice to remember me by—" she held the match within inches of her mouth, looking directly into his eyes as she blew out the flame "—while you're out there roughing it."

He took a step toward the table, and Jerri made a quick move to stand behind the correct chair. "Why don't you sit here, Tyler?" She stood back as she pulled it out for him. "I need to be close to the kitchen, since I'll be serving." *And since I want you to have a good view of everything on to-night's menu.*

"Sure," he said, hesitating a moment before taking his assigned place.

Her hand lingered on his shoulder, and a complete sense of satisfaction settled over her as she realized her plan was working beautifully. His answers had all been clipped, his comments either matter-of-fact or sarcastic, his looks either leering or jittery. She felt perfectly calm now, and here he was acting like... Well, she decided as he shifted to move away from her hand, like a cat on a hot tin roof.

Jerri swished out to the kitchen, then turned toward the stove and out of Tyler's sight. Her steps quickened as she headed for the oven, grabbing pot holders to retrieve the two plates she'd portioned out and kept on "warm" since ten minutes before seven.

When she got back to the parlor, Tyler was studying the wine bottle, turning it toward the candles in an attempt to read the label in the dim light.

"I hope the wine will be all right." She set down each of their plates, then dropped the pot holders onto the coffee table before taking her own place. "It's all I had. Just an inexpensive brand I usually use for cooking."

"I'm sure it'll be fine." His line of sight moved from the food on his plate to the empty jelly glasses and finally, pointedly, to her. "When it comes to meat loaf and 'country crystal,' I think almost anything goes."

He poured the wine, giving each of them precious little before raising his glass to the level of one candle's flame.

Jerri lifted her own glass, returning his silent toast and his carefree smile. And as soon as they had each taken a sip, she poured more wine, filling both glasses half-full.

She picked up her fork and began to eat, then announced that she'd forgotten the butter for the baked potatoes. On each of her three ensuing trips to the kitchen— slow, sensual, convenient trips to get first the butter, then the salt, then the pepper—Jerri made a point of bending from the waist when she stood up and then turning to the side and leaning to drop and eventually retrieve her napkin from the seat of her chair.

Before and after each mission, Tyler smiled at her as if he hadn't noticed a thing. Between trips, he seemed to be busy himself. He was watching every bite she had enough time to take, all the while eating slowly of his own portions, pushing his food around on the plate. Playing with it, studying it, putting his fork down between each bite. Finally she couldn't stand it any longer.

"Is there something wrong, Tyler?"

"Wrong?" he asked casually. "What could possibly be wrong?"

"With your dinner, I mean."

"No, it's delicious. Why?"

"The way you seem to be picking at your food, I thought maybe—"

"No, no. It's wonderful." He put his fork on the plate again. "I'm just making it a point to savor every bite."

"Oh. Well, I'm glad you like it." She chewed another smidgen of meat loaf, then asked, "Did you get a lot done?"

"On what?" As soon as he asked the question, he seemed to realize what she was talking about. "Oh, yeah. I got a good start, anyway."

"What is it you're working on?"

"A new project." He waved his fork. "Something I've put off for a while, but it's time I got it done."

"What kind of a project?"

"Actually, I'd rather not say." He smiled. "Nothing top secret, of course. It's just not developed to the point where I can talk about it."

"Oh," she commented. "Well, that's understandable."

They continued to eat in silence, exchanging polite smiles. Jerri was halfway finished when she noticed that Tyler was finally chewing his last bite of food. She put down her fork and stood, carrying both plates to the kitchen.

"I think I'll have brandy in my coffee, Tyler," she called from the kitchen. "What about you?"

"No, thanks," he answered. "But I wouldn't mind some of that cappuccino you were trying to peddle last night."

To hell with cappuccino, Jerri told herself as she flipped the switch on the coffee maker. She had already prepared it for the plain coffee she thought he preferred, and now that her plan was moving along so smoothly—nearing the pinnacle, she realized, grinning with excitement—she wasn't about to waste precious time making changes.

"Sorry," she called out to him, "but I think there's something wrong with that setting."

When she returned to the parlor, Tyler was still seated at the card table. She held up a brandy bottle, then placed it on the coffee table along with two small glasses.

She took a seat dead center on the sofa and patted the cushion beside her. "I think I'll have my brandy while we're waiting for the coffee." She poured herself a generous dose, then held the bottle over the second glass as she watched Tyler advance toward her. "Are you sure you won't join me?"

"Positive," he said, covering the top of the glass with his hand. "I'll just wait for the coffee. But thanks, anyway." He sat at her right, his spine pressed against the arm of the couch as he gave her an odd look. "So," he stated flatly, raising one eyebrow. "Have you got a bus to catch?"

"No," she answered, her head tilting in curiosity. "Why?"

"I just wondered." Blithely, he lifted a shoulder. "The way you're herding us through this meal, I thought maybe there was someplace you needed to be."

"No," she answered, laughing breezily. "No, I'm here for the night." She scooted closer to him, letting the sofa drag on the jersey covering her bare skin. "Here for the duration, as they say."

Good heavens, Jerri thought, realizing again how clean and manly he smelled, fighting the urge to fan herself as she exhaled noisily. Reaching for her glass, she took a gulp of the potent brandy. It was getting unbearably hot in here, she decided. What would it be like if she'd worn any extra garments under her dress?

Tyler grabbed the jersey fabric, covering the leg that had just been exposed for his benefit. "You're liable to catch cold wearing this, Jerri. Why don't you go put on something more substantial? Jeans and a sweater, maybe?"

"Don't be silly." She grinned at the thought of it. Catch cold? How could she possibly catch cold when her flesh was going to start melting any minute now? "I'm fine, and I want to wear this. After all, I'm a woman. I happen to look good in things that are long and flowing."

"Long and flowing, huh?" he grumbled. "Then maybe I should take you out and throw you in the river."

"Oh, Tyler," she whispered playfully, wiggling even closer. "Come on now. You're just being sarcastic. And obstinate."

"Obstinate?"

"Yes, obstinate, and I know why." She pulled the blue-gray swatch aside again. "It's getting to you, seeing my legs like this."

"No!" He looked down, frowning as he brought the fabric back, trying to cover her left thigh but failing miserably. "It's not getting to me. It's not getting to me at all. In fact..." He glanced down, then rolled his eyes. "I've seen better legs in a bucket of chicken."

"Say whatever you like, Tyler, but I'm not convinced. I saw you ogling them."

"Oh? When was that?"

"You were trying to be subtle about it when I was bringing dinner to the table, but you were practically drooling."

"Yeah, I guess I was." His tone was wry, and his mouth kicked up at one corner as he shrugged his shoulders. "What can I say? I like meat loaf."

"Oh, so it was the meat loaf, was it?" she asked, her question a slow, teasing murmur. "Then why don't you prove it? To both of us. Why don't you just...let me kiss you?"

"No."

"Come on," she whispered, her hand circling his neck, her fingers combing through the hair at his nape. "One little kiss, Tyler. Just one. That's all it should take, don't you think? I mean, you are getting me out of your system, aren't you?"

"Sure." He kept his head back, fighting against the gentle pressure of her hands as she continued to hold him close. "Of course. So why should I let you kiss me?"

"Let's call it the ultimate test, shall we?"

"I don't need to put myself to some arbitrary test." He pried her fingers away from his neck and started straightening his jacket. Considering the sudden, almost suffocating warmth of the room, she knew he had to be hot, but he was just stubborn enough to refuse to take off his suede coat.

"Look, Smoky, I'm trying my best to be a gentleman, but you're making it mighty har—" He stopped abruptly, glancing away as he rubbed his jaw.

Ready to take advantage of the opportunity, Jerri slid her arms around his broad shoulders and crawled onto his lap. Gently she pressed her hip against him, searching for and receiving the evidence of his desire for her, taking the extra measure of confidence she was beginning to need.

"Yes," she whispered, smiling up into his beautiful, darkening blue gaze. "I know I am. That was my intention."

"Jerri!" He tried to hold her away from him. "What's gotten into you?" Frowning at her with a sudden look of suspicion, he gestured toward the brandy bottle. "You've been hitting that stuff all afternoon, haven't you?"

"No," she murmured, smiling slyly. "I'm in charge of all my faculties. But why don't you take charge of them for a while?"

"You are drunk," he said, still trying to keep her hip away from his hardness.

"No, I'm not, Tyler. And we've been over all this before." Her chin brushed against the soft suede before she whispered into his ear. "You're a man, an ordinary man with an ordinary man's needs. And I'm a woman—a woman you just happen to be very attracted to." Her mouth inched even closer, and she smiled as she felt his body tremble beneath her. "So why don't you quit fighting it? Why don't you just give in to what you really want, and let me kiss you?"

"You sound pretty sure of yourself." Still trying his best to appear disgusted instead of aroused, he pulled away from her hot breath and glowered at her. "Who do you think you are, anyway? The finest little filly in these parts?"

"No, Tyler, I don't." She smiled softly, then ran her tongue across her upper lip. "And stop reminding me of all the foolish things I've said to you, because it's not going to change my mind about what we both want. This morning, I got the distinct..." She cleared her throat, pressing herself against him once again. "I got the distinct impression that you wanted to make love to me. Is there something special I need to do to let you know I'm interested, too?"

"Dammit, Smoky, this isn't like you." He took her by the shoulders, trying to hold her back from him. "And I'll be damned if I'll take advantage of you just because you're drunk!"

She ignored the comment, her gaze locking with his. "Is it the dress? All wrong, maybe? Because if the slits aren't high enough, I can take care of that." She reached down, and the sound of a seam being ripped another few inches filled the room.

"Jerri! Stop that." He grabbed her hand. "Now, get a little control over yourself!"

"What kind of a wardrobe does it take to get your attention, Tyler?" A niggling sense of panic started working itself up from the pit of her stomach. She wanted him—desperately, feverishly—but how much longer could she keep up the fight when he seemed intent on making her believe he didn't want her? "What would you like me to wear for you? Spandex pants and a tube top?"

"And now you're getting sarcastic. You've never owned—"

"What, then? I don't mind being flexible, but you'll have to tell me, because I'm not very experienced at this sort of thing."

His spine straightened, and a dead silence hung over them as he watched her and Jerri tried to figure out the expression behind his eyes.

"What does that mean?" he finally asked.

"What?"

"That business about 'not very experienced.'" His tone was level—suddenly, unbelievably level. "Just what does that mean?"

"I told you! Not very experienced."

He grasped her shoulders firmly, trying to remove her from his lap. Somehow she ended up next to him, half sitting, half reclining against the sofa.

"What *exactly*, Smoky? Just how experienced—or inexperienced—are you?"

"What?" she asked, forcing a laugh. "There's one thing about me you don't know? One answer you don't already have?" She flattened her palm against her chest. "Gosh, Tyler! This comes as quite a shock."

"Stop being sarcastic, Jerri, and tell me exactly what you meant by that."

"I'm not being sarcastic, I'm being facetious. There's a big difference."

"And stop dodging the question!"

"All right, then. If you must know, and I gather you must, I'm . . . I'm fairly inexperienced."

"You're—" He narrowed his eyes, his body not moving a muscle as he stared at her. "Are you trying to tell me you're a—"

"What?" she whispered. "You can't even bring yourself to say the word?"

"Geez, Jerri!" He sprang to his feet and started pacing the floor in front of the coffee table. He ran his fingers through his hair, his jaw clenching as he glanced at her time and time again with the most ungodly look of disbelief. Or was it horror?

"Yes, Tyler," she said, her voice a hissing, raspy whisper. "Yes, I'm a virgin. And you can quit looking at me like that, like it's something too ghastly to comprehend!" Jerri scrambled to a sitting position, everything inside her trembling uncontrollably, pain clawing at her as she struggled for words, any words to combat his silence. "Why don't you just go ahead and say it? You were right about me all along.

I am real, but I'm not what you'd call a real woman. So why don't you go ahead and say 'I told you so'?"

"That's not what I was going to say!"

"Oh, no?"

"No. You have no idea what I'm thinking, Smoky, so quit—"

"All right then, tell me I've been a fool, waiting all these years because I thought the first time would only be perfect if Tyler Reynolds made love to me! That I've been stupid to hoard it like it was some...some precious gift or something."

"You're not stupid, Jerri." His breathing was heavy, labored. "For God's sake! I never said you were stupid."

Feeling as if she was dying inside, Jerri watched as he turned on his heel and made for the kitchen.

"Are you leaving?" she screamed, jumping to her feet.

He grabbed his key ring from the kitchen table. "Yes," he said, leveling her a stern look. "And I want you to calm down. I want you to give some serious thought to what you've been trying to do here. To what you're—" He pivoted, yanking open the door as Jerri yelled at him again.

"Tyler? Where are you going!"

"To get myself a pack of cigarettes!" He turned to face her, his voice clear and concise as it boomed across the cabin. "Do you want some or not?"

Barely waiting for the answer she shouted back at him, he slammed the door and was gone.

Chapter Nine

Jerri rolled over, rubbing her swollen eyes, still wrestling to get comfortable on the sofa. In her determination to fall asleep before Tyler came back with the cigarettes, she pulled the blanket over her head and shut out the faint, flickering glow from the stove.

Yes, she told herself as she punched the pillow again. She would show Tyler Reynolds who had willpower. True, she had let him goad her into screaming yes, but now she was thoroughly ashamed of herself. And true, she did want a cigarette, but she'd be darned if she would start smoking again just because of her wounded pride.

Hot, fresh tears rolled down from her eyes, and Jerri threw the blanket aside and reached for the box of tissues on the coffee table. How could she blame him for rejecting her, she wondered, when she had thrown herself at him so blatantly? She had acted no better than that red-haired floozy she'd been jealous of all these years. And now she would rather die than face him again.

"Stupid," she muttered, hurling the now-empty tissue box across the room as she admitted she'd brought all of this on herself. She'd been so hell-bent on following through with her amateurish seduction attempt that she had completely forgotten what Tyler had said only yesterday: that as far as he was concerned, Marty Cunningham was nothing but a tramp.

As she tried to choke back the sobs, she thought back in horror to what she'd admitted to Tyler only seconds before he'd grabbed his keys and left. In all her elaborate planning, she had never included telling him she was a virgin! Her plan had been for him to just take her up on her offer, to simply make love to her and find out for himself. She had wanted him to have proof—physical proof that in this case would also be emotional proof—of how much she cared about him, how very much she had cared about him all these years. She had simply wanted to prove to him that he could trust her.

Just because he'd told her the story of his parents, Jerri had made all kinds of assumptions. She'd based them on what he'd said about his mother without giving one thought to the other women in his past. The Marty Cunninghams and the...

And the mother of his child, she thought all of a sudden. In all the time she had known Tyler, his wife—his ex-wife by now, she assumed—had never been around, never even been mentioned.

Good heavens, Jerri thought. She didn't know the nebulous woman's whereabouts, or even whether she was dead or alive. She'd been so busy analyzing his every word and move that she had jumped on what he'd said about Elise Tyler—never taking into consideration the fact that he seemed to have a healthy attitude about her. At least he had been willing to talk about his mother. But not his wife.

Jerri stood up and made her way to the kitchen. She flipped on the light, still swiping at her wet cheeks, trying to see past her tears as she groped through each of the three cardboard boxes on the countertop.

"Dammit," she muttered aloud. She'd brought everything under the sun—everything except the extra tissues she needed so desperately at the moment. She hadn't used half of what Tyler had referred to as her six hundred pounds of—

Dear Lord! she thought, slumping over one of the boxes. That was something else she hadn't thought about: the way her belongings seemed to bother him so much, the way he had been offended when she'd seemed shocked that "the local yokel made good."

Jerri pressed her hands against her face, a new flood of regrets washing over her as she reminded herself of all the things she hadn't taken into consideration, all the things she didn't know about Tyler. Perhaps, for some reason, her possessions reminded him of his ex-wife. Back when he was young, he'd been struggling financially. What if his wife had wanted all the finer things of life, and he hadn't been able to give them to her? And if that was the case, perhaps his wife had done the same thing as his mother.

Her hand covered her mouth, her heart breaking as she thought about the possibility. Maybe his own wife had run off with the propane salesman—or whoever else had had the means to provide her with what she wanted!

Well, Jerri realized, sniffling as she turned off the light, squared her shoulders and headed for the bathroom, she could go on forever playing what-if and maybe, but it wasn't doing anybody any good.

She unrolled a length of toilet paper and blew her nose, promising herself these would be the last of her tears. And, she continued, finishing her mental pep talk as she turned toward the parlor, this would be the last of her wallowing in self-pity over Tyler's "rejection." He wanted her, she knew that; otherwise, why would a confirmed nonsmoker with a will of iron rush out into the cold and dead of night to buy himself a pack of cigarettes?

No, there was definitely something more to why he'd walked out on her.

Pulling her robe tightly around her, Jerri curled up at the end of the sofa, her legs folded close to her body. She brought the blanket up to cover her knees.

Yes, she decided, raising her chin. She was going to start acting like a real woman.

She would sit up and wait for him to come back. And then she would find out what she needed to know—what she had to know—about Tyler Reynolds.

Fifteen minutes later, Jerri watched in silence as Tyler opened and closed the kitchen door. He stood there for a moment, his eyes adjusting to the dim light before he walked into the parlor and stopped directly in front of her.

When he lifted her face to him, she held her breath for a split second . . . until she felt his warmth, until she saw the expression in his eyes.

The softest smile touched his lips as he leaned to caress her cheek, to kiss her hair before he straightened again and crossed the room. He stoked the fire, adding logs, and then turned toward the easy chair. After tossing a small paper bag onto the end table, he took a seat and leaned back, his long legs sprawled out in front of him as he propped the side of his boot against his knee.

Jerri waited, watching him from across the darkened room, listening while he inhaled deeply, then exhaled.

"Tyler," she finally whispered. "I don't want a cigarette."

"I know," he said, his voice low and steady. "I thought better of it while I was driving around."

"But . . . but there is something else I want."

"I know, I know." A small sound of amusement escaped his throat. "And now that we've both calmed down, I'm ready to give them to you."

"Give what to me?"

"The answers to all your questions. That's why I'm sitting way over here, instead of over there, where I want to be. So why don't I get things rolling?" He settled back, his fingers steepled over his hard, lean stomach. "Yes, yes and no."

She gave him a look of puzzlement.

"Yes, I wanted you to kiss me. Yes, it was getting to me, seeing your legs like that. And no, I wasn't appalled to hear you're a virgin. Just surprised, that's all." He tilted his head, smiling again. "And flattered, if you must know...and I gather you must."

"Thank you, Tyler." Pausing, she let herself enjoy the tingling rush of excitement that raced through her body. "I'm glad to know that. I needed to know that." She returned his light, playful smile. "But actually, there was something else I wanted to ask you first."

"Go ahead."

"Is there something about me that bothers you, Tyler?" Jerri lifted her shoulders before continuing. "Something that reminds you of someone else, maybe?" She stopped for another moment, realizing she didn't even know the woman's name. "Like, for instance...Samantha's mother?"

"That's not a simple yes-or-no question. But it was the next subject I planned to cover." His hand moved down the length of his thigh. "First of all, you were right about 'excess baggage,' and about none of it having anything to do with you." He leaned back against his laced fingers, his eyes never leaving hers. "And in answer to your question, yes, for a long time now, because of a few surface things, I've been trying to tell myself you were just like Pauline. But you're not. Not at all."

She remained silent, listening as he told her about the apparent similarities that had made him think she was another Pauline, then about his reasoning for denying his feelings for Jerri because of those similarities...because he hadn't wanted to be hurt again.

As she listened and watched, Jerri realized that even though Tyler was sitting across the room from her, she had never felt closer to him than she did right now. She had never felt happier than she did at this very moment, knowing that all these years he had felt the same way about her that she had about him—but more than that, knowing that he had finally resolved his reasons for fighting his attraction to her.

"How long were you together, Tyler? You and Pauline?"

"Not very long," he said, his dry answer followed by a short, bitter laugh. "Her family didn't approve of what they called my questionable background. Still don't, as a matter of fact. As it turned out, keeping company with me was Pauline's way of defying her parents, plain and simple."

"How...how cruel."

"No, not really," he said. "We were both immature, and I think I had my reasons for 'keeping company' with her, too. Her folks were socially prominent, old money, and I guess I wanted to show the Reynolds family—the whole world, maybe—that I was as good as the rest of them. My dad had just died, and I was still angry inside, resentful of the way he'd been treated like an outcast for so long—because of me, I thought at the time. It wasn't exactly reasonable thinking, but back then, that was the way I looked at it."

"None of it sounds unreasonable to me," she murmured. "Especially when you and Pauline were both so young. And it's a shame you had her parents' disapproval to deal with, too...along with everything else. That couldn't have made your other problems any easier, knowing your wife's parents didn't like you."

"She was never my wife, Smoky." He watched her closely, as if he were testing her for a reaction. "History sometimes repeats itself, and in this case, it did." When she lifted her eyebrows, showing him she was curious but certainly not horrified, he went on. "Pauline was naive, and by the time she knew she was pregnant—much to her dismay—it was too late for an abortion. I asked her to marry me, but she laughed in my face. Literally.''

There was no expression at all behind his eyes, Jerri decided. And she felt a deep sense of relief, knowing he had come to terms with it a long time before now. Knowing he wasn't still bitter over being rejected by a selfish, immature girl.

Pauline, Jerri decided, was a fool. "Did she just give Samantha to you, then? Just like that?"

"With a little pressure, I guess you'd call it. It didn't take much. I made a few threats; she got a little nervous."

"Then Samantha doesn't know her mother? She's never seen her or—"

"No," he answered, his tone matter-of-fact. "Pauline died in a crazy auto accident a couple of years after Sam was born. It was so wild and reckless, in fact, that you'd have to say she brought it on herself. And even if she'd made it through the accident, considering the way she was living, she probably never would've amounted to much. The way I look at it, there was only one decent thing she did in her whole life." He smiled, a soft, caring, heart-stirring smile. "She gave birth to a wonderful little girl. And then she did the right thing by giving her to me. For that, I'm grateful to her."

Jerri watched as he reached up, his big hand rubbing his face, wiping away the smile that had touched her soul.

He glanced her way again, giving her a sudden look of intensity as he continued. "I've said this before, and I'll say it again. When I was younger, there was a lot of this stuff I hadn't figured out. It bothered me then, but it doesn't now." He tilted his head. "And even though some people still look down their noses at me, I have no regrets. I've always known that Sam was the best thing that ever could've happened to me. It took a few years, but the responsibility of raising her eventually forced me to think these things through, to bring a sense of order to my life."

Realizing he was leading up to something more important, she waited without a word. And in that exact moment, while she waited for him to continue, Jerri realized
she was no longer infatuated with the perfect Tyler of her
girlish daydreams. She was in love with the real Tyler—a
man of infinite, tender strengths and understandable human frailties. A man whose body and soul she wanted to
experience, to share with her own.

"And if any of this bothers you, Smoky—" He stopped,
clearing his throat. "Let's just put it this way. I'm not usually a man of many words, but I made it a point just now to
answer your question fully, because there were certain things
I thought you should know about my life, before..."

"Oh, Tyler," she murmured, her heartfelt words reaching out to him, wanting to touch him. "How could it possibly bother me? Knowing what you've done, and how
much you love your daughter? Knowing how very much you
loved her and wanted her even before she was born?"

Earlier Jerri had promised herself there would be no more
crying, but she felt a single warm, joyful tear rolling down
each of her cheeks. "How can that possibly upset me?" she
whispered, smiling into the flickering darkness. "How can
it do anything but make me care about you even more?"

"Think about it for a minute, Jerri," he answered bluntly.
"It wasn't so noble, really—not considering my own upbringing. What if my dad hadn't wanted me?"

"Be modest all you want. But if nothing else, I think
you're wonderful just for telling me, just for thinking I had
the right to know about it... before you make love to me."

He rolled his eyes toward the ceiling. "That's not so noble either, honey, considering what's been going on in that
head of yours." He cleared his throat. "I was jittery enough
about this without having to worry about all the doubts you
had about me—about the way I've been treating you. Most
of making love is up here." He touched his temple. "And I
figured there were things that were crowding your mind,
things that had to be cleared up and gotten out of the way.

"Since I'm the first man you've chosen to make love with, you need to be able to trust me enough to relax with me. If that doesn't happen, I'll fail you. I won't be able to make this what it should be for you. So you see, I'm not being noble. I'm just . . . looking out for my reputation."

"Oh. Is that what it is?" As she watched his beautiful blue eyes, Jerri realized she might as well face it. Everything Tyler did only made her love him more. He was treating this moment lightly, on purpose, to keep her from feeling nervous. And she loved him for it.

"Yeah." His voice was a low, husky growl. "Now come here."

"Why?"

"Because I've been without you long enough. Too long. Because if I don't touch you within the next couple of seconds, I think I might die."

And, she decided as she moved across the room, closing the space between them, she knew everything she needed to know about Tyler Reynolds—to trust him, to give herself to him completely, to take completely of what he had to give her.

She stood close to him, beside the chair, and he simply reached up to take her hand, rubbing it with his strong, sure, gentle fingers as he smiled. Odd, she thought, the kind of feeling she had now: knowing they wanted each other, knowing they were soon going to have each other. Yet there was no edge of frenzy. Mingling with the desire she felt for him was the most wonderful, unbelievable sense of inner peace. She never would have thought it possible to feel like this.

His hand still around hers, he guided her in front of him, on top of him. She straddled his long legs, her knees pushing against the back of the big, comfortable chair. Her hands moved to stroke his back, and he cradled her face in his hands. He kissed the corners of her mouth, then held her away from him, leaving only the slightest distance between their faces. She breathed deeply, taking in the scent of him.

"I'm sorry I walked out on you like that," he whispered. "Forgive me?"

"Yes. Yes, of course. I'm just sorry I made you feel like you had to leave. I'm sorry I turned you off by—by acting like a blatantly obvious floozy."

"Nothing you could ever do would turn me off," he said quietly. "You can be blatantly obvious with me any time you like. As often as you want." He shook his head. "That's not why I left. I left because I needed a chance to think, to get some kind of control over myself." He released his gentle hold on her face. "I left because I was a wreck."

Her eyes brightened, and she smiled knowingly as she slowly unfastened three snaps at the front of his shirt. While weaving her fingers through the soft, crisp mat of hair, Jerri continued to watch him. She would never forget this night, she decided. This moment. The dancing light of the fire, their hushed voices in the near-darkness. The flame of desire she saw in his eyes. The warmth of his palm as he covered her hand, holding it against the wild, powerful beat of his heart. The look of his loving, teasing smile.

"Why?" she asked. "Why were you a wreck?"

"That announcement you made." He rubbed his jaw, grinning sheepishly as he made the confession. "I don't mind telling you, sweetheart. I got a little nervous just thinking about it."

"I'm sorry," she whispered. "I never meant to tell you that. I wanted you to find out for yourself."

"For God's sake, Jerri," he said quietly. "Why?"

"Because I thought if you knew beforehand, you might not want to..."

"Take advantage of you? Spoil your innocence?"

"Yes," she murmured, her voice hesitant as she went on. "I was afraid you might turn me down. I decided that if you found out afterward, then it would eliminate all that worry and just...make you happy, I guess."

He lifted her hand from his chest, holding her fingers against his lips as his gaze locked with hers. "It does make me happy. It makes me happier than I ever could've imagined. But I'm glad you told me."

"Why?"

"Because even though it made me nervous, I needed to know."

"Are you still nervous?" she asked timidly.

"No. I think I'm over it now."

"Good," she whispered, "because you don't need to be. I was so worried about what you'd think of *my* performance, I never realized you'd be worried about what I thought of yours." She laughed softly at her own naiveté. "And it doesn't really matter anyway, Tyler, because all I ever wanted was to *be* with you."

"And that's why I came back. Because I decided that's what I've been wanting all this time, too. To be with you. I don't want to have intercourse with you. I don't want to make love to you." She opened her mouth, ready to reassure him that she knew what she was doing, that she knew what she wanted, but he covered her lips with his fingers. "I want to make love *with* you. I want to be with you. And if the physical act of making love comes into it, that's fine; I hope it does. If it doesn't until later, that's fine, too. It wouldn't be easy, but I could deal with it." He cupped her chin, his thumb moving tenderly across her cheek. "So let's make a pact, huh? If it happens, it happens. Neither one of us worries about anything. Okay?"

"Okay."

"Here," he said. "I brought you a present."

She took the small paper bag he handed her, then opened it. A smile touched her lips when she saw what was inside. Since he knew she had never had to think about birth control before now, he had taken care of it for her.

He gave her a brief, wry smile. "That's so you won't have anything to worry about. In case it does happen."

"Oh, Tyler," she whispered, taking the package out of the bag. "This is the sweetest, most thoughtful gift you could ever..." She blinked once as she realized the box wasn't tiny. Standing up, she turned the front panel toward the light of the fire. "How—how many are in here?"

"All right," he admitted flatly. "That's just in case it happens... twelve times."

"Twelve times?" she asked, her eyes rounding as she smiled at him in disbelief. "Tonight?"

"God, no!" Laughing, he stood and swept her into his arms. "Be gentle with me, will you, woman?" he asked as he carried her toward the bedroom. "At least leave me breathing, huh?"

Grasping the box, she put her arms around him and held him tight, whispering against his collarbone. "I'll be gentle, darling. I promise."

As he carried her into the bedroom, she realized this was the moment she had dreamed of for so long. And now, more than anything, she wanted to know the moment was real. "Tyler?" she asked, her voice quiet and hesitant. "Could we... turn on a light? I want to be able to see everything. I want to be able to see you."

"Mmm," he said in agreement, smiling down at her. "I don't want to miss anything, either."

He set her down, near the bed, and she started to untie the sash of her robe.

"No," he said, stopping the movement by grasping her hands. "Don't move. Don't do anything until I get back."

He turned to leave the bedroom. But his scent lingered, enveloping her senses like a velvety caress. She watched as he walked to the kitchen and flipped on the light, then shed his suede coat and returned to stand in front of her.

"How's that?" he asked, gesturing toward the soft, warm glow spilling in behind him.

"Perfect," she murmured. "But don't you want me to take this off? Or... or wear something else?" She ran her palm along the blue chenille. "This can't be very sexy."

"Honey, this is the sexiest outfit I've ever laid eyes on." He lifted his brows, looking shamelessly rakish. "Ever since the first time I saw you in this thing, I've wanted to get your gorgeous body out of it and down on this bed—or any other surface that happened to be handy."

"You mean . . ." She glanced downward, then smiled up at him in sudden disbelief. "You mean 'Old Blue' excites you?" she asked, her quiet words filled with astonishment.

"No." His gaze never left hers, but she felt his hands as he released the sash from around her waist. "You excite me."

Her breath seemed to be trapped in her lungs. "So that's what was bothering you when you came back today? When you told me to put on something 'decent'?"

"Uh-huh. I was afraid if you left it on, I couldn't be held responsible for what I might do to you." His fingers slid under the faded blue lapel, bringing the robe past her shoulders so that it fell to the floor. Then his hand took her neck. And he leaned toward her to trail sensual, feather-light kisses along her temple. "I was afraid I might get *in*decent with you."

She felt the gentle sureness, the expertise of his touch and his mouth. Her fingers lost their grip on the package he'd given her, and it fell onto the nightstand.

He reached to turn back the linens for her. She slipped underneath, feeling the cool, crisp sheet as it dragged against the warmth of her soft T-shirt. Keeping the covers over her bare legs, she studied every movement he made—every slow, deliberate movement of his hands and his body as he began to undress.

As he released the snaps on his cuffs and loosened his shirttail, her eyes worked to memorize his broad, muscular chest and the dark pattern of hair that formed a provocative V into his jeans. His hands moved to the buttons below his lean waist, and she watched, spellbound, as he drew the denim down his powerful thighs. He stood before her, the light radiating from behind him as he prepared to join her on the bed.

"Please, Tyler. Don't stop now. I want to see...all of you." When he took off the last scrap of clothing left on his body, she swallowed the air that had been lodged in her throat, then touched her tongue to her suddenly dry lips. Her gaze traveled upward, from his magnificent body to his eyes. "You're beautiful," she whispered, her voice full of wonder.

"You're beautiful," he said in return, the length of his hard body now pressed against her softness. He lay alongside her, almost on top of her, as he gazed down into her face. "You take my breath away." His mouth came down on hers, branding her, capturing all of her senses in a kiss that seemed to reach deep down inside her, tugging at everything in her body. Her soul.

His fingers were twining through her hair, and hers through his. And when she felt him tremble, she experienced the most incredible surge of happiness. Happiness that his strong, hard, masculine body would react to her kiss, her touch, in such a way.

"Tyler?" she asked, gasping for air. "Would you like me to stop talking?"

"Oh, no," he said. "Absolutely not. I figure this is the best kind of foreplay for a woman like you."

"And what kind of a woman am I?"

"The damnedest, most inquisitive woman I've ever met." His hands were traveling smoothly, slowly, along the length of her legs. Up to her hips. To the sides of her breasts. "With every question, every answer—" His voice was low and husky. Inviting. "With every word, I can feel you getting hotter."

"I don't think it's the talking." She couldn't seem to stop taking in quick, jerky gulps of air. "I think it's the way you're touching me. In the most interesting ways, the most interesting places."

"Uh-uh," he murmured. "Not the most interesting places. I haven't gotten to the most interesting places yet." He found the hem of her soft white T-shirt, then reached underneath and brought it over her head and away from her body. "I want to touch all of you."

With excruciating slowness, his hands skimmed up along her burning-hot flesh to cup the weight of her breasts. "My God," he whispered, "you are beautiful."

The adoration in his eyes, the strength and gentleness of his touch, made her tense with desire, and she watched as his mouth descended to her shoulder, then to the roundness of one throbbing breast. His lips closed over her, his mouth and his tongue drawing first on that tight, sensitive nipple and then the other. She moaned his name as she held his head to her body.

Her voice was quivering and barely audible. "I want to touch you, too, Tyler. All of you."

Wordlessly he guided her toward him. He held her hand in place, pressing it against his arousal. And it seemed only natural for her fingers to close over him—exploring, tracing its shape, its length. Her eyes widened as he throbbed against her palm, and she released her hold on him.

His gaze was still intent on hers, and he smiled. "Don't worry, Smoky. I assure you, I won't break." Keeping her locked in the tender strength of his arms, he rolled her onto her side, their faces only inches apart. He brought his body closer to her then, his hardness straining against her. "There's nothing to be embarrassed about. You don't have to be timid with me."

He lifted her chin, his eyes searching hers. "And if I do anything that bothers you or frightens you, all you have to do is tell me."

"I'm not frightened." Her voice was a plaintive whisper, and she had to struggle for every breath. "I'm aching for you." She brought her leg over his, sliding it up and down, feeling the provocative friction of his hair against her smoothness. "I feel like I'm hot and liquid and..."

He reached between her thighs—finding her, stroking her, making her leg move faster, up and down along his. "Yes," he murmured. "Yes, you are."

"And there's this . . . this pressure. This throbbing heaviness inside me." She swallowed hard. "Like a slow-burning emptiness, deep inside, aching to be filled."

"That's good," he whispered. "That's definitely good." He continued to rub her, his strokes quick and sure and steady.

"I'm so excited, Tyler. I want you to—" She took him in her hand again, the rock-hardness of him causing her to draw in a sharp breath. She exerted more pressure on him, her hand moving along his length, her thumb and her nail grazing slowly over the tip of his arousal.

"Oh, God." His hand moved away from her, his body reacting with a wild spasm that he seemed to control almost as quickly as it had hit him. "Sweetheart?" he said, his palm closing over her hand, stilling its movement. "You have to stop that."

"Am I doing it wrong?"

"No," he whispered, a smile playing across his lean, rugged features as he shook his head. "No. You're doing it—" he took a deep breath "—absolutely right. That's why you have to stop."

In a sudden, desperate movement, she rolled onto her back and brought him with her, pulling his face down to hers. "Please, Tyler," she begged, her eyes boring into his. "Please! I want you to make love with me. Now."

He laced his fingers with hers, spreading their arms out to the edges of the bed. His dark blue gaze raked over her, worshiping her, and while he held her there, pinned to the bed, the sheer weight of his body seemed to make her breathing become less jerky and shallow.

"That's it, sweetheart," he whispered, his lips moving to the column of her throat. "Relax. Let yourself enjoy it."

Closing her eyes, she released her breath in a long, leisurely moan as she felt his hands slide down the length of each of her arms, felt his kisses on the sensitive area where her neck joined her shoulder, felt his fingers moving into her hair.

"Mmm." He uttered the sound against her flesh, and she opened her eyes as he reached for the nightstand.

Feeling his full weight on top of her again, she smiled softly, in sweet, blissful anticipation.

"Jerri?" he said quietly. "Promise me you'll tell me if it hurts too much, and I'll stop."

"All right," she whispered, her heartbeat lurching wildly as she studied the look of concern, the intensity in his beautiful eyes.

His mouth came down on hers then . . . and seconds later, he entered her. His lips, his tongue, felt as tender and loving and slow as the movements he made inside her body. She tensed against him as he held her, as she bit her lip to keep from screaming against the quick, sharp surge of pain. Pain that she welcomed . . . because it was over with, at last. Pain that was also joy . . . because it was Tyler who had given it to her, and that was how she had always dreamed it would be.

She moaned into his mouth—in relief, in happiness—and his thrusts became more forceful, more steady and sure and incredibly rhythmic. Her hips rose to meet him, over and over again, her tongue twining with his, and she suddenly felt herself . . .

"Tyler!" she whispered frantically, her voice pleading, and his movements halted. "Oh, God, I am frightened." She wrapped her arms completely around him, holding him tight, clinging to him. "I feel I might be . . . going over the edge." She sucked in a quick gasp of air. "Like I might faint or, or—"

"Oh, sweetheart," he whispered, letting her keep her hold on him. "That's okay. It's the way you're supposed to feel." His soft, hot breath fanned her hair. "You just have to let yourself go. Enough to let it happen."

Her fingers loosened their grip on him, and he raised up on his elbows. He steepled his hands atop her hair, and when his eyes met hers, she saw the reassurance in his smile...felt the reassurance of his mouth as it skimmed the outline of her lips.

His movements started again, ever so slowly, his gaze never leaving hers. Time was nonexistent as she let herself become lost in his eyes. As she heard his desire-roughened voice from what seemed like far away. As her body reacted violently, gloriously, to the mind-shattering tremors of ecstasy....

She moaned, crying out with every breath, her gasps rushing out—hitting against the hard wall of his chest. She felt his body tense completely, his muscles tightening, and then she heard his own release as he cried her name.

They held each other, their breathing still gasping and ragged, and she marveled at what had just happened. She had never felt such total love and sharing, such total give and take. She held him tighter, reveling in the feel of him as he stayed inside her, enjoying the rise and fall of his chest, loving the warm strength of his muscular body against her softness.

Minutes passed, and she listened as their breathing slowed gradually. In unison.

"Well?" he finally whispered.

"Well what?" she asked, laughing softly against his neck as she realized he was mimicking the dialogue they'd shared in the parlor after that first incredible kiss.

"Well?" He raised up and smiled devilishly, keeping a firm hold on her hips as he rolled them over. "How was it?"

"It was definitely worth waiting for," she whispered, her tongue sliding across her upper lip as she smiled down at him. "It was everything I ever dreamed it would be—and more."

Dear Lord, she wondered, would this be the way it would always be with him? It was such a wondrous combination: heart-wrenchingly serious and deliciously fun. And neither quality would be nearly as precious to her without the other.

"And what else?" he asked. "I can tell there's something else."

"It was everything I could've ever hoped for." She paused dramatically. "Except..."

"Except?" Pretending to be outraged, he gave her a playful slap on the fanny. "Except what?"

"Except that I wish it wasn't over with." She pressed her face against his throat, whispering to him. "Can we do it again?"

"Yes, sweetheart," he said, and she felt the rumble of laughter in his chest as she lay on top of him, her lips grazing the shadowy stubble on his cheek as he amended his answer. "Yes, we can—if you think you can wait a few minutes. I'm just a man, you know. An ordinary man."

"Yes," she said reverently, her heart threatening to burst from the happiness inside her. "And I'm a woman now. A real woman."

His expression turned grave, and he cradled her face in his big hands. "No, Smoky. You always were. You didn't need me for that."

Tyler watched her as she smiled and said nothing in return. She slid downward then, releasing him from the inner warmth of her body.

God, he thought, folding her into his arms and nuzzling her pale brown hair. She was so beautiful. So ready to share herself with him. So willing to trust him.

Tyler closed his eyes, dragging the sweet scent of her, the scent of their passion, into his lungs. And he let out a long sigh as he realized his instincts had been right.

After she had told him she was a virgin—that she had saved herself specifically for him—he'd left for a lot of reasons. He'd had to get away from her long enough to figure out a few things. Long enough to lecture himself about what he did or didn't have to tell her.

And while he was driving around, he'd decided that he owed her the basics: the cold, hard facts of his life that couldn't be changed. He'd told her enough about his past for her to know whether she could accept those things, the way he had so long ago. He had told her enough so that he would know, before they made love for the first time, whether she would be able to trust him enough to enjoy it.

And now, holding Jerri in his arms, remembering the drugged look in her eyes when she'd cried out his name over and over again, he was glad he'd done it that way. He was damned glad he'd decided to wait on telling her everything there was to know about him. He'd done it for her because this night was for her.

Just then he felt her stirring against him, felt the brush of her bare, still-taut nipples as they skimmed across the hair on his chest.

Yeah, he decided, his body tensing with desire as he gazed down and saw the wanton smile on her lips, nobility could wait. There'd be plenty of time for it later.

For now, all he wanted was Jerri. To be inside her again, surrounded by her. To feel her beautiful body beneath him, to see her gray eyes fixed on him...adoring him. To hear her soft, throaty voice as she moaned, begging him to—

"Tyler?" Her leg moved, putting just the right amount of pressure on the most sensitive area of his body. "I get the distinct impression," she whispered playfully, "you've given up on trying to be a gentleman."

"Yes, sweetheart." He drew her mouth close to his, still intensely aware of the silky-smooth stroke of her leg. "I just can't help it. You make it too hard."

Chapter Ten

You told me it would be wonderful, Tyler, but it's so much more. It's absolutely, breathtakingly... perfect.''

Tyler stood behind her at the top of the hill, his arms folded over her upper body to envelop her as she leaned back and relaxed against his chest. Wordlessly both of them gazed down at what had been his favorite view for as long as he could remember.

Located less than five miles from the cabin, Nirvana Lookout was on the very edge of his own property. But it had once been a place where, as boys, his dad and his Uncle Charlie had played together. When the ranch had been split between the two of them, this side had become his dad's. And from the time Tyler was nothing but a boy himself, he'd loved this portion of the ranch more than any other.

He rested his chin on Jerri's soft, shining hair, and she snuggled against his down-filled vest. Her arms were at her sides, her hands grazing the faded blue denim on the outsides of his legs.

"And you were right about something else," she murmured. "It's like nothing I've ever seen before."

Her touch, he thought with a smile, was like nothing he'd ever felt before. He had decided that last night, as soon as she touched him—even before they'd made love.

"I can't imagine it being called anything but Nirvana Lookout," she said. "It's so blissful, so peaceful and serene." Pausing for a moment, she inhaled a long, full breath of air. "And that smell is heavenly. What is it?"

He kissed the top of her head, sighing deeply after he took in the flowery, ever-present scent of her. "Gardenias," he whispered against her hair.

"No, darling." Laughing softly, she tilted her face up toward him, and the felt brim of his Stetson brushed against her before she looked back down. "I'm not talking about me, I'm talking about whatever it is in the air. It's . . ." She inhaled deeply again, and from beneath her jacket and sweater, he felt her breasts straining against his folded arms. "It's like damp earth. And burning leaves somewhere way off in the distance. Could someone be—"

"I don't think so, but for some reason it usually smells this way. That's one of the things I've always loved about it. That and the fact that it's just what the name implies. It's unfettered, uncomplicated by anything worldly." His chin moved, stroking her hair. "And even though the sight and the smell of it are familiar, it never seems to lose its newness."

"That's what it is," she said, her voice full of wonder. "Like it's nothing but God and the heavens and the rolling hills. And us. Like it was created especially for us to share, and even then, just for this brief moment."

Until now Tyler had never shared this spot, this view, with anyone else—except, of course, with his dad and his daughter. Until now, he realized, he had never wanted to share it with anyone else.

Her hands moved up to his forearms, and without any warning she broke his hold on her. "Let's go to the bottom," she said enthusiastically, pulling her unzipped jacket close to her as she sprinted away from him. "I want to see it all. Everything."

Tyler shoved his fingertips into his pockets, his feet planted firmly apart as he stayed where he was, enjoying the view only Jerri could provide. After a series of leaps and bounds, she stopped on an outcropping a few yards down from where he stood.

The morning had started out cold, but the air was already tinged with warmth from the sun. It was one of those cool, crisp, mild winter days so abnormal for anywhere else, so normal for many parts of Texas, and Jerri was hugging herself as she lifted her face to the bright, clear blue sky.

"Come on," she said, turning around suddenly, giving him a come-hither look that was hard to resist. "After being cooped up in that cabin, we could use the exercise."

"Uh-uh," he said, shaking his head. "I can't do it. You go ahead if you like, but I don't have the energy for it."

"Well, why not?" she asked, grinning up at him, looking like the epitome of sweetness and light and innocence.

"You know damned good and well why not." He pasted a look of disgust on his face. "Because of what you put me through God-knows-how-many times last night and again this morning, that's why not." His dark brows lifted. "A man can only take so much 'exercise,' you know."

She tilted her head, her eyes teasing him right back. "I can't imagine what's wrong with you, Tyler." She turned, raising her arms in a gesture that said "go figure," and started picking her way down the side of the hill. "I, personally, have never felt more invigorated."

"I can see that." His voice carried easily in the quiet, midmorning air. He knelt down, one knee touching the rocky ground, his forearm balanced on his thigh as he addressed his comment to her gorgeous backside while she continued her descent. "I'm beginning to think you're some kind of vampire, sapping every ounce of my strength and keeping it all for yourself."

"My poor darling," she said over her shoulder, her tone cheerful as she went on. "But doesn't it make you feel wonderful—knowing what you've done for me? This morning, for the very first time, I woke up wanting something besides a cigarette." She stopped and turned around, looking coy as she beamed up at him.

"So that's it, huh?" He rested his chin against his open palm, his eyes shooting playful daggers at her. "Is that all I am? Nothing but a substitute?"

"Well," she said flatly, nonchalantly, propping her hands at her sides. "I must admit, from the vast amount of experience I've had since last night, your lovemaking does seem to be addictive. I guess I'm just—" she shrugged her shoulders "—replacing one bad habit with another."

"Be careful, woman, or I'll cut you off—make you go back to chocolate cake and bubble gum."

"Idle threats." She pivoted and went back to her downhill journey. "Nothing but idle threats."

"Ha!" he yelled. "Just wait till we get back to the cabin. When I fall flat on my back on that bed, you'll see who's—"

"Careful now, Tyler," she called over her shoulder, her tone flippant as she interrupted him. "That sounds more like a promise than a threat."

He laughed, watching her disappear from his line of sight before he lowered himself onto the ground. Stretching his legs out in front of him, he crossed one boot over the other. His hands went behind him, pushing his hat up over his face as he leaned back, his fingers forming a cushion against the hard earth.

For what seemed about the millionth time, he thought about what a wonderful combination she brought to their lovemaking. Give and take, innocence and eagerness, tenderness and lust. He had a feeling it would always be that way—that she, like this very spot, would never lose that sense of newness.

He had expected her to be shy or reticent, but she had surprised him. Each and every time they'd made love, she had been about as hesitant as a kid who'd just discovered another package under the Christmas tree.

As the thought crossed his mind, he heard a squeal coming from down the hill. And then her excited voice floated up to him:

"Tyler! Wait till you see what I've found!"

He laughed under his breath, realizing that was one of the things he loved most about her—that inquisitive nature of hers. She wanted to know everything. It was as if every minute of every day she was on this eternal quest for knowledge. Probably because of her background, her schooling, it was a way of life for her.

"Hi," he heard, then felt his Stetson being lifted away from his face. She was sitting on her folded legs, leaning over him, smiling down at him.

"I'm really glad you suggested I bring my easel," she went on, raising her eyes and looking around her. "This place, this view, is absolutely awe-inspiring."

"You're awe-inspiring."

"I'm serious, Tyler. There's an illustration I want to do for the book, and now I'm anxious to get going on it. I told you, you've inspired me." She sat back on her feet, sighing deeply. "I still can't get over it—how much you've made me realize about myself. I think I even know now why I hung on to my silly crush on you for so many years."

"Oh?" he asked, his words hushed. "Why was that?"

"I think maybe I was afraid," she said pensively, "afraid that if I quit dreaming about an illusion and let some real flesh-and-blood man get close to me, then I might end up falling in love with him. And he might end up being the *wrong* man." She smiled sheepishly, then lifted her shoulders. "Maybe it felt safe in a way, being in love with some kind of a dream."

"When did you decide all this?" he asked, wondering if he really wanted to hear the answer, but knowing he had to ask.

"In the parlor last night, before we made love. When you were telling me about your life." She looked so peacefully happy, he thought. So pleased about her revelation. "I decided then that I didn't need my silly illusions anymore, because I knew the real Tyler Reynolds."

He swallowed hard. "You don't know that much about me, Jerri."

"I know enough," she said quietly. "I know you're a wonderful man. I know that I feel like a real, live, flesh-and-blood woman now for the first time in my life." She gently placed her hand on his shoulder, then put her head against his chest before she whispered, "I know I'll always love you for that."

Dear God, he thought. *What have I done?*

He breathed deeply, his palm moving over her hand, holding it tightly against his body as he closed his eyes to the sunlight. At the most vulnerable time of her life, he had chosen not to tell her the one thing about him that she might not be able to accept. He had been terribly unfair with her, picking and choosing what she ought to know about him when she was willing to share everything she had with him, when he knew everything there was to know about her.

And now, he decided with an overwhelming pang of regret, how could he admit that he hadn't been totally honest with her? That he wasn't nearly as noble and wonderful as she thought he was?

How could he possibly tell her that she was still in love with an illusion?

Tyler cleared his throat, then realized Jerri was holding something, pressing it against his chest. "What've you got?" he asked, lifting his shoulder.

"Look," she said quietly, raising herself up and giving him the object. "I think it might be a fossil of some sort."

"Oh, yeah," he said as he held up the heart-shaped rock. "It's a clam fossil. One of the smaller ones. This place used to be covered by the sea, so these things are all over the place around here." He pointed to a thin ribbon of water in the distance. "There're even some dinosaur tracks right over there in Hondo Creek. The creek bed's solid rock now, but it was mud at one time."

She watched him for a moment, then cupped his hand, ready to take the clam fossil out of his palm. "Your...your hands are like ice, darling. Here." She guided his palm toward the bottom edge of her sweater. "Why don't you warm them on me?"

"Please, Jerri," he said, trying to cover his sudden mood of remorse by smiling and teasing her. "Have mercy on me, will you? Just this once?"

He glanced at the hardened nipples straining against her sweater, aching to touch her but realizing his conscience wouldn't allow it. He had convinced himself he'd acted solely on her behalf the night before, but now he realized how selfish his motives had been. Deep down, he'd known damn good and well that she could accept the facts from his past, that she wouldn't judge him by the things he'd had no control over. He had known she would still admire him. He had probably known, instinctively, that she would decide he was even more wonderful.

A flood of guilt rushed over him as he realized how carefully his mind must have planned it. Because he had wanted her so fiercely, he had chosen what to tell her so she would still want him. He had done what he'd had to do to keep from jeopardizing his chances to be with her. To make love with her.

"Come on, Smoky. Why don't you let me put my hands somewhere safe? Here, maybe?" He hurried to put his hands in the pockets of her unzipped jacket, and the crinkling of cellophane tore into the morning quiet. He drew out the noisy item, holding it up in the air.

"Oh, for heaven's sake!" she said, taking the half-empty pack of cigarettes from him and crushing it. "I never thought to check while I was packing. These must have been in my pocket since last winter."

"Uh-huh. Sure." He winked at her, took the crumpled pack and shoved it into the pocket of his down vest.

"I'll get your painting supplies," he said, glad for the opportunity to stand up. "You don't mind if I watch you work, do you?"

"No," she said quickly. "No, of course not."

"Good." He turned and headed for the Jeep to get her supplies and his sleeping bag. "I hope you're not getting hungry yet. If you can wait till we get back to the cabin, I'll fix you something special."

"I take it back, Tyler," he heard her say from behind him. "I thought I knew you, but I don't. Not at all."

He spun on his boot heel, staring at the serious expression in her eyes. "What does that mean?"

Looking pointedly at her wristwatch, she finally glanced up and gave him a wry smile. "I thought you were a big macho man, and here you are planning brunch."

"Yeah," he said, pushing out a laugh. "But I'll tell you one thing. It damned sure won't be quiche."

After unloading the easel and helping her set it up, Tyler turned to the huge, centuries-old live oak tree that dominated the landscape. He spread out the sleeping bag and propped his head on the jacket she had taken off and folded.

He looked at his watch, frowning as he noted that in only a couple of hours, it would be noon. What was his so-called sense of honor going to do now? he wondered. He let out a sigh as he lowered his wrist, and then he noticed Jerri watching him from the other side of her canvas.

"On the way back to the cabin," she asked, her voice sounding almost hesitant, "will you take me to the creek and show me the dinosaur tracks?"

"Sure," he answered, attempting to smile as he rubbed his tight jaw. "No problem. We'll head back just as soon as you're through there."

Jerri stood back and studied her work. Gripping her paintbrush in her right fist, she brought her left hand to her throbbing temple.

She was glad she'd positioned the canvas so that Tyler couldn't see it. What was supposed to have been a portrayal of serenity had turned into something that appeared to be straight out of the mind of a maniac. This morning's pastoral sky, on canvas, was filled with jagged slashes of dark color. Storm clouds, lightning. And it was no wonder—since every nerve in her body was screaming for nicotine.

No, she decided. Not just screaming. Begging. Groveling! At this point, she would make any kind of a deal, promise anything, sign whatever. She would commit herself to a year in the state mental ward for just one of those cigarettes Tyler had blithely stuffed in his pocket.

She rolled her eyes skyward, gritting her teeth as she realized the stupidity of that particular thought. Not much of a deal, she told herself acidly, considering the fact that if she didn't get a cigarette within the next thirty seconds at the most, she would undoubtedly have to be locked up in a rubber room, anyway.

Out of the corner of her eye, she caught Tyler's movement as he lifted his arm and, for the umpteenth time in however long it had been, checked his wristwatch. She quickly shifted her weight onto her left foot, using the canvas to block their views of each other.

"Dammit," she muttered under her breath, gritting her teeth again. If he studied her any longer, she decided, if he as much as looked at that blasted watch of his one more time, she might just—

Might just what? her mind screamed. Wrap her fingers around his throat? Strangle him with her bare hands?

Maybe. The way her adrenaline was pumping now, she figured she could take him—and if she thought for one minute that he had a book of matches on him, there wouldn't
be any maybes about it.

And, she told herself vehemently, since he had brought
this attack of nerves on her in the first place, she wouldn't
feel the least little bit of remorse. If he hadn't been so
damned silent and pensive ever since she'd told him she
loved him, her mind never would have started churning
about a—

Dear God! she screamed inwardly. Strangling him! What
was she thinking of? What had gotten into her?

As quickly as she asked herself the question, her frazzled
mind furnished the answer. It was a sickness: a disgusting,
clawing addiction that was robbing her of every ounce of her
sanity. And it wasn't just excruciating mental anguish, it was
physical torture. Every inch of her body was in pain, she
realized all of a sudden. Even her hair follicles seemed to be
hurting!

No, she lectured herself, balling up her fists and biting
hard against the insides of her cheeks. She was not going to
drop everything and rush over to wrestle that crumpled pack
of cigarettes from Tyler—and she wouldn't scramble around
searching for the two sticks she'd fantasized about rubbing
together!

She might always be a slave to her feelings for Tyler
Reynolds, but she'd be damned if she would continue to be
a slave to smoking. And if Tyler didn't like the fact that she
loved him, then that was his problem, because she didn't
regret her words, not for one minute.

There was no way she was going to take them back, no
matter how much they seemed to bother him. She couldn't
even if she wanted to, she realized.

And she hadn't even said, "I love you, Tyler." She hadn't
said it in those exact words, as if she were begging him to
jump in with an "I love you, too." She had simply wanted
to be honest with him.

When she sensed how solemn and quiet he was afterward, she had even tried to lighten the atmosphere by joining in with his teasing. But ever since then, she hadn't been able to stop thinking about the way that he had refused to touch her when she'd offered him her warmth.

And that, she now admitted to herself, was exactly when this ridiculous anxiety attack had started building inside her. She had even wondered if when he promised her a special meal today, back at the cabin, he might be repeating what she had claimed to be doing just last night.

For all she knew, the special meal, along with everything else they'd shared since the night before, might be nothing more than "something to remember him by," something she could cling to and dream about after he went off into the wilderness.

She glared at the canvas, as if she could bore a hole first through the horrible painting and then through him. Well, she told herself, if he wanted to keep checking his watch—to calculate exactly how long it would be until his time was up and he could leave—then that was fine. He could check the blasted thing another thousand times if he wanted to, because she wasn't going to let it hurt her. And she certainly wasn't going to let it drive her back to a habit she'd promised herself she would quit.

As she caught sight of his long legs advancing toward her, Jerri took a quick gulp of air. And when he walked around the easel to stand behind her, she ignored him while pretending to choose her next color.

"Whoa!" he said, his tone playful. "I'm no art-therapy expert, but I'll bet I've got this illustration figured out. Boy, if this thing doesn't scream 'inner turmoil,' I don't know what does. You've done a great job, Smoky."

Feeling his hands as they came to rest on her tense shoulders, she wanted to pull away. But she seemed to be frozen in place. Unable to turn around and look at him, she spoke through gritted teeth. "I wish you'd quit calling me

Smoky," she said evenly. "Whether you believe it or not, I've given up cigarettes. Forever!"

"Maybe so, but—"

"Not maybe so, Tyler! Positively so."

"Yeah, but I can still call you Smoky, because it never had anything to do with cigarettes." He laughed softly as he started kneading her shoulders, but the tension only mounted. "You're trembling," he said, his tone changing, becoming quiet and concerned. "What's wrong, sweetheart? Are you cold?"

"No!" He started to wrap his arms around her but she twisted away from his hands, whirling around and backing away. "And don't you 'sweetheart' me, either!" she said, her voice almost a hiss as she glared up at him.

"Now calm down, sweetheart," he said, then corrected himself. "Calm down, Jerri. You're gonna be okay." He started advancing toward her, his movements extremely slow. He held up his hands, his tone unbelievably placating as he kept talking. "Trust me, now. This'll be over in a few minutes. You're having withdrawal symptoms, that's all, but if you'll stop fighting it and try to—"

"I am *not* having a nicotine fit!" She held up her hands, warning him not to come any closer. She wanted to scream and cry and strike out at him. Instead, all she could seem to do was scream. And tremble uncontrollably. "There's no such thing as a nicotine fit, and you know it!"

"Look, Smoky. I know there is. I know what I'm talking about."

He had stopped dead in his tracks, but she couldn't stop shaking. It was making her even more furious, the way he was treating her like a child having a momentary tantrum. The way he was speaking so softly, trying to pacify her with his voice as he went on.

"Listen to me, sweetheart. It takes at least three days to get the worst of this out of your system, so—"

"Which is certainly more than I can say for you!" She glared at her watch and then back up at him. "If I'm not mistaken, the twenty-four hours you asked for is almost up. And since you've obviously done what you wanted to do—dug up all my faults and gotten me out of your system—let's just get this stuff packed up so you can hit the road!''

She yanked the painting off the easel, slinging the canvas in the direction of the Jeep while he stood there staring at her. Her entire body was still quaking, and she kicked the easel until it collapsed on the ground.

"You've gotten my attention," he said quietly, his feet planted firmly apart and his arms crossed in front of his chest. "So why don't you go ahead now? Tell me what you're getting at."

"You know exactly what I'm getting at," she answered, her hands on her hips as she glowered at him. "You've already accused me of being a dreamer and not a doer. And then this morning when I told you I didn't know those cigarettes were in my pocket, you as much as called me a liar. Over and over again, you've accused me of having no willpower, and I'm tired of it." Still furious, she took the few steps necessary to close the distance between them, then jabbed his chest with her index finger. "You don't know me at all, or you'd know that I'm every bit as determined and strong-willed as you are—which is probably why it's a good thing you *have* gotten me out of your system. We'd be a terrible combination!"

Tyler captured her hand, pressing her fist against his chest and then folding her into the strength and warmth of his powerful arms. "Oh, Jerri," he whispered tenderly. "Who says I've gotten you out of my system? I'm beginning to think that's an impossible feat."

He nuzzled her hair, his hot breath fanning it as he kissed the top of her head. Her trembling didn't cease, not even when he lifted her chin, his eyes searching hers. He gave her a soft, loving smile before he continued.

"And if I'm not mistaken, we made a damned good combination last night." He lifted his eyebrows. "And again this morning."

She stiffened, her fist making contact with his chest. "I'm talking about *out* of bed, Tyler! You see what I mean? Most of the time, we're not even on the same wavelength. And when we are on the same wavelength, we're too much alike." She dropped her forehead against the cool cushion of his vest, her voice sounding mournful as she whispered, "We probably wouldn't last six months."

His big hand spanned her face as he turned her head, pressing her cheek against the strong wall of his chest and holding it there as he caressed her, his fingers threading into her hair. She felt rather than heard his light chuckle before he spoke.

"That's what they said about rock and roll—and look at how long that's been around."

"Oh, Tyler," she murmured pathetically, "please don't tease me, not now. I'm serious." Her fingers dug into the flat, hard muscles of his back. "I...I want you to see me— to understand and appreciate me—for what I am, whether it's for my good qualities or my not-so-good ones."

"I do, sweetheart. Believe me, I do." His index finger went under her chin, and he tilted her face up. "Come on, now." Taking off his vest, he wrapped it around her shoulders. He held her against his side, under the shelter of his arm, as he led her toward the sleeping bag. "We'll talk in a minute, but first let's get you over this crisis. You quit smoking, what? The night before I got here, right?" She nodded, her hand around his waist as she clung to him. "That's two-and-a-half days ago. You're probably going through the worst of it right now."

He kept her hand in his as he stretched out, guiding her gently into his arms and holding her tightly beside him, almost beneath him. "I'm sorry, honey," he murmured against her ear. "You've been so brave that I just didn't see this coming. You were doing so well, and there was so much going on between us."

Jerri took a long, deep breath, realizing she had been treating it the same way. She let the air out of her lungs, feeling its warmth as it touched Tyler's neck and came back to her. Whether it was due to the sheer weight of him or the gentle strength of his voice or both, she didn't know, but the trembling slowly began to subside.

"I knew you were telling the truth about those cigarettes, and I shouldn't have teased you. I should've known my timing was rotten."

"No, it—"

"Shh," he whispered. "Let me do the talking for a while. You just try to relax." He pulled her closer. "I've got some not-so-good qualities myself, you know. And I guess teasing is one of them. I'm used to relating with a twelve-year-old girl, for the most part. Maybe I haven't made this clear, Smoky—" he lifted his face, his gaze intent on hers "—but you're the first woman I've ever really let into my life."

Her chest tightened, her heart swelling with joy, her breath catching in her throat. She couldn't speak; all she could do was return the loving look she saw in his eyes.

"So," he whispered, "do you think you can put up with an old bachelor who doesn't always think before he speaks? Who teases you unmercifully sometimes?"

"Yes, Tyler." She held on to him, pulling him closer as the words came out in a whispered rush. "Oh, yes. I love your teasing, I really do. But I saw you looking at your watch and . . . and studying me. And then I got this crazy notion in my head that you were—"

His soft laughter interrupted her. "All I wanted was a simple yes-or-no answer. You're supposed to be trying to calm down, remember?" He smiled and shook his head, then folded her up tightly in his arms again. "And I know why you got excited. I know, sweetheart, so you don't have to explain." He rolled over, letting her lie across his chest as he kept his firm, comforting hold on her. "I also know this nicotine withdrawal is tough going, so you don't have to apologize." He brushed a light, sensual kiss across her hair. "You worry too much, Smoky. Just be quiet a minute and let me hold you. Let me finish what I need to say."

With slow, tender strokes, he rubbed her back. "If you haven't already convinced me that you're determined and strong-willed, you might as well hang up your dancin' shoes—because if you haven't proven it to me in the last forty-eight hours, you never will. And if we're alike in some ways, is that really so terrible? In case you've never thought about it before, strong people can take turns being strong." His voice caressed her. "Sometimes I get mighty tired of being strong, don't you? Once in a while, don't you want to lean on someone else? Be babied just a little?" She felt his smile. "And in case you haven't noticed, when it comes to you ... Let's just say you have a knack for bringing out the weaknesses in this strong will of mine."

"I do?"

"Yes, you do," he said. "You know damn good and well you do, so quit acting like it comes as a big shock."

An unknown amount of time passed, and as she felt herself beginning to relax, Jerri let her mind replay his beautiful, meaningful, tender words. Before the last calming shudders left her body, she even remembered the words they had exchanged while she was screaming at him.

"Tyler?" she finally whispered against his neck. "Why do you call me Smoky? I mean, if it's not because of the cigarettes, then why did you ever start calling me—" She stopped the question, enjoying the rumble of laughter she felt in his throat.

"Nothing slides by you, does it?" She shook her head, listening and smiling as he went on. "It was because of your eyes. Those beautiful, mysterious, smoky-gray eyes. I could never figure out what was going on behind them, and it made me damned mad that I couldn't seem to stop trying."

"Really?" she asked, her face beaming with astonishment as she sat up to look at him.

"Yes, really," he stated matter-of-factly, then grinned as he laced his fingers and placed them under his head. "The first time I looked straight into 'em, I said to myself, 'You could get in trouble here, Reynolds. Mighty big trouble.'"

"Why?" she asked quietly, her expression reflecting both curiosity and joy—joy in knowing that all those years he had been just as intrigued by her as she had been by him.

He laughed again, then rubbed his jaw. "Hell, Jerri, I don't know. All I know is that I thought . . . well, I guess I said to myself . . ." He put his hands back behind his head, glancing up to the sky. "'Now, those are the kind of eyes a man could get lost in—and never find his way out again.'" He raised his shoulders off the sleeping bag, looking embarrassed all of a sudden. "I don't know, something like that. Something kind of . . . sappy and stupid."

"Oh, Tyler," she whispered. "That's the most beautiful thing you've ever said to me. You . . . you make me so happy." She swallowed the lump that had formed in her throat, her eyes never leaving his as her hand grazed his chest, then moved downward to skim his lower body. "I want to make you happy, Tyler," she whispered. "Let me make you happy. Let me . . . baby you."

"Right here?" he asked, laughing. "Now?"

"Yes," she answered. "Right now. Right this minute."

He paused for a moment. "Okay," he said hesitantly. "But first, there's something you have to know about me."

"What?" she asked, the movement of her hand stopping abruptly. She blinked once, her eyes growing round as she studied the solemn expression in his dark blue gaze.

"I hate to admit this, but— Well, I guess you're bound to find out sooner or later, so . . ." He tossed the fallen vest aside, then put his hand on hers, holding her palm against his arousal. "I can only 'do it again' so many times, sweetheart, before I'm totally useless to you." The corner of his mouth slanted upward into a wry frown. "Maybe even dead."

"Oh, darling," she whispered, breathing a sigh of relief as she smiled and decided to play along. "You worry too much." Her hand moved leisurely, provocatively, beneath his, and her voice took on the tone of a nurse dealing with a fretful patient. "And this is for you, remember? Not for me."

"Oh?" he asked, lifting his dark brows.

"Well, all right," she answered, trying to make the statement sound more like resignation than an admission. "Maybe it's for both of us." She moved his hand aside, patting it gently before she started unfastening the top button of his jeans. "But it'll be okay, I promise. You just have to trust me."

Her hands were trembling again, she realized, but for a different reason now. It was her desire for Tyler—this quick, aching, burning desire for him and him alone. And the realization was making it difficult for her to breathe, much less to tease and undress him. Her fingers moved to the second button as she ran her tongue across her lips. "If I do anything that hurts you, just tell me and I'll stop." She smiled then. "Okay?"

"Well..." His body tensed, his beautiful gaze locking with hers as he reached for her, his fingers moving into her hair. "Okay," he whispered, returning her playful smile even though his breathing was already ragged, almost out of control. "But be gentle with me, Smoky. I think ... I think I really am ... getting ready to die."

"No, Tyler," she murmured, "no." God, how she loved hearing his low, husky voice when he called her Smoky. How she loved feeling his long, muscular body tighten every time she touched him. Still smiling, she leaned over to brush her lips tentatively against his. "Trust me, darling. Just relax now... and let it happen."

Chapter Eleven

Tyler cradled her against his side, their sated, bare bodies wrapped in the folds of the heavy sleeping bag.

He reached under the fabric, his free hand enveloping one enticingly warm breast. Her nipple was beginning to lose its hardness, but it tightened again in response to the light, grazing pressure of his thumb, and she covered his fingers with her own, pressing them against the now-slowing beat of her heart.

He gazed down into her desire-clouded gray eyes and then settled back, staring at the live-oak branches overhead as his mind drifted back to some of the other times he'd spread out a bedroll in this exact spot.

"After a hard day's work," he said, "my dad and I used to just tie up the horses and camp out here sometimes—right under this old oak." He turned his head, his jaw brushing her ash-brown hair aside before he kissed her temple. His forearm pointed toward the gnarled, overhanging limbs as he held her neck snug in the crook of his arm, and a faint smile touched the corners of his mouth. "I wish you could've known him. He would've loved knowing you."

"Why?" she murmured.

"You want a list?" he asked playfully, knowing the answer before she nodded her head. "Because you're you, mainly. Because my life's been too intense for quite a while now, too serious, and you make me want to laugh. And smile. And *talk*, so that I can give you long lists and satisfy all your million-and-one questions."

"What else?" she whispered secretively. "I can tell there's something else."

He laughed, then decided to leave the teasing behind. "Because I was his only son, and you make me unbelievably happy."

She snuggled her face against his neck, letting out a sigh that felt like a warm, feathery kiss on his throat, then slid her leg over his with leisurely, silken smoothness. His body tensed as her fingers made a sensuous journey through the hair on his chest, working their way across and upward. She brought her light touch to rest on his shoulder, and he reached up to stroke the warm flesh of her forearm as they held each other in silence.

In that moment Tyler was glad she had her face pressed against his throat so that she couldn't see the solemn look he knew was in his eyes. Never again would he be able to look at this spot, this hilltop, without thinking of her.

She was already worried about their differences. That he knew without a doubt, thanks to what she'd told him during her nicotine crisis. He had managed to soothe her fears about their likenesses, but he'd conveniently skipped over their differences.

She was the most loving, caring woman he'd ever known, so knowing just how different they really were probably wouldn't bother her. But there was always that remote chance that she would be disappointed in him, that to her, his reasons for putting off his education all these years would sound like nothing but feeble excuses. That she might decide she was still in love with an illusion.

His mind started churning again, practicing what he would say. What he knew he had to say in order to play fair with her. It was what he'd been doing earlier, when Jerri had caught him glancing at his watch. He hadn't been planning to leave, the way she'd thought. No, he'd been deciding how he could word it: *Well, Smoky. We're not exactly in the same ballpark, the two of us. I was a high-school dropout, and...*

Dammit! That last phrase, in particular, had sounded like the title of some cheap B movie. But none of the other possibilities had sounded much better.

He couldn't seem to think straight anymore. All he could do was stare at the landscape surrounding them. If he lost her now, he thought with a long, deep sigh, how could he ever bring himself to this spot again? And if he told her everything there was to know, how could he be absolutely sure that he wouldn't lose her?

"Tyler?" she whispered. "What are you worried about?"

"Nothing," he answered quickly. "What makes you think I'm—"

She laughed softly, interrupting him. "Because I won't have any skin left on this arm if you keep rubbing it like that." She leaned over and kissed his hand, bringing the motion to a stop. "And that hard, handsome, sandpapery jaw of yours has been working a mile a minute."

"What's that got to do with anything?"

She shook her head slowly, giving him a chastising, knowing grin. "In case you haven't realized it, darling, I'm beginning to learn a few things about you. When you start clenching that jaw, it means one of two things."

"Oh?"

"Yes," she answered, her tone smug. "It either means you're angry or you're stewing over something. And considering what we've just been doing under this lovely old oak, I think I'm pretty safe in ruling out anger."

He feigned a look of disgust. "So who died and made you Sigmund Freud?"

"Sigmund Freud," she answered flatly. "So why don't you just go ahead and tell me what you're stewing about?"

"Nothing, really." He shrugged his shoulders. "I was just thinking about the lousy timing on this project I've got going right now. It'll demand my full attention for quite a while, and I was just wishing I'd gotten it out of the way a long time ago, that's all."

"You really do have a project going?" she asked.

"Yeah. I told you that the other day." He ran his fingers through his dark hair, then shook his head. "God, that was just yesterday, wasn't it?"

Amazing, he thought, the changes that could take place in a matter of hours. It was approximately one short hour ago, in fact, that she had told him that she loved him. And as soon as she'd whispered it, he'd realized that it was exactly what he wanted to hear.

And now that he knew how she felt about him, he knew something else. He knew he couldn't tell her anything that might change her mind. No, he decided all of a sudden, he wouldn't do anything to tamper with that. And if that was pure selfishness on his part, then so be it. Because this was one time when he was going to make damned sure that history didn't repeat itself.

"Darling," she whispered, drawing the word out. "You're still stewing."

"No, I'm not. I'm thinking, that's all." He covered her fingers with his palm. "I was just thinking that I've sort of gotten used to having you around."

He felt her hand tense for a split second. Then it relaxed again, and she raised herself up on one elbow and murmured, "Ohh?"

"Don't be coy, Jerri. It doesn't suit you."

"Oh, all right," she stated flatly, settling down again, skimming her cheek across the hair on his naked chest. "Go ahead."

"Well, I have an idea. At first I thought the timing was really lousy—because of the projects we've both got going right now—but maybe this could work out just fine for everybody."

He moved downward, brushing his lips across the flat smoothness of her stomach before he looked back into her eyes. "What was I talking about?" he asked, trying to appear nonchalant.

"You were talking about our projects." Her tongue touched her lips momentarily. "And about something that could work out just fine for everybody...whatever that means."

"Oh, yeah." He shifted his weight, reaching over to cover her bare chest. Her body, he decided, was one hell of a distraction. And he needed to be able to think clearly, since this idea had only started forming a few seconds before he'd brought it up in the first place. "Look, Smoky, I'll be honest with you. You've worn me out to the point where my brain isn't working too well. Give me another minute to think about this, will you?"

"Sure," she answered quietly, smiling as she snuggled up to him again. "No problem."

Considering that insatiable curiosity of hers, he knew damned well she'd be asking for details about his "project." He needed to have his wits about him, so that he could gloss over the project part as quickly as possible—and move right on to the good parts. The convincing parts.

And there was probably nothing to worry about, anyway. After all, she loved him—she'd been in love with him for a long time—so why wouldn't she say yes? But, he reminded himself, maybe there were one or two angles he hadn't thought of yet....

Her heart, Jerri realized, had been threatening to leap straight out of her throat ever since Tyler had said the words she had yearned to hear: "I've gotten used to having you around."

And even though she'd been dying for him to explain exactly what that meant—even though visions of a woody, Jerri and Tyler's woody, had been dancing in her head—she had also been determined to keep it light. He'd said that his life had been too serious for too long, and it had thrilled her to know that she made him want to smile and tease. He gave her such incredible excitement and warmth and fun, and despite an almost overwhelming sense of anxiety, she had wanted to draw out this moment.

Yes, Jerri told herself, smiling as she watched him, she wanted to enjoy every second of what could be the beginning. The beginning of a whole lifetime of excitement and warmth and fun.

Her fingers reached out, tracing the faint line along his eye, and her mind drifted back to that first time she'd seen him, leaning against an old oak much like this one. His scar, she'd decided that day, made him look like a bandit. And now, all these years later, she wanted nothing more than for Tyler Reynolds to be *her* bandit.

She wanted to be beside him, in his bed. She wanted to be the woman he yearned for, the woman he reached for in the dark...just as he had when he'd woken up at some unknown point the night before.

He cleared his throat, looking devastatingly serious again. This, she decided, was probably the most difficult thing he'd ever done in his life. There had to be something she could do to make it easier for him.

Talking about business, she remembered, had made him more comfortable at the kitchen table only yesterday. And ever since last night, both of them had been dealing with nothing but new and raw emotions. Just then she recalled his words about "lousy timing" because of his project; their relationship had obviously come at a bad time, business-wise, and he was a man who took business matters seriously.

Yes, she decided quickly. She would calm his fears about business matters in relation to her. Then perhaps it would be easier for him to get on with the real issue at hand: *emotional matters* in relation to her.

"What sort of project is this, anyway?" she asked, trying to sound perky but not too perky, interested but not snoopy.

"Geez, Jerri," he said, laughing playfully. "It's no wonder you were still a virgin. You get a guy so worn out from answering questions, he can't possibly have enough energy left over to do anything else." His head moved into the crook of her neck. "That's not what I want to talk about, anyway. I want to talk about this idea I've got. This suggestion."

Jerri smiled at Tyler's edginess.

"I was thinking it would be nice for you to come back to the ranch with me. It would work out perfectly for everyone, I think, for a lot of reasons. You want to work on your book, and you'd have a lot of peace and quiet and serenity."

He stopped talking for a moment, and simply held her close.

"Cotton's getting on in years," he added, "but I haven't taken any steps to hire a housekeeper. I haven't wanted to hurt the old guy's ego because he thinks he runs the place just fine all by himself, but actually, Sam and I jump in and do the extras when he's out running errands. He still works too hard, though, and I feel like he needs to be enjoying his later years." He cleared his throat again. "I've been thinking about that a lot lately. And once he sees how nice it is to have a woman around the house, maybe it would pave the way for me to hire someone."

Didn't he know, she wondered, that he didn't need to convince her? She wanted to be asked "properly," of course, but the way she felt about him, Tyler could mutter "Will ya, huh?" and she would gladly follow him to the ends of the earth. How could she not be happy at his ranch? With him?

"And there's something else I've been thinking about," he said. "I've got this important dinner party coming up in a couple of weeks. Pauline's parents are coming over to celebrate their granddaughter's thirteenth birthday. You're a classy dame—'' he laughed under his breath ''—and we could all use a few lessons in manners and refinement. In fact, I'm a little worried about Sam in that respect. She's still a real tomboy, which isn't surprising since she's been around nothing but men all her life. So maybe it would help if she had the influence of a good woman. A lady.''

Jerri remained silent, simply smiling and listening as he piled on one good reason after another.

''I have a friend who's a publisher of textbooks, and I could put you in touch with him after you're a little further along with your idea. That might not be the right contact, of course, but it would be a logical place to start, and—''

''I didn't major in business, darling.'' She laughed softly. ''But are you using some kind of a marketing technique on me?''

''No,'' he answered, laughing in return as she nuzzled closer to him. ''Okay. Maybe it is a sales pitch of a sort, but I was only trying to point out all the possibilities. All the advantages.'' He swallowed hard. ''I was just thinking maybe you could stay and finish your book. That's what you want to do, so why don't you do it? I know you're worried about your expenses, but that's no problem. I'll be glad to take care of those.''

Jerri's heart seemed to plunge into her belly. Tyler hadn't been talking about spending a lifetime together, as she had yearned for. No, he wasn't talking about forever or marriage. He was simply talking about cohabiting for a while. While it was convenient for both of them.

When he reached over to lightly stroke her cheek, Jerri erased that particular possibility from her mind. This couldn't be just a simple little liaison, meant to satisfy everyone's biological needs. No, she didn't know everything about Tyler Reynolds, but she darned sure knew how he felt about certain things. He was an honorable man—a man with an impressionable daughter at home.

And maybe that was the problem, Jerri decided sadly. Maybe his high moral character, his sense of honor, was exactly what was behind this proposition. And if that was his only reason for making it, then she knew it would break her heart.

"Well?" he asked. "What do you say, Smoky? How does that sound to you?"

"It sounds rather cut and dried, but maybe I missed something. You want me to come home with you—" she inhaled deeply, her eyes searching his "—so that I can do windows?"

"Of course not. I never meant you'd be expected to do any of the—"

"Why, then? To teach you and Sam the difference between a soupspoon and a salad fork?"

"Well, that couldn't hurt." He laughed self-consciously. "But I can't say it's my primary reason for—"

"Whatever happened to being honest with each other?"

He didn't seem to have a ready answer.

"All right, Tyler," she whispered. "Let me be honest with you, then. I think I know why you're doing this." She sat up and drew her sweater over her head before she looked at him again. "We've been teasing about my virginity, but I know you're a man who takes his responsibilities seriously. And I think that as of last night, in that lumpy old bed, I somehow got added to that list of responsibilities that can't be taken lightly."

"Good God, Jerri," he said, his tone quiet but incredulous. "What are you talking about?"

As she watched him sit up and pull on his shirt, she knew she had to ask. Had to know if he was making this gesture because he thought he owed her something for what he'd "done" to her. "I'm talking about the fact that maybe you feel you've tainted me. And I'll tell you something, Tyler. I don't feel that way at all—not for one minute. I wouldn't change anything that's happened in the last forty-eight hours. I made love with you because I wanted to, and I got every bit as much as I gave. I'm a big girl now, so you can just take me off your damned list." Her voice had started trembling, and she stood and yanked on her jeans. "You can just stop feeling guilty and obligated to me for something that I went into with my eyes wide open!"

When Tyler grabbed his Levi's, Jerri turned and made for the Jeep, leaning against the support of its hood as she buried her face in her hands.

"No, sweetheart," he whispered from behind her. "No, that's not what I'm feeling." He turned her around to face him, then lifted her chin. "Okay. I will be honest with you. That's what I should've done from the beginning, instead of hurting you like this." His arms moved past her hips, pinning her against the Jeep. "I'll tell you exactly how I feel about your virginity, and I'll make it simple. I'm damned glad you waited for me all those years. I'm damned glad you waited long enough for me to wise up and realize how long I've been waiting for you."

His serious gaze held hers as he went on. "I'm asking you to go home with me because after forty-eight hours, I can't seem to remember what life was like before you. And worse than that, I can't imagine what life would be like without you." He took a step backward, but his eyes stayed on her. "I gave you that long, ridiculous list because I think I've fallen in love with you, but asking you to go home with me is— It's all I can offer you right now." He closed the narrow space between them, then cupped her face in his big hands. "I don't know what else to say."

"Oh, Tyler," she whispered, sheer happiness rushing through her because of what he'd said. About loving her. About realizing how long he'd been waiting for her.

He took her into his arms, holding her close against him. In that moment, as her hands moved around his back and she clung to his tall, strong body, she couldn't help thinking about the two women who had hurt him in the past. And the people who were a part of his life now—the people who looked down their noses at him because of his "questionable upbringing." And Samantha's grandparents, who still didn't approve of him and who would be bringing their disapproval when they attended Sam's birthday party.

She wanted to look up into Tyler's eyes and assure him she wasn't any of those other people. She wanted to tell him that she was Jerri, that she would be proud to spend a lifetime with him—if only he would ask. That he could trust her not to hurt him.

But she knew she couldn't, because that was something he needed to realize for himself. Trust was something she couldn't force him to have, especially when he'd been treated badly by so many people. Her heart went out to him, but she smiled hopefully as she thought about what he'd admitted to her earlier: that she was the first woman he'd ever really let into his life. He had said it himself, and that statement alone was enough to make her realize she had good reason to hope.

Yes, she decided all of a sudden. There was only one thing she could do. If it was time he needed, she could give him that. Time to learn to trust in her love for him.

Yet she knew she couldn't leave herself wide open to the pain she would feel if he never saw her for what she was. As much as she loved Tyler Reynolds, she couldn't wait forever. She had to set a limit of some kind for his sake as well as her own. After a little more time together, if he didn't learn to trust her, a million years wouldn't make any difference, because there would never be any hope for true happiness between them.

"What do you say, Smoky? Will you go home with me?"

"Yes, Tyler. I will, at least until after Sam's party. But I can't promise I'll stay indefinitely to finish my book."

"But—"

Jerri reached up and put her fingers to his lips. "Please, Tyler. Let me finish."

She thought quickly and came up with her own list: actual factors that would sound logical. "When I talked about expenses and obligations, I was talking about more than groceries and the rent. I have a contract with the museum, an obligation I can't just ignore.'' The owner of the museum was a reasonable and caring man, though, Jerri reminded herself. She was positive that if the need arose, she could work something out with him.

"And there's something else," she added. "I'm trying to set aside a little money for my mother's retirement. It's not much, but she's done so much for me—she's practically lived her whole life for me, and I want her to have some money she can spend on a few extravagances just for herself. I know that may sound silly to you, but it's something that's very important to me."

"No, sweetheart," he replied. "That doesn't sound silly at all. I understand."

"Thank you for understanding." Her voice was hushed, reverent. "For asking me to go home with you. For being honest with me." She smiled up at him, her eyes on his breathtakingly pensive blue gaze. "For loving me."

He looked serious for another few moments. And then, without warning, he grabbed her hand, depositing her into the passenger seat.

"Let's get going, woman. I've got things to do."

"Like what?" she called to him, laughing as he rushed back to the tree, filling his arms with the unrolled sleeping bag and then her easel.

"Like packing up all your creature comforts," he said, making a second trip to throw together her painting supplies. "I'm not sure if the boat will hold everything, but I'm glad I brought it with me. It'll make a great trailer."

He dumped the items into the back seat, then gave her a brief kiss and a wink that made her thankful she was already sitting down. "Before we get going," he added, "there's one thing I should warn you about. Right now."

"What's that?" she asked, smiling at the rakish grin on his face.

"After I get through hauling all six hundred pounds of that stuff, I may not be the man I once was."

"Mmm. I'll take my chances." She touched his cheek and laughed. "You worry too much, darling."

No, Tyler decided as he walked around to the driver's side. He wasn't actually worried. He was simply doing what he thought was best.

What they needed was time. Some time together would show her that they could get along, that they could make a relationship last. Time together would point out their similarities instead of their differences.

He would tell her everything she needed to know, but not just yet. He would simply postpone it for a while. And, he reminded himself once again, it would be better for Jerri if he did wait. She was a bundle of new sensations and emotions right now, not to mention a bundle of raw nerves while she fought her way through the worst part of kicking the cigarette habit.

Yes, he would simply wait until after he had taken his college entrance exams and gotten himself enrolled. The timing would be better for Jerri, and it certainly wouldn't hurt his case, either. When she saw that he was taking responsibility for an earlier mistake in judgment, when she saw that he was actually doing something concrete about it and not just dreaming, she would no doubt look at it differently.

Yeah, Tyler assured himself as he gunned the engine. Jerri would get the whole truth. Just as soon as he felt sure she was ready to hear it.

Chapter Twelve

"See?" Samantha said, her long blond hair shining in the afternoon sunlight, her brown eyes looking almost animated. "That wasn't so hard now, was it?"

"No," Jerri answered, following the girl's example by hanging on to the tree limbs and situating herself against one of the giant branches high above the ground. "It was fun."

"And this really is your first time?" Sam's brown eyes were wide, as if she couldn't fathom such a thing. "You've never climbed a tree before? Never, ever, *ever*?"

"Never, ever, ever," Jerri confessed, her heartbeat still racing. And it wasn't just fun, she admitted inwardly. It was downright exhilarating.

"I wish the county stock show was next weekend instead of this weekend," the girl said, employing a habit Jerri had noticed almost as soon as she'd met the preteen over a week before. Samantha seemed to change topics of conversation about as easily and quickly as she would a pair of tennis shoes.

"Why would you wish that?" Jerri asked.

"Because if the stock show wasn't until next weekend, then I'd be off school *next* Friday instead of today. And next Friday would be a lot better."

"Why?" Jerri asked innocently, as if they hadn't discussed what one week from today would be at least a hundred times already. "What's so special about next Friday?"

"Guess," Samantha said.

"Report-card day?"

The girl only rolled her eyeballs.

"Garbage pickup?"

"Not even close."

"Oh, I remember now," Jerri said. "It's your birthday, isn't it? I keep forgetting, though—how old will you be?"

"Thirteen," Sam said, her tone mockingly patient.

"That's right. Twelve going on thirteen. A very good age to be. A momentous age, I'd say."

"You know what'd really be good right now?" Sam asked, licking her lips. "An apple with peanut butter on it."

"Ughh!" Jerri said, grimacing. "That sounds horrible."

"Oh, it's great. Wait'll you taste it." Sam scrambled quickly down the tree. "I'll be right back."

Shaking her head and laughing, Jerri watched her sprint toward the house. Had she, too, been that excited about turning thirteen? She honestly couldn't remember.

Squirming to get comfortable against the scratchy branch beneath her, Jerri kept one hand wrapped around a limb. Seeing the rambling yet contemporary ranch house from this distance made her think about seeing it for the first time, over a week ago, from the passenger seat of Tyler's Jeep. He'd insisted they leave her car at Beth's house because he had plenty of vehicles she could use if she needed one. So she had made a quick call to Beth from the pay phone at The General Store. She hadn't told her best friend much: just a heartfelt thanks for sending Tyler to the cabin, along with a promise to call her as soon as there were any further developments.

She flattened her palm against her chest, remembering the sense of excitement and anticipation she'd felt that afternoon. Tyler hadn't really had to introduce her to Samantha. They already knew each other slightly. But he had introduced her to Cotton, and while everyone was gathered around in the den, he'd mentioned casually that Jerri had just stopped smoking and that he'd asked her to come to the ranch and stay awhile. Since Cotton and Sam had already been through the same experience with him, Tyler had pointed out, he knew they could all help Jerri stay on the right track.

On the drive from the cabin to the ranch that day—which seemed like months ago instead of only nine days—she had wondered how he was going to handle the introductions. And even though he'd made it sound as if they were nothing more than old friends, she was glad he'd handled it that way. She hadn't wanted Samantha and Cotton to think she was being pushed on them.

Jerri only hoped that when Tyler made his statement about her staying for a while, his reasoning had been the same as her own. Whether it had been or not, though, it appeared to be working. They were all getting along famously and becoming fast friends.

Jerri glanced at the wide expanse of kitchen windows, watching Cotton's shadowy form as he helped Sam with her preparations. It was too far away to see them, but in her mind she could visualize his white hair and those pale blue eyes that sparkled and danced when he spoke. They were the kind of eyes that were almost piercing, as if they could see right through to your soul.

Leaning leisurely against the rough branch behind her, Jerri smiled as she realized she was beginning to think of Cotton as the grandfather *she* never had. He was an old-fashioned kind of man, very relaxed and straightforward, who enjoyed life to the fullest in his own unhurried way. He had special endearments for everyone. He referred to Tyler as "the boy," which she really got a kick out of, and Samantha was "the young 'un," and Tyler's bottling-company foreman was "that young buck," despite the fact he was recently married and probably in his thirties.

Cotton already had his own special endearments for her, too. He called her either "Miss Jerri" or "sugar," depending on the mood of the moment, and he seemed to love telling her colorful tales from his younger days. Most of them were lively stories about him and Big Sam, who had indeed been nicknamed for his stature, when they were breaking horses, breaking cows for milking and trapping bobcat and beaver. Cotton had even taken to drawing her little diagrams to show her how the different animals' tracks looked while he explained how and why the trapping was done.

She had to admit she had never been happier, never felt more at home. She loved it here, in the midst of their daily activities and their family closeness, and had decided she would gladly stay forever—if only Tyler would ask her.

Closing her eyes, Jerri moaned as she moved left and right, using the rough branch behind her as a back scratcher. These had been the happiest nine days of her life, she reminded herself, still smiling. And missing Tyler...his warmth, his constant teasing, his lovemaking...was the only thing that had kept them from being totally idyllic. He hadn't been gone from the house at all, yet he'd been closeted away in his study, working day and night on his project. She opened her eyes, glancing toward the study window again, wishing Tyler's desk was within view but knowing that it wasn't.

Maybe his long hours of work would slow down soon, she thought, since tomorrow was going to be his big day. It was the day he'd been preparing for, the day of his project's important initial meeting.

And how could she fault him for being a good provider for his family? she asked herself. For putting his ranch and his business first at times when he knew he must? She couldn't think badly of him for being responsible. That was one of the things she loved most about him.

And maybe it was for the best that Tyler had been busy, she reminded herself. Not only had it given her time to get to know Cotton and Sam on her own terms, without any of it feeling forced, but it had also provided her with the chance to get a lot accomplished on her book. She had refined her outline and had even started sketching out chapters. It was all still very patchy, but she was getting more excited about it by the day.

And Tyler seemed to be just as excited about it as she was. Several times during meals, which seemed to be their only time together lately, he'd asked Jerri how the book was coming along. And when she'd shown him copies of her old outline and her new one, wanting his advice because she trusted his business and marketing skills, he'd seemed genuinely impressed with the improvements she'd made. He had even promised to look over her new outline more carefully as soon as his meeting was over, on the off chance that he might be able to offer a suggestion or two.

She'd been thrilled that he'd taken such an interest in her idea. He was, after all, a concerned parent, and that was exactly the kind of person her book was meant to entice.

All in all, she was feeling happier and more confident than ever.

And she was feeling very womanly, too, she reminded herself, her fingers skimming lightly along the limb she still held. Even though they hadn't been able to be alone together, every time she and Tyler were in the same room, he seemed to make love to her with his eyes. And in the midst of the rest of the family, she had noticed something that amazed her. Something that made her feel more womanly than ever.

When he was upset with Samantha one day—she'd been experimenting with makeup and had gone a bit overboard—his jaw hadn't flexed. Not even once. And that's when it had dawned on Jerri that she, Jerri, might be the only person, the only female, who had that kind of an effect on him. That realization had made her feel special. It made her feel powerful in her femininity, knowing that only she could affect him that way.

Samantha's blond head appeared below her, and Jerri watched the girl's ascent, marveling at the ease with which she shimmied up the huge tree, even with the flap of a paper bag clamped between her teeth.

"I brought us a soda, too," Sam said after she wiggled into place and unfolded the top flap.

"You take it," Jerri said, holding out her hand to refuse the aluminum can as the girl tried to give it to her. "I'll be fine. I don't need anything to drink."

"With *peanut butter*?" the preteen asked, her tone aghast. "Yuck! Maybe you can do it, but not me." She took a long swig. "Daddy always takes me to the fair at the stock show, but he says he's too busy to go tonight. Cotton says he'll take me. You wanta go, too?"

"Why not?" she asked, thrilled to be asked but trying not to sound gushy about it. "That sounds like fun."

"Jerri?"

She smiled as she heard Tyler's voice calling her, then turned her head and saw him standing inside the open window of his study.

"Will you come here a minute, please?"

"Sure," she yelled, then leaned forward and grabbed hold of two limbs. As she started downward she took it slowly, making sure of her footing against each junction of branch and tree trunk. Hearing Sam's laughter above her, she decided to show at least a modicum of bravery by jumping the last few feet of distance to the ground. And she fell right smack on her bottom, leaving Samantha giggling at her as she stood and brushed off the seat of her jeans.

"Hey, kid!" she said, glowering up at Sam playfully. "I'm new at this. Be nice to me, or I'll—"

"What? Fire me?"

"Yeah!" she said, giving her a cocky smile. Sam had offered to be her "secretary," and Jerri could tell she was proud to be helping with the book. But the girl was also enough like her daddy to tease Jerri by grumbling about her being a slave driver.

"Big threat," Sam replied. "I'm really scared."

"I can see that," Jerri said, laughing as she whirled and ran to the house. By the time she opened the door to Tyler's study, she was nearly out of breath.

"Hi!" she said, her heartbeat racing even faster just looking at him.

"What the hell do you think you were doing out there?"

She blinked once, confused over the note of anger in his question. "I was climbing a tree. I'd never done it before, so Sam was teaching me how."

"And is that your idea of teaching her how to be ladylike?" he asked, his voice gruff. "Romping around with her? Reliving your childhood?"

He took a seat then, leaning back against the leather swivel chair.

Jerri's fingers stiffened, clutching the doorknob, but she kept her voice steady as she glared at him. "I'll be right back," she said, then pivoted and made for the kitchen.

"Cotton?" she asked when she arrived. "Do you know just how many hours 'the boy' has had himself chained to that desk today?"

"I can't tell you down to the minute," the man said, his head ducked inside the open refrigerator, "but I woke up this mornin' around four and smelled the coffee brewin'. So I reckon he got up just before then. Why do you ask, sugar?"

"Because he and I are fixing to have a little talk, and I wanted to know whether I should let him have it with both barrels or just one." She smiled back at him before turning on her heel.

She returned to the study, closed the door and pressed her spine against it.

"I'm going to answer that question calmly and rationally, Tyler, because I know how tired you are. And because I don't believe for one minute that you asked me here for want of my tutoring abilities. If it weren't for those two factors, though, I wouldn't be nearly so kind. So I suggest you hear me out."

Without a word, he propped his boots on the edge of the desk and crossed them at the ankle.

"I am not *re*living my youth. I'm simply doing some of the things I was afraid to do as a child—and quite frankly, to put it in two-bit terms, I'm enjoying the hell out of it!" She pushed away from the door. "Beyond that, as far as I'm concerned, it's been a real eye-opener for you and Sam to teach me that I don't always have to do what other people might want or expect of me. That I don't always have to act like the perfect lady in order to be a lady."

While she paced the floor in front of him, he simply watched. As if he were too weary to protest or argue.

"In case you don't realize it, Tyler, being a lady is not wearing frilly white dresses and crossing your ankles properly while you sip your tea. It's not something you can even put your finger on. It's—" She pointed toward the tree. "It's a state of mind! Samantha may be a bit of a tomboy, but inside she feels like a young lady. She's a wonderful girl—to use your own words—and I won't have anything to do with trying to change her. I'm crazy about her just the way she is."

He pushed out a sigh, then rubbed his jaw. "Are you through yet?"

"No, Tyler. I'm not through. I'm trying my darnedest to understand why you have this chip on your shoulder. You seem to hold disdain for society people, yet you want your daughter to act like a proper little lady. Sam is well behaved and well mannered when she needs to be, but she's also a child and should be allowed to run and play."

Jerri stopped pacing then and stood still, crossing her arms in front of her as she looked him directly in the eye.

"And if her grandparents look down their noses at you, then that's their problem. As far as I'm concerned, it's also their loss. And no amount of manners and refinement on your part or Sam's is going to make them anything but a couple of fools." She lifted her chin high. "I'm through now."

"Good." He stood up and crossed the room, then folded her into his arms and kissed her. Involuntarily, her hands slid around his lean waist, and she felt herself melting against his tall, muscular body as she held on to him.

"What—" she swallowed once, trying to control her uneven breathing "—what was that all about?"

"That was my way of saying I'm sorry," he murmured. "Apology accepted?"

"No," she whispered, "not yet. Do it again, and we'll see."

His lips brushed one corner of her mouth, then the other, before he kissed her passionately...lingeringly. Beautifully.

"I don't know why I barked at you." He raised his head and sighed. "Except that I've been feeling guilty as hell."

"Why?" she asked, confused by the grave expression in his eyes.

"Because of having to ignore you like this."

"Don't be silly, darling. I know it can't be helped."

"No. And it's temporary. I promise you that." He propped his chin against her hair. "Give it another week, huh? After that, if I can get past your secretary, things will be better. You'll see."

She laughed at his reference to Samantha's diligence, then fell silent as she let herself enjoy his reassuring warmth. How good it felt to be in his arms.

He let out one brief sound of amusement, then glanced away. "Now I know why boxers train the way they do, before they go into the ring." His gaze moved to hers before he smiled. "This abstinence stuff makes you mean."

"My poor baby," she whispered. "You're not mean, you're exhausted." She snuggled closer to him. "Is there anything I can do to help?"

"Yeah," he answered abruptly, holding her at arm's length. "You can leave me with this fighter's edge I've built up. This...meeting is supposed to take a full day, but if I go in there feeling like I do now, I can probably get through it in fifteen minutes flat." He reached up, gently stroking the edge of her face with his thumb. "What do you say we go out tomorrow night? I'll take you out to dinner, and then—" he wiggled his eyebrows "—if you're in a blatantly obvious mood, I'll take you dancing...and let you polish my belt buckle."

"Mmm. That sounds heavenly." She kissed her fingers, then pressed them tenderly to his cheek before she headed for the door. "Now get back to business, if that's what you have to do, and stop your worrying. When it comes to me, you don't have anything to feel guilty about. Okay?"

Tyler stood there, frowning with resignation before he turned toward his desk.

Jerri waited until she heard him mutter "okay." And then she smiled and left him to his work.

Chapter Thirteen

Jerri closed the narrow-slatted blinds against the late-morning sunlight, then leaned over to kiss Samantha's cheek.

"Well," she said to the girl, "I'm just glad your stomach wasn't bothering you *before* we went to the fair last night. I wouldn't have missed it for anything."

"Me neither!"

She touched the pad of her index finger to Sam's nose. "And you know what my favorite part was?" she asked, hoping to distract her from her discomfort.

"What?"

"When you and Cotton took me to watch your girl-friend Amie while she washed her lambs. I still can't believe it!"

"Why not?" Sam asked. "They had to be clean or they never would've won any ribbons at the stock show."

"No, not that. What I meant was, I still can't believe she washed them at the car wash, of all places. And that everyone else in Bandera County seemed to be doing the same thing.'' Jerri laughed as she visualized the busy, coin-operated facility and the proprietors rushing around to clean up after everyone. ''But at least I know the rules now. Pigs have to stay inside the trailers while they're being washed, whereas sheep get to come out.''

''Makes sense, doesn't it?'' the girl asked, grinning. ''Pigs are too squirmy and slippery to—'' She stopped then, wincing.

''Here,'' Jerri said, taking the tepid hot-water bottle from her tummy. ''Let me refill this for you. That'll make you feel better.''

She closed the door behind her and headed for the kitchen. For Samantha's sake, she was glad that the house was unusually peaceful this morning. Tyler had left for his meeting before anyone else had risen, and Cotton was out tending to the few horses that had been kept on the ranch almost solely for his pleasure.

After refilling the bottle, Jerri replaced the stopper and gazed out the window just as a dark, sleek, shining Cadillac approached the drive then angled toward the front of the house. Not wanting the doorbell to disturb Samantha, she went through the den and on to the front door.

She watched through the panel of stained-glass windows alongside the door as an elderly woman stepped out of the car. Clutching her handbag, the woman adjusted a gorgeous, full-length mink coat that looked as if the poor, unsuspecting little animals had been custom-bred for her—the coat's soft, silvery color was only one or two shades darker than her perfectly styled hair. As the woman closed the car door and walked toward the house, carrying herself with graceful elegance, Jerri noticed how aloof and reserved she appeared to be.

Placing the hot-water bottle close to a vase on the entry table, she opened the door. And that was when she saw the woman's eyes. Despite the chilly look behind them, her eyes were the same deep brown as Samantha's. This, Jerri real-

ized, must be the woman who had never approved of Tyler
Reynolds.

"Hello," she said, extending her hand. But the woman
only stood there and studied her. "I'm Jerri Davenport, and
you must be Samantha's grandmother. Mrs...."

"Mrs. Hart," the woman answered, looking puzzled.

"I'm sorry. Come in, won't you?" She stood back to let
Mrs. Hart enter. "Let me take your coat." *Please!* her mind
added, and Jerri bit the insides of her mouth to keep from
giggling from a sudden attack of nerves. This woman, she
realized, would not appreciate such a giddy, impulsive attempt at humor.

"Thank you," Samantha's grandmother said, her chin in
the air as she shrugged out of the fur and handed it to her
with what seemed like great reluctance.

Being careful with it, Jerri turned toward the entry closet
to find a padded hanger and tuck away the expensive coat.
She felt even more edgy all of a sudden, realizing she needed
to explain her presence here in a diplomatic and discreet
way. She needed to let Mrs. Hart know she was neither a
total stranger nor an irresponsible flake. If not, she knew she
would never be able to approach the subject of the night
before and why the woman's granddaughter was subse-
quently bedridden.

And now, too, Jerri realized why Tyler had felt so uncomfortable with her own formality. It didn't matter that
her reasons had been different; it was nevertheless unnerving.

She closed the closet and turned around, smiling. "I'm
sure you're here to see Samantha," she said airily, "but if
you don't mind my taking a few minutes of your time, I'd
appreciate being able to introduce myself properly." With
a wave of her hand, she indicated the sofa.

The woman took a seat at last, smoothing the folds of her
wool dress, and Jerri straightened her own sweater as she
moved to Tyler's favorite chair, which seemed comforting
somehow. "I'm Jerri Davenport," she repeated, placing her

hands flat against her denim-clad thighs and trying to keep them still. "I'm not sure whether you know Beth Ferguson, Tyler's cousin, but I'm her best friend."

"No," the woman responded. "I don't believe I know Ms. Ferguson."

"Well, I've known Samantha and Tyler for about seven or eight years now, because of my friendship with Beth, and Tyler was kind enough to offer me his guest room for a while. Actually, I live in Houston. But I felt I needed a little serenity and seclusion while I'm working on a book I hope to have published someday."

"Oh," Mrs. Hart said stiffly, looking a bit more at ease. "How nice, dear." Her spine finally made contact with the throw pillow in the corner of the sofa. "What kind of a book is it?"

"It's about art therapy for children, so Samantha's been a big help. She's a very sweet, bright little girl." Jerri leaned back, feeling a bit more comfortable herself. "She's done everything she can to help me. To make me feel at home here. I know you and Mr. Hart must be proud of her."

"Yes," she said, a soft smile touching her lips. "She's always been such a precious child." The smile changed then, a haunted look clouding her brown eyes. "Very selfless and loving. We feel extremely fortunate."

"I know she feels the same about you and your husband," Jerri said quietly, her heart going out to the woman as she watched the expression in her eyes. Was Mrs. Hart thinking about her own daughter, she wondered, and the way Pauline had so easily given up such a special child?

"Well," Jerri said, smiling more brightly, "I know you want to see Samantha, but I think I should tell you she's in bed at the moment."

"Oh, no! Is she ill? She was feeling fine when I talked to her on the phone yesterday."

"No, no. She's not really ill. She's just not feeling very well. Uh, Mrs. Hart, I don't know how to say this, except to just say it." She swallowed hard. "Well, we went to the fair last night, and after we got home, Samantha started her period. Her very first period." Mrs. Hart's formal stance was making this an uncomfortable explanation, even though the topic was a natural part of all women's lives. "You're her grandmother, of course, and I would never presume to tell you how to handle this. I just thought you'd like to know, before you went in to see her, how I've been handling it."

"Oh," she stated flatly, looking rather embarrassed. "Well, thank you, dear. That's very thoughtful of you."

"She's having a few cramps—mild ones, I think—but the feeling is a little new and confusing to her. I thought it would be best not to treat it as an illness, per se, but as a normal progression in her life. I don't know how you feel about these things, of course, but..." She was beginning to rattle on, but she didn't want Mrs. Hart to go in there babying Sam when Sam obviously didn't want to be babied. "Well, I just thought you'd be happy to know that, despite the cramps, she's not the least bit frightened. She had some knowledge from her friends, of course. And it seems that Tyler has talked to her about this part of her life, but considering the fact that he's a man, I knew it couldn't have been easy for him to discuss this sort of thing at length, so—"

Jerri stopped, seeing the haunted expression as it came to the woman's eyes again. And a deep sense of regret washed over her as she realized what she had done: her wording had only reminded Mrs. Hart of her daughter's absence from Samantha's life.

"Well," she went on, trying to relieve the awkward silence, "I just wanted to let you know that I took it upon myself to ask Samantha if she had any questions. And then I answered them as best I could. I hope that doesn't bother you—me being a total stranger to you, and you being her grandmother."

"No, no," the woman replied quickly. "On the contrary, I'm glad you did. I think you handled it very well."

Jerri stood up, fighting the urge to sigh in relief. She picked up the hot-water bottle, and both of them walked through the hall and into the bedroom.

"Grandma!" Sam squealed as soon as the door opened. "I'm glad you're here. You'll never guess what I've got!"

"What?" the woman asked, her smile glowing with pride as she walked over and kissed the girl before sitting on the edge of her bed.

"Cramps!" Sam said excitedly, almost reverently. "The *real* ones!"

"Well!" her grandmother gushed. "And before your thirteenth birthday, too. Isn't that wonderful?"

"Yes! And I'm so glad it happened *before* my party! Jerri says she got her very first period the day before Thanksgiving. And that meant her next one was during Christmas! Wouldn't that be just horrible?"

"Not so horrible," Jerri said, laughing as she handed her the water bottle. "I lived to tell about it, didn't I?"

She turned toward the hallway, leaving the two of them alone now that she knew all was well. Before she closed the door, though, she heard Sam's excited voice:

"Jerri says I probably won't have cramps every month. But they're really not so bad. Do you remember what it felt like, Grandma? The first time you had cramps when you were..."

Lucky for her, she decided, smiling on her way to the kitchen, that Sam was at least including her grandmother after her little stream of "Jerri says this, Jerri says that."

Thirty minutes later, Mrs. Hart walked out of the bedroom. And when Jerri glanced up from her lunch preparations, she noticed that "Grandma" was absolutely beaming.

"Thank you, Jerri—" the woman actually used her real name, instead of calling her dear "—for taking care of my granddaughter, for putting her mind at ease about all this."

"It's nothing, Mrs. Hart. Really."

"Why don't you call me Phyliss?" She reached out and squeezed Jerri's hand between hers. "And don't say it's nothing. You've taken time out of your work—your book—to see that she's all right, and I'm grateful to you for being here when she needed you."

"I'm happy to do it. She's a fine little girl." She returned the pressure of Phyliss's hand and smiled. "But I guess I shouldn't call her a little girl anymore."

"That's right. She's turning into a fine young woman, isn't she?"

"Yes, she is," Jerri agreed. "I know Tyler would be proud to hear you say that."

The woman stared at her for a long moment, a strange, quizzical look in her brown eyes before she finally spoke. "Yes, he would, wouldn't he?" Her voice lowered even more as she glanced away and continued. "He's done a wonderful job of bringing her up."

Jerri blinked, surprised. Phyliss Hart had uttered the statement so quietly that it seemed she was making the admission to herself and no one else.

The elegant-looking woman straightened to her usual posture then and squeezed her hand once more. "Well," she said, starting toward the den. "Thank you again, Jerri, for everything!" She stopped at the front door and turned to her. "I'm looking forward to seeing all of you at Samantha's party next week. And I know Walter—Mr. Hart—will be anxious to meet you, too." She walked to the car, giving a wave of her fingers. "See you then."

With that, she got into the car and started the engine.

Jerri stood in the open doorway, her hand raised motionless in the air, her eyes wide with astonishment as she watched Samantha's grandmother drive away. And it wasn't until the Cadillac turned onto the main road that she realized what the woman had forgotten: the fur coat that, less than an hour before, had seemed to be Phyliss Hart's most prized possession.

In the den that evening Jerri threw her arms around Tyler before he lifted her into the air.

"I assume this means your meeting went well?" she asked, grinning before her bare toes found the carpet once again.

"I'm not positive yet, but I think it went *real* well." He grazed her lips with a kiss. "So," he whispered seductively. "Are you ready to celebrate?"

"Of course," she murmured, "but instead of going out, I thought maybe we could stay here and be alone together."

"Alone? Just exactly how do you propose to work that?"

"Well," she answered, "Cotton went out earlier with a couple of friends. It seems that on Saturday nights, things really get hopping, and the three old bucks 'got a hankerin' to go into town.' They must have gone to the big dance, because on the way out of the house he mentioned something about wearing the ladies out on the dance floor." She lifted her gaze toward the ceiling, then back to Tyler. "Men!"

His rakish blue eyes questioned her. "What about Sam, though? Where's she?"

"Fast asleep."

"Already?" He glanced at his watch, looking worried all of a sudden. "She's not sick, is she?"

"No," Jerri answered, not wanting to give Tyler the news about his daughter just yet—not until he'd had a chance to share his own good news of the day. "Just exhausted, that's all. She and I stayed up late last night. We were too excited to sleep after our big night on the town."

"Women!" he muttered disgustedly.

She gave him a gentle slug on the arm. "So what do you say, big guy? Are you ready for some good old-fashioned necking right here in your own den?"

"That sounds terrific. What are we waiting for?" Tyler took off his sports coat, then took a seat in his favorite chair and ran his palms down the snug, dark jeans covering his thighs. Jerri turned around, her back to him. Straddling one leg and then the other, she removed his dress boots and set them aside. And when she turned back to face him, he brought her down to his lap.

"So," Jerri whispered, sighing as she relaxed against his hard chest. Terrific was too mild a word, she decided. Just being close to him felt heavenly. "Why don't you go ahead, darling? Tell me all about your meeting."

"I don't especially want to talk about it. I'm just glad that it seemed to go well—and that it's over with." He lifted her chin. "And now that we've exhausted that subject . . . Ever since I got home, you've been dying to tell me something, so why don't you go ahead and spit it out?"

"Well, okay," she admitted. "I just wanted to tell you there's another reason I needed to stay home tonight. It's actually . . . a female-type reason."

"Ahh." His hand moved to her belly then, rubbing it gently. "My poor baby," he murmured compassionately. "I'm sorry you're feeling rotten."

"No, I'm feeling fine. Just fine." After stilling the movement of his hand by covering it with her own palm, she narrowed her eyes. "No, Tyler. I'm talking about the other female in your life."

He appeared to be thoroughly perplexed. But then he looked stunned, and his eyes rounded. "You're kidding."

"No, darling. I wouldn't kid about a thing like that." She shook her head, amused by the stricken expression on his ruggedly handsome face. "It's true. As of late last night, your daughter is indeed a young lady."

"Why didn't you tell me last night?" he asked, his tone reflecting his concern.

"Because today, of all days, I didn't want you to be worrying about her. And she's doing just fine. In fact, she couldn't be happier. I think she's thrilled to be blossoming into womanhood, as they say."

He stared at her, a blank look in his eyes, and finally grimaced.

"Now come on, Daddy!" She slapped his hand. "You see why I didn't tell you sooner? You're already worrying about her."

"Oh, I'm not worrying about *her*. I'm sure she'll do fine." He lifted his brows. "No. I was worrying about 'Daddy.'"

"For heaven's sake, Tyler. Why?"

"Because it just dawned on me how old she's getting to be. And for some reason, it struck me that it won't be long before I'll be worrying myself silly. Oh, not about her. I trust her. I just don't trust those boys." He frowned wryly. "Those boys who are bursting into manhood, as they say."

"Oh, now," she whispered, turning her cheek and pressing her face against the cool, crisp fabric of his shirt. "It'll be okay. You'll see." She held him close, smiling blissfully as she squeezed her eyes shut and visualized the scene. When that day finally rolled around, Jerri hoped she would be at his side, in his bed. In their bed. Someday, if Samantha was late getting home from a date, she hoped more than anything else in the world that Mr. and Mrs. Tyler Reynolds would be comforting each other. That they would be holding each other in the dark, giving each other warmth and strength as they watched the glowing hands of the clock...as they worried about *their* daughter. Together.

"Smoky?" he asked, hearing the soft, velvety purr that slipped past her lips. "You're not falling asleep on me, are you?"

"Oh, no. Too much happened today. I'm too excited to sleep."

"Good God," he whispered, laughing. "What else happened?"

"I met someone new, that's all. Guess who it was?"

"Guess who?" he asked, and she felt him shake his head. "You've been hanging around your secretary too long."

"Just a minute. I'll give you a hint." She scurried up from his lap and across the room, grinning as she opened the closet to point inside.

"All right," he stated flatly. "What'd she look like?"

"You *do* know whose coat this is, don't you?"

"Of course. How could I not know?" He frowned bitterly. "I also know how proud she is of that damned thing."

"But you said, 'What did she look like?'"

"Yeah." He sighed and leaned back against his laced fingers. "What I meant was, what'd she look like when she left here? How bad did she look after you wrestled her to the floor and took that precious coat away from her?" He gave her a scolding glance. "I hope you weren't too rough on her, Smoky. She's in pretty good shape, for an old broad, but you've definitely got the advantage of youth and—"

"No!" she said, laughing. "That's what I'm talking about, Tyler. Phyliss Hart was so happy and excited when she left here, she actually forgot her coat! Can you imagine? She never even called about it afterward."

"That could only mean one thing, then. She realized it later and had a heart attack. She's been in intensive care all this time, or she would've been on the phone about it way before now."

"For heaven's sake, Tyler. I'm serious."

"I know. So am I. That woman has never even let me get within striking range of that extravagant coat." The frown left his face, and he smiled devilishly. "Listen, sweetheart, I have an idea. Why don't you spread that thing out on the floor." He lowered his voice, whispering to her from across the room. "Let's make love on it. And then we'll give it back to her."

"Good grief, Tyler," she whispered back at him. "Don't be such a shameless lech!" Jerri started to close the closet, but she couldn't resist the urge to reach inside for just a moment or two. Running the back of her hand along the ultrasoft fur, she sighed dreamily. "It probably would feel wonderful, wouldn't it?"

"Yeah," she heard from behind her. "I do believe it would. So how 'bout it?"

"No," she chastised him firmly, shutting the door and then taking her place on his lap again. "Now stop trying to distract me, because I want to tell you about this." She put her arms around his wide shoulders. "Before Grandma Hart left, she actually started warming up to me. She doesn't know about you and me, of course, but I think she actually approves of me. And you know what else? I don't think she's ever really disapproved of you. I think she's been treating you the way she has because of her pride."

The frown was back on his face. "She's got plenty of that."

"Oh, come on now, Tyler. We all do. You certainly do."

"I do not."

"You do, too." She clamped her fingers around the back of his neck. "Now stop arguing with me, because I need to tell you what I've realized about all this. I was always stiff and formal with you because—" She glanced up toward the ceiling and frowned in mock resignation. "Well, because I was mesmerized by your very presence, okay?" Her gaze moved back to his, and she returned his sudden smile. "I was so crazy-wild about you that I always just froze up inside. But I'd be willing to bet that Phyliss Hart's had her own reasons for being cold when she's around you. I think I know what the problem is, and right before she left here today, I think she was beginning to understand it, too. I think she's been motivated by a sense of guilt."

"Bull," he said bluntly. "What's guilt got to do with anything?"

"Think about it for a minute, Tyler. Maybe she's been feeling guilty all these years—about a lot of things. The way Pauline treated you, for instance. And the way *they've* treated you."

He only lifted his shoulders.

"Look, Tyler. I think she realized today that she admires you, that you're the one who's always been there for Sam. But maybe she's just been too proud to admit that to you, of all people, because if she admitted she approved of you, then that might mean she was admitting she disapproved of her own daughter. And in turn, that might mean she'd done something very wrong—as a mother."

He gave her a sidelong frown, as if he'd just decided there were a couple of screws loose and rattling around in her brain.

"What I'm trying to say is, deep down she knows you've been a wonderful father." Jerri wasn't going to tell him about Mrs. Hart's admission. She knew he deserved to hear that from Phyliss herself, no matter when that might be. "All I'm saying is, there's always hope. Maybe she'll start realizing that it doesn't really matter who's been right and who's been wrong and who's to 'blame.' All that matters is that she has a loving, caring granddaughter who's being raised by a loving, caring father. And if she realizes that, maybe she'll be able to drop her stubborn sense of pride and get on with life as it is now."

"I don't know," he said, sighing wearily. "All I know, Jerri, is that whatever her motivation has been—pride or guilt or whatever—it doesn't really matter, because Phyliss Hart is the way she is. Today's a prime example: anytime Sam mentions my plans to be gone, she conveniently drops by. She can't abide being in the same house with me, but she turns that around and acts like I've forbidden her to come here." He leaned back, staring at the ceiling as he breathed deeply and ran his fingers through his hair. "And all I know is that I hate that. I hate it."

"And that, my darling, is because you've got *your* pride," she said softly, her heart going out to him as she detected the sadness he felt.

"And you know what I say to that?" he asked, lifting his head and abruptly changing the mood by leering at her playfully. "I say that if Sigmund Freud had been here for the last God-knows-how-many minutes, he would've fired your gorgeous, shapely ass for that particular analysis." His hand moved around her, to the area in discussion.

"Well, I disagree," she said with feigned arrogance. "I think Sigmund would be darned pleased with my analysis." Phyliss Hart, Jerri reminded herself, had clearly stated that she was looking forward to seeing all of them the following

Friday night. "And you just wait until Sam's birthday party. I think you might notice a difference in that woman's attitude toward you."

"Fat chance."

Jerri noticed that the same bitter frown was on his face again. The topic of Phyliss Hart truly bothered him—she knew that now, beyond a shadow of a doubt. But she also felt a great sense of hope that the situation would be changing soon, possibly on the night of the party.

For now, though, she would drop the subject rather than spoil his evening. This was a night for celebration. They had both been working hard for the past week and a half, and she would make it a point to keep things light for the rest of the evening.

"I'll bet you're starving," she said, "after nothing but that horrible chicken à la king they always serve at those meetings. Come on. Cotton fixed a nice dinner, but I didn't eat. I waited for you."

After they had finished their late meal, Tyler swept her into his arms and carried her back to the den. "Stay right here till I get back," he whispered, laying her on the sofa and then brushing her lips with the gentlest of kisses. "Don't move."

"Where are you going?"

"To shave." He ran his hand upward, along the dark, stubbly growth that Jerri had always considered nothing but sexy. He lifted his brows as he continued. "I'm not about to let you squirm out of that promise you made about necking on the sofa—but I don't want to tear up your face." He touched her cheek. "I'll look in on Sam when I'm through shaving. I won't be long."

A few minutes later, Tyler stood in front of the bathroom mirror, humming under his breath as he worked the straight razor over his face.

He felt sure he had passed his entrance exams, but that didn't make him nearly as happy as just getting them out of the way. That was the one condition to enrolling in a cou-

ple of days. Verification of taking his exams would allow
him to start attending classes as a "special student" in another week. Later on, when Trinity received notification of
adequate test scores, his status would change to that of a
"regular student." But that was nothing more than a change
on paper.

All that counted right now, he reminded himself, was that
he was one step closer to enrollment, which meant he was
one step closer to being totally honest with Jerri.

Tyler pulled on his shirt again, leaving it to hang free as
he left the bathroom. When he stopped to check on Sam,
she was sleeping soundly. He smiled as he looked down on
her and realized what an eventful twenty-four hours his own
daughter had just been through. He picked up the glass of
water that was balanced dangerously close to the edge of her
nightstand and turned to leave the bedroom, shutting the
door behind him.

"I still can't believe my little girl's old enough to be—"
He stopped dead in his tracks, staring at Jerri stretched out
lazily on the sofa. Staring at the cigarette she held poised
between her lips—and at the smoke trailing upward from its
lit end.

"Jerri!" If it hadn't been for Sam sleeping in the other
room, he would have been yelling. Instead, his voice hissed
at her from the entrance to the den. "What the hell do you
think you're doing?"

She glanced at him, looking maddeningly blasé. "I just
wanted to see what it was like, that's all. Everyone talks
about how great it is, propping yourself up afterward and
smoking a cigarette, so—"

"For God's sake! That's after you make love. Not after
one innocent little kiss!" He crossed the room in nothing
flat, his shirttail flying. Glaring down at her, he yanked the
cigarette out of her hand and quickly dropped it into the
drinking glass. "After you've worked so hard at this, why
the hell would you—"

The cigarette, he realized all of a sudden, hadn't sizzled when it hit the water.

"What's—" He fished it out of the glass. The phony cigarette fell from his fingers, and he plunked the glass down on the end table. "Why, you little . . ." He stared at Jerri as she rolled off the couch and onto the carpet, holding a throw pillow over her face to muffle her uncontrolled laughter.

"Of all the dirty tricks!" He landed on top of her, pinning her to the floor, and uncovered her face.

"And you said I had no sense of humor," she finally managed to say. "What do you know, mister?"

"Oh, I'll get you for this. You've got a lot of nerve, laughing while I'm in the middle of a—"

"I'm sorry, Tyler. Really! But I can't help it. You should've seen your face! It looked just like Sam's and mine last night when we saw this boy at the county fair. He was about five years old, and our jaws dropped to the ground when we saw him puffing on one of those things!" She kept right on gasping for breath. "It looks real, doesn't it? With that fake smoke coming out the end?"

"Hell, yes, it looks real. You almost gave me a seizure! And you can't talk your way out of punishment, so just—"

"No, Tyler! No, no. Sam made me do it. She did! She bought it with her own money from that booth at the fair, and she made me promise I'd pull this trick on you!"

"Well . . ." He smiled down at her, loosening his grip on her wrists, enjoying the friction of her warmth and softness against the hair on his chest. "Maybe I'll have mercy on you, woman. But just this once, and only because—"

"Are you two having fun?" they heard from the kitchen doorway.

"Oh, Sam," Tyler said, rolling off Jerri. He snatched up the throw pillow and shoved it behind his head, lounging back against the carpet and trying to look casual. "Hi, honey," he said, fastening the bottom snaps on his shirt. "I thought you were asleep."

The girl gave him a small, knowing smile. "I can see that."

Jerri scrambled to a sitting position, running her fingers through her hair. But somehow, she resisted the impulse to place her hand against her thudding chest.

"Your dad really fell for this joke, Sam!" Her voice bubbled over with enthusiasm as she grabbed the cigarette and held it in the air. "He was convinced it was real. You should've seen him! He was furious with me there for a min—"

"Yeah, I sure was," Tyler interrupted, his laughter short and stilted. "That was just a second ago. I got so mad that I started attacking her, trying to take it away from her."

"Uh-huh," the girl said, rolling her eyeballs. "Sure." With that she turned toward the kitchen, and they heard the refrigerator door being opened.

Jerri turned to Tyler, her expression deadpan. "Well, I see she's got her father's charming, dry wit."

"Yeah," he mumbled under his breath, rubbing his face. "And if I ever find out what she did with it, I'll beat the livin' daylights out of her."

They both glanced up then to see Samantha standing in the doorway again. This time, she held a glass of juice in her hand. "I'm going back to bed now," she announced to both of them. She turned and started down the hallway toward her room, sending a final message over her shoulder. "I'll be asleep in a couple of minutes, Daddy—in case you wanta take that cigarette away from her again."

Jerri fell straight back against the carpet, slamming her eyes shut. Then she opened them again, only to see Tyler stretched out beside her, his mouth closed to stifle his laughter as he watched her reaction.

"My, my," she said, taking several deep, long breaths and finally pressing her palm against her now-calming heart. "This has definitely been an eventful day, hasn't it?"

"Yeah," he said, putting his arm around her. They remained on the floor, in happy silence, for another few minutes until Tyler spoke again.

"Yesterday was pretty eventful, too. I just haven't had the chance to tell you about it."

"Tell me about what?" she asked.

"An interesting new development that has to do with your book." His blue eyes were now wide and smiling. "Good news, I think."

She blinked, staring at him excitedly. "What are you talking about, Tyler?"

"You know that friend I was telling you about? The one who publishes textbooks?" She nodded before he explained. "I took the liberty of sending him a copy of your outline."

"But you haven't even been out of the house to speak of. How did you—"

"The day you gave it to me, I had Cotton run it over to my attorney's office in San Antonio. They have a telex machine."

"You are so sneaky!" she said. "So is he interested in the idea? This publisher friend of yours?"

"Whoa! You're getting ahead of me. He told me—"

"When did you talk to him?"

"Last week. I called him the day we got here. And then he called me back last night, right after you left for the stock show."

"But he couldn't have had it for more than—"

Grinning, Tyler covered her mouth with his hand, then took it away as soon as her lips stopped moving. "Geez, Jerri. Do me a favor. Save your questions till the end, will you?"

"Okay, okay. I'll shut up!"

"The first time I talked to him, he said he was sure the idea wasn't right for him. But he knew of an editor who might like it. So as soon as he got the outline, he passed it along to that person: Anne Something-or-Other, an associate editor at a reputable publishing house who also happens to be a personal friend of his. And he called last night to say she was excited about it. Very excited. She wants to see something more concrete as soon as you've got it ready. In fact, she wants you to keep her posted from the ground up. I guess that's in case either one of you runs into a snag or—" He frowned, pretending to be disgusted with her. "Okay. You can ask questions now."

"No!" She threw her arms around him. "I don't want to ask questions. I want to scream, I want to yell!"

"For God's sake, don't do that! Sam'll think I really am attacking you. She'll be in here trying to save you from the beast."

"Oh, darling," she whispered against his throat. "That was wonderful of you, to do that for me when you were so busy with your own work." She swallowed against the lump in her throat. "I love you, Tyler."

"And I love you, Jerri." He lay there, perfectly still, holding her against the strong, steady rhythm of his pulse. When she felt the tightening of his jaw, she looked up at him just before he spoke again. "And now that Sam's promised us some privacy, I have something important I need to talk to you about."

"What?" she murmured, smiling softly. Her heartbeat suddenly began racing again. But this time, a building sense of anticipation seemed to be making it race completely out of control.

"Well, I thought maybe you should know what's going on with my work right now. True, this project is at least off the ground. But I'll be honest with you, Smoky. It's definitely looking long term. It'll be keeping me away from home quite a lot, in fact. But I was thinking, well, you've got your long-term project, too. I know how important your book is to you, so maybe it wouldn't seem like I was neglecting you or—"

He cleared his throat, and Jerri thought she would surely die while she waited for him to continue.

"And now that this editor is really interested in it, it seems to me it'd be a great idea if you'd just stay on and finish it. You seem to be able to get a lot of work done here, and—"

"Oh, Tyler." Jerri blinked against the threat of tears. She had never felt such a plummeting sensation. Such a dive from sheer blissfulness to devastating sadness. "Is that what you think? That you have to line me up with an editor? That you have to buy my presence here?"

"No, sweetheart," he murmured. "Of course not. I just wanted the conditions to be perfect for you, that's all."

"Is that how I've made you feel? That I wouldn't stay unless the conditions were perfect?"

"No." He tilted his head, his soulful gaze touching hers. "I just didn't want you to leave."

He slowly ran his fingers through her hair, then lifted his eyes in a look of self-recrimination. "When I drove in tonight and saw your car parked outside, I guess it just stuck in my mind. I guess it made me wonder if you were..."

"Oh, darling," she whispered as she realized how foolish she had been. Despite her many courses in psychology, she hadn't seen what was so apparent here. All Tyler's life, women had been leaving him. And the entire time he and Jerri had been together, she'd been giving him those same messages. Either she had been asking Tyler to leave, or she had been telling him she was only staying with him temporarily. Now, too, she realized why he'd insisted that she didn't need her own vehicle while she was here.

"You wonderful, silly man," she murmured, smiling up at him. "My car's here because Beth and Doug are getting ready to go on their vacation. They didn't want it left unattended outside their house for the next couple of weeks, so Doug and one of his friends delivered it this afternoon. But that's the one and only reason.

"Darling," she went on, "let me tell you why I've been here all this time. I've been here because I've wanted to be here."

Her fingertip grazed the faint scar that was so much a part of him. "My book is important to me, and I have been working hard on it. But your promise of a contact with an editor was not my prime motivation for coming home with you. For staying with you." Dear Lord, she thought, he had the most beautiful, loving, soul-wrenching eyes. He could say more with those eyes than most men could say with a thousand words. "I agreed to come home with you because I thought maybe you needed some time. Some time to believe how much I really, truly love you."

"Oh, sweetheart," he whispered, pulling her into his arms and holding her as close as he could. "I know that. I've always known that." His hand moved tenderly along the back of her neck, sending electric charges rushing through her body. "I've just been feeling so damned guilty. Because you deserve more than these short-term promises I've been giving you. And believe me, Smoky, I want to give you more, but I can't do it just yet. I have my reasons, so do you think you can stick by me for a while longer?" He held her back from him, his gaze intent on hers. "I know you'll understand when I make my announcement the night of the dinner party."

"Oh, Tyler," she whispered, pulling him against her as she closed her eyes and smiled with overwhelming joy. She didn't want to say another word. All she wanted to do was hold him and etch this breathtaking moment in her memory, so that it would be with her forever.

She wanted to keep the firm and reassuring rhythm of his heartbeat against her own. To revel in the happiness, the closeness she felt with him at this very—

Jerri drew away from him slightly, reluctantly, when she heard the sound of the television that had just been clicked on in Samantha's room. She groped for the fake cigarette. Granted, it had been a flimsy cover, but it was better than nothing.

Tyler obviously knew what she was doing. He propped himself up on one elbow and shook his head in amusement. "Seeing you holding that thing sure brings back old memories."

"What old memories?" she asked, stretching out on her back to watch him.

"Good old memories of that Christmas dance. And you waving a cigarette around, trying to look sophisticated."

"Oh, that. That was stupid." The corner of her mouth tilted up into a self-derisive frown. "And don't remind me, because every time I think about that night, I think about Marty Cunningham. And every time I picture you and that floozy all snuggled up together on the dance floor, I get—" she rolled her eyes "—green with jealousy. There. I've admitted it."

"You didn't need to be jealous, you know. Even with her flaming red tresses, Marty Cunningham couldn't hold a candle to you." He took the phony cigarette away from her, studying it at length. "Or maybe I should say Marty couldn't hold a cigarette to you."

"That's a lousy pun, Tyler."

"Is it? I thought it was pretty good. Pretty appropriate, too, considering what you did to yourself that night." Smiling, he touched the glowing end of the pretend-cigarette to her hair.

Her mouth dropped open, and she stared at him in disbelief. "Beth told you about that, didn't she? I'll kill her!"

"No, Beth didn't tell me. She didn't have to." He lifted his brows. "Marty's big hairdo made mighty good camouflage. The whole time I was 'snuggling up' to her, I was actually ogling you."

"Oh, no," she moaned, dragging the pillow over her face again. "I can't believe you saw that! I want to die!"

"Come on now, sweetheart. You ought to be damned glad I saw it."

"For heaven's sake, Tyler," she moaned, her voice still muffled. "Why?"

"Because even though I wouldn't admit it to myself for a long time, I think that's exactly when I knew deep down that I was a goner."

She peeked out from under the pillow, her eyes wide and full of awe. "You did?" she whispered.

"Uh-huh," he admitted. "And what about you?"

"What about me?" she asked, the words sounding breathless.

"Oh, I know you've always had the hots for me.... But when did you know for sure?"

"Well." She took in a gulp of air, her mind still reeling from what he had just told her. "It was a series of things, actually."

All of a sudden, she noticed that Tyler was beginning to look tired. "Are you sure we have time for this?" she asked playfully.

"We'll make time. I want to hear the whole list."

"Well, okay. If you're sure."

"Oh, yes," he whispered. "I'm sure."

"Well," she said, smiling as she thought back. "I think it struck me for the first time when you came storming into the cabin, insisting on your twenty-four hours. Demanding that I give you equal time to get me out of your system." She touched her tongue to the corner of her mouth. "And then, it hit me again when you were packing my six hundred pounds of conveniences into the boat—moaning and bitching and complaining the whole time, but never letting me carry one thing."

He waited patiently, a smug grin on his face.

"But until yesterday I don't think I knew for sure, beyond a shadow of a doubt, that I was an absolute goner."

"Yesterday? When yesterday?"

"At breakfast, when Cotton told you how nice it was having me around. You looked me straight in the eye, and then you winked, which makes my knees go weak, anyway. And then in that slow, sure, sexy voice of yours, you said,

'Yeah. I'd say she's about as handy as the pocket on a shirt.'"

It still made her smile, made her feel light-headed, just thinking about it. "Now tell me, darling. How can a poor, defenseless woman resist a man like that? A man who can describe how he feels about her in such eloquent terms?"

"Mmm." He leaned over her then, settling his masculine strength and weight against her breasts. "You always were a pushover for my two-bit phrases."

"Call it a two-bit phrase all you want, mister," she murmured slowly, "but it felt like a thousand-dollar sentence to me."

His mouth came down on hers then, his warm tongue parting her lips, his hand brushing aside the hem of her blouse. The volume of the television changed a fraction, and Tyler rolled onto his back and tried to control his breathing. In another few moments, he sighed deeply. Tiredly.

"Go to bed, darling," she said gently, standing and taking his hand. "I'll go tuck Sam in. And then maybe I'll slip into your room just for a minute and tuck you in, too. How does that sound?"

"Like a dream," he whispered as he got to his feet. "Will you change into something less decent first, though?"

"Like what?" she asked, lowering her voice as they passed through the hallway.

When they reached the threshold of his bedroom, he leaned against the jamb. "I've got—" he brought her fingers to his lips "—this sudden hankerin' to see you in 'Old Blue.'"

She smiled, beaming up into his beautiful, dark blue eyes. "That sounds dangerous, darling." She moved her hand, brushing the back of it across his freshly shaven cheek. "But I'll definitely think about it."

She turned away from him at last, and as she opened the door to Sam's room, Tyler winked at her. And her knees went weak....

Tyler undressed quickly and got into bed, smiling as he thought about the upcoming Friday night. Only six more days, and he'd be able to tell her. And as soon as she heard what was going on in his life, she would understand why he wanted to wait awhile, until he'd at least gotten a decent start on changing things. He closed his eyes then, amazed that he could still smell the gardenias. She had never been in his bed, yet the scent of her lingered like one of her caresses, floated around him like a warm . . .

Thirty minutes later, when Samantha had finally drifted off again, Jerri stood over Tyler's sleeping body.

She knelt on the thick carpet next to his bed, then sat back on her folded legs and adjusted the blue chenille. She couldn't bear the thought of waking him. He was exhausted, and neither one of them would have been able to go through with it, anyway.

No. They wouldn't have shared his bed. Not tonight, not with his daughter in the next room, and certainly not when they had such a short time left before they could share it proudly, happily. Legally.

Only six more days, she thought, her heart singing with joy, and he would be announcing their upcoming marriage to his family. To the thirteen-year-old girl who would soon be Jerri's daughter, too.

She smiled as she stood up, leaning to touch his hair. She had waited a lifetime for this. To feel the promise of a life that was warm and rich and full. To share the rest of her life with the man she loved.

Yes, Jerri told herself as she began edging out of the quiet room, still smiling softly and watching him. Six days was precious little time to wait for something as wonderful as that.

Chapter Fourteen

Jerri stood in the bright, sunny kitchen, filling her cup with freshly brewed coffee from the day's second pot. Her over-excited nerves didn't need more coffee today, of all days—but her mind seemed to need its warm, soothing effects.

The back door opened, a soft wave of chilly air touching her as Cotton sauntered into the kitchen.

"Hey, sugar." His light blue eyes twinkled in her direction. "What's got you grinnin' like a possum?"

"Just the fact that it's finally Friday." After adjusting the hem of her sweater, she squared her shoulders and added a logical explanation for her glorious mood. "It's the day we've all been waiting for. And that reminds me, Cotton. Is there anything else I can help you with before the party?"

"I can't think of a thing. We've done it all, I reckon, or else it won't get done. I've even got my roast ready to go in the oven." He opened the refrigerator and proudly pointed inside. "I had this 'un cut special. It's a beauty, isn't it?"

"It certainly is!" Jerri tried to show the proper degree of respect for the plastic-covered roast, although her mind was much too busy with other things. Tyler had been out on business virtually all day every day since the previous Sunday afternoon, so his study was available. Fully intending to work, she had gotten up this morning and spread out the chapters of her extremely rough draft all over his once-tidy desk, but she was beginning to think it was wasted effort. Thanks to the building excitement she felt about tonight, not to mention the fact that his study seemed to hold not only the scent of leather, but also the lingering scent of Tyler, she couldn't seem to concentrate.

"Well," she added, picking up her coffee cup. "I'll be in the study for a few more minutes, and then I'll run into town for the flowers and the other last-minute things. But I'll check with you before I go, in case you think of anything else you need."

She watched him thumb through the mail he'd brought in, then realized there might be something in the stack for her. Since she used the museum's address for her correspondence, she had called the receptionist a few days before and asked her to forward anything that looked either personal or urgent.

"Anything for me, Cotton?"

"Yeah, there sure is." He fished out a postcard, then turned it around to show her the picture. "Looks like some tropical island."

"Great!" she replied. "It must be from my mother. She works on a cruise ship." She abandoned her coffee cup in the sink and took the postcard he handed her. "Thanks," she said, grinning as she headed for the study.

After closing the door, Jerri flipped over the colorful card and read the message.

Dearest Jerri,
Lo and behold, your hunch was right. Howard *is* in-

terested. Very interested. And I'm beginning to see how interested I am in *him*.

We went out on a date last night—dinner on St. Croix while in port. Can you believe it, honey? Your old mom has a boyfriend, of all things, and is feeling like a kid again!

We're having a great time together, so thanks for sharing your bout of "woman's intuition."

Love you,
Mom

"Well, isn't that just wonderful?" she murmured out loud.

Yes, she decided, still smiling happily as she moved to Tyler's desk and read the postcard again. This was indeed going to be an eventful day all the way around.

Hearing the ring of Tyler's private telephone line, the one that rang only in this location, Jerri lifted her head. The multibutton phone linked the household, the bottling company and the study, and Jerri stared at the one flashing light, wondering if this particular call might be from Tyler's publisher friend. Or better yet, the editor who was interested in her work.

Probably not, she decided on the second ring, realizing it was ridiculous to hope for that many fantastic events in one day. She would simply follow what she knew to be the regular house rules and let the recorder pick up the call.

Still, she thought on the third ring. It could be about her book. There was always that possibility, and if it was a call for Tyler, she could certainly make sure he got the message.

She pushed the flashing button, managing to snatch up the receiver before the fourth ring. Not knowing exactly what words to use in answering, she decided on a phrase that would at least sound businesslike.

"Mr. Reynolds's office," she stated. "May I help you?"

"Yes," came the reply. "This is Bob Woodman at Trinity. Is he in?"

"Not at the moment, Mr. Woodman," she answered. "But I'll be happy to tell him you called. Did you say Trinity? Trinity University?" Perhaps that was Tyler's alma mater.

"That's right."

"And the number?" she asked, grabbing a nearby scratch pad and pencil.

The man rattled off the number, and she barely had time to jot it down before he continued. "But we can probably save a call here. Just tell him that regarding the request he filed with our office last week, we're sorry, but it's been denied." She wrote down "request denied" as he went on. "If he has any questions, of course I'll be glad to discuss them with him. He probably has my extension, but if you'd like to make a note of it . . ."

She repeated the extension number he had given her, then straightened. As the next official-sounding question started out of her mouth, Jerri realized she was asking it out of pure curiosity. "And which department is that, Mr. Woodman?"

When the man answered her question, she gave the phone a quizzical glance and mumbled, "Thank you. I'll be sure he gets the message."

Jerri settled against the big swivel chair, thoroughly perplexed. Why on earth, she wondered, would Tyler have filed any sort of request with Bob Woodman's office at Trinity University? She had thought perhaps it had to do with alumni matters or that Tyler might be teaching or attending some kind of a special marketing symposium. But what kind of dealings would he have with admissions?

She shrugged her shoulders, deciding it was silly to waste time on guessing games. She had too much to do for that. She would simply ask Tyler about it later.

Glancing at her wristwatch, she realized it was noon—almost time to pick up the flowers for Sam's party. She gathered her file folders, making one neat stack, and glanced up as she heard the door being opened.

"Hi, sweetheart!"

"Oh, hi, Tyler," she greeted him enthusiastically, realizing her smile must be beaming. "I'm glad you're home early for a change!"

He tossed his Stetson aside, and she couldn't help gawking at the button-front of the provocatively faded Levi's that were her favorites. Then she forced her gaze upward and realized what she was still holding in her hand. "Oh, wait a minute. I don't want to forget about this." As he closed the door behind him, she tore the handwritten message from the scratch pad. "I just took a call for you."

He took the slip of paper from her, and she noticed the odd look in his eyes when he scanned it quickly and tucked it into his shirt pocket. "Thanks." His expression changed to a nonchalant smile then, and he nodded toward her file folders. "You look mighty busy."

"No," she answered, laughing. "Just spinning my wheels, that's all. I've decided to give it up for the rest of the day." She lifted her hand, gesturing toward his pocket. "I'm just curious, darling. Why would you be getting a call from Bob Woodman? I don't want to sound nosy, but he said he was a coordinator for—"

"Look, Smoky. I didn't want to tell you this just yet, but I got a call from Bob Woodman because the spring semester starts next week, and I'll be attending."

"But how can you do that, Tyler? How can you take on a college course when you're so busy with your project?"

"Not a college course," he said immediately. "Courses, as in four years' worth. A full load." His eyes never left her puzzled gaze. "That *is* my long-term project."

Her mouth fell open, and Jerri searched her mind for some sort of logic behind all this. "I can't believe it. You mean you'll be a freshman?"

He gave a short, bitter laugh. "Probably the oldest one on campus."

"I'm sorry, Tyler, I don't mean to act so... This comes as a complete surprise, that's all. I just assumed you'd gone to college years ago." Another thought occurred to her. A thought that was even more confusing. "Don't get me wrong. I'm proud of you for wanting to further your education. Very proud. But I don't understand why you'd want to do it this particular way. You've made a huge success of your life—your ranch, your businesses—and you're probably the smartest man I know. If you want to sharpen your skills, why don't you just take some correspondence or evening courses instead of attending full time for the next four years?"

"Listen, sweetheart." He held up a placating hand. "It's not as bad as it sounds. They've denied my request to live off campus, but that rule only applies for the duration of freshman year, so after that—"

"Only?" she asked, her tone incredulous. She pointed in the direction of the bottling company on Tyler's property. "You have a ranch and a business to run, so just how much time do you expect to be able to devote to a family? Why would you choose to spend so much time away from your daughter? From me?"

"But that's exactly what this is all about, Smoky. All my life I've fallen short in this one area. I want to be more than what I've always been. I want that for myself and my daughter—and now, for you, too!"

Jerri's spine stiffened, pushing against the leather chair. She could never remember feeling so stunned. So hurt. And when she asked the question that had to be asked, her voice was unbelievably quiet. "How can you think so little of me, Tyler? That my feelings would change just because of a bit of a difference in formal education, of all things?"

"That's just it, Jerri! It's a lot more than a bit of a difference. It's a tremendous difference, and all I'm asking for is a little patience. I need a little time. A chance to narrow that gap."

He walked around the desk then, spinning the chair around and bending a knee to lower himself in front of her.

"Look, sweetheart," he whispered tenderly. "You can't ask me to shove this aside. For too many years now, going to college has been my dream." His hand moved past her knee, spanning her leg. "You, of all people, understand what that's all about."

"Yes, Tyler, I do." She covered his fingers with her own, holding his palm in place against her thigh. "And if this was truly your dream, I'd be all for it. But as far as I can see, it's your obsession. It goes right along with that chip you still seem to have on your shoulder. And I think you need to do some soul-searching about what really motivates you."

Her voice sounded faraway. And sad. "I always thought you were your own man, Tyler. I thought you did what you knew was best and to hell with how the world labeled it. But now I wonder if I've been all wrong about you."

Heartsick and disillusioned, she glanced away from him to the stack of file folders, then smiled softly as she looked back into his serious dark blue eyes. "But I'll tell you something else. I'm grateful to you, Tyler. Because you've taught me to be my own woman." Her fingers squeezed his tightly. "Thanks to you, I realize now that I hold my fate in my own hands, that I'm the only one who can make my dreams come true. I'm going to finish my book, come hell or high water. I know now that I want to do it, that I have what it takes to do it. Even if I have to work day and night, I'll—"

"But you don't have to do it like that, sweetheart. There's no need for you to work day and night, and we can at least be together on the weekends." He smiled and lifted her chin. "I've made sure everything's going to be perfect, for both of us. There's no reason why you can't stay here and finish your book. Not anymore." His finger grazed her cheek as she looked at him questioningly. "You don't have to worry anymore, because it's all been taken care of. I've bought out your contract with the museum."

Jerri's emotional state swung abruptly from sadness to anger. Fury. "You know what, Tyler? You've just hit on the real problem here. Your real problem." Using her feet, she pushed the rolling chair backward, away from him. "You still can't accept me for what I am! I'm capable of hard work and making my own dreams come true, but you don't believe for one minute that I can do it without your help!"

"I do, sweetheart." He seemed puzzled by her attitude. "I bought out your contract because I *wanted* to help."

"Did you?" she asked, completely enraged. "It seems to me that, if anything, it's just another one of your bribes. First you gave my outline to that publisher without my permission—and now this!" She glared at him, her fingers grasping the chair's leather arms. "Do you think I'm so pretentious that I have to be paid to stay here? To love you?"

He stood up, rubbing his jaw, and moved across the room.

"No, Jerri," he said, sounding exasperated with her as he gazed out the window, his hand propped against its frame. "I don't think that at all. I just don't want you to realize someday that we're too different. That I'm not everything you want me to be."

Jerri stared at him, shocked by the statement he'd made in such a matter-of-fact way. Didn't he know those differences were a vital part of her love for him? Didn't he know he was already everything she wanted him to be?

She watched as he started pacing back and forth across the room. Her heart ached to reach out to him, to erase the worried look from his eyes.

"Tyler?" she said softly. "Let me tell you something right now." She swallowed a gulp of air, trying not to cry. "You may never allow yourself to believe this, but I love you just exactly the way you are. Perfect and imperfect, good and bad. And that's all I'm asking of you in return: to love me the way I am."

"We've been over this before," he said, pushing out a weary sigh. "I do love you the way you are."

"You do not!" she said, her voice rising. "If you did, you would've been honest with me from the beginning. You would have discussed this infernal project with me, so that I could have told you it doesn't matter to me!"

Again he started wearing out the floor in front of her, raking his fingers across his scalp.

"Look, Smoky." He stopped, standing perfectly still as he watched her, his gaze intense and unwavering. "It matters to me! And I was going to discuss it with you, but I put it off for a good reason. I've let this thing go for too many years now, and I just wanted to get my entrance exams out of the way and get myself enrolled. I figured that way you'd see that I was really doing something about it, instead of just dreaming. I thought you'd be happy."

He looked at her in disbelief, his fingertips making contact with his chest. "I wanted you to be proud of me. Is that so terrible? I wasn't trying to be deceptive, I only wanted to have everything set up and ready to go. And that's the *only* reason I was waiting until tonight to—"

Jerri gasped, her hand flying up to cover her mouth. And then she heard a sound coming from her own lips. A pathetic sound that was almost a whimper.

"What's wrong, sweetheart? What—"

"Don't you dare 'sweetheart' me," she moaned, her words slow and distinct, her heart feeling as though it had just been ripped to shreds.

"What did I do?" he asked, his eyes reflecting what looked like concern.

Tears flowed down her cheeks, her hand clutching her tight chest. "You just did me a big favor," she whispered. "The biggest favor of all. You just let me know what a first-class fool I've been." She swallowed the lump in her throat. "All this time, I assumed your announcement tonight was going to be about our marriage. Instead, it's nothing but a proclamation—for the benefit of Pauline's parents!—of your being accepted into Trinity. Of your attending a fine, fancy, private school."

He stood there protesting, but she didn't hear a word. His pride was standing between them. It tore her apart, realizing that nothing she could do or say would change the way he felt.

He had given her no choice, she decided sadly. She had to leave him now. Because if they stayed together the way things were, it would only make them both miserable in the long run. And she couldn't bear the thought of that, for his sake as well as her own.

Her mournful gaze lowered to the desk top. She picked up the postcard, her eyes swimming with tears as she glanced at the message that had made her so happy for her mother. Yes, she told herself, clutching the card with renewed determination. She wanted her life to be different. She had no desire for a future of feeling empty and alone, and Tyler had just told her exactly how he felt: his pride wanted college more than he wanted her.

She refused to live like her mother had for so many years, hanging on to an impossible dream!

Jerri lifted her chin, dreading what she had to say, but knowing she had to say it.

"This dream of yours is nothing more than your stubborn pride, Tyler." Her words were even. Precise. "And I'll be damned if I'll put my life on hold for it. I'll be damned if I'll wait around while you decide whether I think you're good enough for me. If you can't love me the way I am, if you don't love me enough to prove it to me right now, then I'll just get out there and find some man who will!"

There was a strange look in his eyes. A look she had never seen before. But she wasn't going to let it deter her from what she knew she had to do. And, she reminded herself, she wasn't going to let him hurt her any more than he had already.

"What did you expect me to do, Tyler?" she asked angrily. "Stay on indefinitely as your resident author? As a paid nanny for your daughter?"

"Don't start getting sarcastic with me!" he yelled. "For God's sake, Jerri! I never meant I expected you to wait until I *graduated*."

"Oh, no?" she yelled back at him. "And once we were married, what did you think I wanted to do? Spend our evenings in lively discussions of the *classics*?" She didn't miss the look of disgust he shot her way. "Well, I've got news for you, mister! Maybe we are too different, because I had this crazy notion we'd be spending at least some of our time making little brothers and sisters for Sam!"

"Maybe you could be a bit more reasonable about this," he said through clenched teeth, "if you'd stop with that lousy sarcasm you call up every time you—"

"And maybe you could be more reasonable, if you'd stop working that damned jaw!" She returned his sudden glare. "You'll never understand, will you, Tyler? To hell with the book, to hell with everything else. All I ever really wanted was you and Sam and one measly little station wagon with wood on the sides!"

"Is that what you want?" he asked, looking totally perplexed by her statement. "Because if that's all you want, I'll buy you one. What color? What make and model? Just name it and I'll—"

"Dammit, Tyler!" she screamed. "It's not something you have to buy for me. It's not even something you can put your finger on." The postcard waved in the air as her hands flew up. "It could've been used, for heaven's sake! I would've been happy to make the payments on it myself!"

He stood there looking more befuddled than ever, and Jerri became more furious as the thought of money reminded her of what he'd done. She snatched up her stack of file folders, her voice low and determined.

"And I'll pay back every cent it cost you to buy out my contract, even if I have to wait on tables and scrub floors to do it. I'll mail you the first installment tomorrow, as soon as I get back home."

As she stormed past him, he tried to stop her. But she wrenched her arm away from his grasp.

"Oh, don't worry, Tyler. I'll stick around for your precious dinner party tonight. Not because of you or your announcement or Pauline's parents, but because it's Sam's birthday. I love that little girl, and I wouldn't disappoint her for anything in the world!"

After pivoting on her heel, Jerri yanked open the door. She turned her head again, just long enough to give Tyler her own announcement.

"But I'll be out of here before the crack of dawn."

Chapter Fifteen

Tyler was stretched out, one boot propped on top of the other, his ankle on the arm of the new sofa.

He took his forearm away from his eyes, glancing around him at the living room of the condo, complete with all the comforts of home. It had been only five days ago—Sunday afternoon, to be exact—that he'd found and leased this four-bedroom high-rise unit overlooking the Trinity campus. Like a fool, he'd decided they would need it: for times when Jerri, Samantha and Cotton wanted the four of them to spend the weekend in San Antonio together, instead of in Tarpley. And now, for the past three or four days, he'd been buying and hauling and setting up all the creature comforts so that no matter where Jerri was, here or at the ranch, she would always feel as if she had a real home. He had wanted her to have that, thinking it was what she'd always wanted.

But what did she want? he asked himself again. When she got started with that sarcasm, he never knew what it was she was getting at, and it drove him crazy. Even now, a couple of hours after their big blowout, he was still trying to figure out exactly what had thrown her into such a rage back at the house, and what he could do to make her understand what he had to do.

And why should that come as such a big surprise? he wondered, rubbing his tense jaw. He was still trying to figure out his own thinking over the past few weeks, and especially over the past few days. Four days ago, when he'd registered and bought his textbooks, it had dawned on him that he wasn't as excited about starting college as he had once thought he'd be, but he had tried to boost his spirits by admitting inwardly that he was proud of himself. Just as he had hoped Jerri would be.

Groaning wearily, he pushed himself up from the sofa and walked along the hallway, stopping in the one bedroom that was still unfurnished: the bedroom that eventually would have been theirs, if only Jerri had agreed to stay long enough to decorate this room the way she wanted it.

Hell, he thought, rubbing his hands tiredly over his face. She wasn't even giving him another twenty-four hours. She had acted like he was a jerk—a stupid jerk she couldn't wait to get away from. And maybe he was, judging by the way he was still trying to fit together the pieces she'd thrown at him all at once this afternoon.

Staring at the empty bedroom, he found himself thinking about how wonderful it was to be with her. In and out of bed she was all the things he ever could have hoped for. Everything she did in life she did with an intensity and an enthusiasm that had always flat-out astounded him. She could be a true lady or a passionate, eager little spitfire— and anything and everything in between.

A true lady. Tyler laughed then, shaking his head as he remembered their fight about Sam being "ladylike." It had been exactly one week before, when he'd been feeling guilty for not telling Jerri the whole truth. He could still picture her standing there in his study, telling him just exactly what she thought about it.

God, how he loved the way she always stood right up to him. The way she gave him hell whenever she thought he was dead-wrong about something. And he'd been wrong that day, without a doubt. Everything she'd said about being a lady was right on target.

Leaving the bare bedroom, he roamed back to the living area. "Empty," he said out loud, glancing around the perfectly and completely furnished room.

Yeah, he decided, empty was also a state of mind.

Tyler moved to the glass doors leading to the balcony, a long sigh echoing through the room as he reached into his breast pocket for matches and—

Good God, he reprimanded himself, was this the point he'd set himself back to? His fingers touched the slip of paper in his pocket, and he pulled it out, glaring at the damned telephone message that had started all this in the first place: "request denied." If Woodman hadn't called, none of this would be happening. He wouldn't be losing her now.

"Uh-huh. Sure." He stuffed the message back into his shirt pocket, frowning with resignation as he thought about Jerri's words the previous Saturday night. It didn't matter what was right or wrong or who was to blame. What mattered was life—as it is now.

And in that respect, there was only one thing he knew for sure. There was one area of his life he couldn't ask Jerri to accept, because he hadn't been able to accept it himself.

He gazed out the window, a glum look on his face as he stared unseeingly at the park across the street. It was the view of the park that had made him choose this particular high-rise complex. That and the fact that it was so near the Trinity campus. His eyes swept the stately buildings before moving back to the greenery. He could see almost the entire campus from here, including the administrative offices and—

A reflective flash of sunlight darted across his line of sight, catching his eye. Tyler studied the source for a moment, then took one more look around the room.

He smiled. A slow, broadening smile of realization. Glancing at his wristwatch, he calculated exactly how much time he had left for what he needed to do between now and five o'clock.

Yeah, Tyler assured himself, it was still a couple of hours before closing time. He quickly turned on his heel and grabbed his hat, grinning smugly as he walked out of the condo and locked the door behind him.

Jerri stood in front of the guest room's mirror, assuring herself that the ice bags and extra makeup had done their duty. She had cried almost the entire afternoon, in this very room. But at least now, she decided, she had shed every possible tear. Now she could make it.

If only there were something she could do to hide the look of despair she saw reflecting back at her. Unfortunately that was something no amount of makeup could conceal.

Not wanting to risk another confrontation with Tyler, one that might upset Samantha on her big day, Jerri had decided to wait in her room until Phyliss and Walter Hart arrived. Turning to the side, she straightened the lines of her simple, fitted dress: the only nice dress she had packed for this trip. She studied the silvery gray wool, wishing this could be some ordinary Friday night in the future. A night when it was cold enough for a fire in the master bedroom's large, inviting fireplace, with her wearing blue chenille and Tyler wearing—

She turned away from the mirror, staunchly reminding herself that she couldn't be wishing and hoping. Not any more.

A brief knock sounded at the door and Samantha entered, quickly racing across the room to hug Jerri.

"Hi, there," she said, loosening her hold as she realized she was hugging Samantha far too tightly. "Happy birthday, honey." She brushed Sam's curly blond hair with a kiss, ready to cry again as she reminded herself that Tyler's child might have been hers, too.

Inwardly, she reprimanded herself once more. She couldn't be wishing and hoping. And she couldn't allow any self-indulgent tears. She wouldn't. She would keep her emotions to herself. After all, until only a few short weeks ago, she'd had a lifetime of practice.

She lifted her cheek from atop the girl's head. For one night—the night of Sam's birthday party—she could call on those years of training. For one night she could push her own pain to the back of her mind.

"So," she asked abruptly, trying to sound bright as she held Sam back at arm's length and smiled. "I was resting earlier, but I heard you leave with your daddy. Did he take you to see your surprise birthday present? The one he's been keeping a big secret from both of us?"

"Uh-huh," the girl said slyly. "And guess what it is?"

"Give me a hint."

"I'll give you three hints. It's long and sleek and really fast."

"A Maserati," she said quickly, as if it couldn't be anything else.

"No!" the girl said, thrown completely off guard by the comment. "A greyhound!"

"Well, that's pretty silly, isn't it?" She feigned a look of disgust. "I mean, you don't even have a driver's license yet, so why on earth would you need your own bus?"

"A *dog*," Samantha answered, rolling her brown eyes and then grinning. "And you knew about it all along, didn't you?"

"Uh-huh," she answered. "I confess."

"Have you seen her?" she asked, her eyes rounding.

Jerri nodded. She had been there when Cotton returned from the airport the day before with the animal in tow. And Jerri had thought it a wonderful gift: a greyhound that hadn't proved to be a winner of races but that needed a loving home and the space to run free. An adoption, of sorts.

"Isn't she beautiful?" Samantha asked breathlessly.

"She's absolutely gorgeous. The most beautiful dog I've ever seen."

"And you'll never guess what I'm gonna name her," Sam said, bubbling over with excitement. "Never, ever, *ever*."

"Probably not," she said, laughing. "So why don't you just tell me?"

"She's gray, just like your eyes, and Daddy said that's why he calls you Smoky." She grinned sheepishly. "So I'm gonna name her Little Smoky, after you. Do you like that?"

"Oh, yes," Jerri murmured, gathering Sam to her again and holding her close. "Yes, I love that," she whispered. "And I love you."

Samantha's arms were around her waist, squeezing her. "I love you, too, Jerri."

"Thank you. Thank you, Sam." As she took a deep, ragged breath, the doorbell chimed. "You go ahead now and greet your guests. I'll be right behind you."

"Okay," she said happily, then bounded out of the room.

Jerri lifted her face and smiled as she moved into the hallway, telling herself she would force her mind to dwell on Samantha's sweet, loving gesture, instead of on the harsh finality of this night.

She arrived under the arched doorway that connected the hall to the den just in time to look across the big, contemporary room and watch an exuberant Sam as she opened the front door. Phyliss Hart leaned to kiss her granddaughter and then straightened to approach Tyler, who was standing directly behind his daughter. He was wearing a Western-cut suit, complete with a vest, and Jerri had never seen him looking so tall and strong and handsome. Just seeing him in that color, the darkest shade of navy, was enough to take her breath away. To make her pulse throb uncontrollably.

"Hello, Tyler," Mrs. Hart said, looking self-conscious as she smiled and reached for his outstretched hand. "It's really good to see you." The woman returned his handshake, and for only a brief moment, she put her free palm over their clasped hands. "You're looking wonderful. How have you been?"

Her light touch on his hand had been such a small gesture, yet Jerri noticed that Tyler's face had registered momentary shock.

"Fine, Phyliss. Just fine." He cleared his throat. "Thank you for asking."

Jerri realized her hip was almost hugging the side of the doorway, as if she could fade completely out of sight if she were allowed to stay in this spot all evening. Moving away from the jamb toward the center of the archway, she watched in silence as Tyler continued to visit with his guests. This would be her last opportunity to simply study him.

He seemed to be making a point of not glancing in her direction, and Jerri reminded herself of her promise. To put on a happy face and keep it there. To get through this evening without upsetting anyone else no matter how badly she was hurting inside.

And now, looking at Tyler, she realized she had to put up a brave, happy front. She loved him so much. She would always love him, and if this night was going to be the start of a new relationship between him and the Harts, she wanted that for him. It was her turn to be strong.

Her mind went back to that glorious morning at Nirvana Lookout, when he had babied her through her nicotine crisis. That had been the last time they had made love, and it seemed so very long ago.

Dear Lord, she thought. How she ached for him. Even now, knowing she had to leave him, she still wanted him with a fierceness that was frightening.

Would it always be this way? she wondered, her fingers touching her lips as she watched him move to the wet bar. Would this burning desire for Tyler be a clawing, aching sickness that would stay with her for the rest of—

"Hello, Jerri," Phyliss Hart said, her tone warm and open as she approached. "You should wear that color all the time, dear. It's the perfect complement to your smoky-gray eyes.''

Mrs. Hart smiled as she went on. ''Not that you didn't look lovely in your jeans and sweater the other day,'' she said, as if she thought her earlier statement might have offended Jerri.

If only Phyliss knew that the very mention of smoky gray had only served as another painful reminder of the day she'd been thinking of when the woman walked toward her.

''Thank you, Phyliss.'' Jerri forced a friendly, carefree look. ''And I've been wanting to tell you how beautiful you look in that gorgeous coat. We—I mustn't let you forget it again when you leave tonight.''

Tyler turned to look at her, with what seemed a non-expression on his face. And when he went back to his conversation with Walter Hart, she realized he had heard her comment. A bittersweet smile touched her lips as she thought about his suggestion that they make love on that coat, as she thought about the way he had teased because he was hurting.

After Mr. Hart had helped Tyler with the predinner cocktails, he delivered Jerri's drink to her and introduced himself with enthusiasm. Tyler watched closely while they exchanged pleasantries, and then he asked everyone to gather around. Jerri moved to the sofa. Even though everyone else was standing, she knew she couldn't manage it. Not now.

And, she reminded herself, she was glad to be slightly behind the rest of the group. Especially while she watched Tyler as he lifted his glass in a toast, especially when she wanted to avoid his serious blue gaze but couldn't seem to do it. His eyes, she reminded herself, had always had the power to draw her to him.

Tyler smiled just before he began to speak. ''This party is in honor of my daughter on her birthday. And even though I'm sure nothing's ever going to be the same around here from this day forward, I'm proud to say that I now have a teenager on my hands."

Noisy congratulations seemed to be in order, and Jerri joined in with the applause part of it. She kept her eyes on Tyler, though, and the proud expression on his face. How could she love that about him? she wondered. How could she love that fierce sense of pride when it was the very quality that was making it impossible for her to spend a lifetime with him?

"Go ahead, Daddy," Sam broke in, unable to stand still. "Say the rest."

When the hugging and talking died down, he continued. "Earlier today, my teenager—" father and daughter exchanged a private smile "—assured me she wouldn't mind sharing a little of the glory here tonight. So first of all, I'm proud to announce that after leaving school so many years ago, I've finally completed my high-school education."

Dear God, she thought, her heart going out to him as she stifled a moan. She had never dreamed Tyler hadn't finished high school. At last, she understood his fixation about their difference in educational backgrounds. But, she reminded herself sadly, this new information didn't change anything, because the problem separating them had nothing to do with education.

Tyler was watching her for a reaction, she realized. And even though the news had stunned her, she smiled softly to let him know that she was genuinely proud of his accomplishment. To assure him that even after she was gone from his life she would always admire him.

After the Harts each took a turn at shaking his hand, Tyler went on. "And now, I've been accepted into one of the best private universities in the country." He held up one palm, indicating that he wanted to continue. But instead, he crossed the room and pushed the intercom buzzer on the bottom panel of the telephone.

Jerri glanced around the room, realizing that he was signaling for Cotton to join them. And her heart sank even

further as she thought of the wonderful old man, as she reminded herself of what was happening here. She was being
forced to leave Tyler Reynolds and every facet of his life she
had yearned to share. She had grown to love everyone he
loved.

Why had she offered to stay for this party? she wondered, a fresh note of alarm building inside her. What she
really wanted to do was to leave this house now, with the few
pieces of herself that were still intact. Instead she would have
to sit here while Tyler continued with his announcement.

She had never dreaded anything so much, she realized,
watching him as he returned to finish speaking. In a few
sentences, he would be destroying the future she had hoped
they would have together. His announcement would be the
harsh and absolute end. And she knew that when the end
came, her heart and soul would break into a million extra
fragments.

"I'm very proud of being accepted," he was adding now,
while she forced herself to avoid his gaze. "I applied to
Trinity because I always thought that a college degree would
earn me a degree of respectability. I felt that that piece of
paper was what I needed to make my life complete."

The wording of his sentence grasped her attention, her
undivided attention, and Jerri stared up into his serious-
looking eyes before he spoke again.

"But thanks to some advice from a wise and wonderful
friend, I've finally learned that self-acceptance, feeling
empty or feeling complete, isn't something you can put your
finger on or something you can hang on a wall. It's a personal state of mind." He smiled at her then. "This friend of
mine has helped me open my eyes to what I am, to what I've
been all along. She's helped me make an important decision."

Jerri felt numb. The problem, she realized now, hadn't
been his pride or the fact that he couldn't accept her for
what she was. No. Tyler hadn't been able to accept this one

thing in himself. And now that he'd figured that out, what important decision was he talking about?

"Instead of attending college I'm going to stay here at home, where I want to be and where I belong. I'm going to hold my head up and continue to be what I think I've always been: an honest man, a decent boss. A loving, caring father. If I haven't proved myself in those areas by this point in time—" his eyes caressed her with a soft smile "—then I figure I might as well hang up my dancin' shoes right here and now.

"As for my goals for the future, there's one thing I'd like to accomplish. With me tonight is my real dream—the woman I love. I've finally realized that if I throw that dream away, no amount of education's going to make me anything but a fool. So if she'll give me a chance, I'd like to prove that I love her for exactly what she is. If she'll have me, I'd like to be with her while she makes her own dreams come true. To help her with them if I can."

If she'll have me? Jerri's mind replayed the words, trying to decide exactly what they meant. She blinked her eyes and tried to focus against the tears that were welling up behind them. She knew Tyler loved her, she had never doubted that. But she had been through this torment twice before. What would she do this time if he was only asking her to stay on again?

"Join me, please, in a toast to the woman who's helped me see what's important in life." Tyler smiled hopefully, soulfully, as he raised his glass and continued, his eyes never leaving hers. "I'll give her some time to give me an answer. I think I can hold out for…oh, I'd say twenty-four seconds would be just about all I—"

Just then, everyone turned to the approaching sound from beyond the den's wide expanse of windows. And Jerri's heart seemed to stop beating as she saw the shiny new Woody that had slowed to a halt under the glow of the outdoor lights.

Cotton got out of the station wagon and stood proudly beside it. He smiled and waved at them, then took out his handkerchief and started buffing away at a nonexistent smudge on its windshield.

Jerri's hand flew to her mouth, and she tried not to cry as she looked at Tyler. Her words were pleading and hushed. "But...but I can't let you—"

"It's not a bribe, Smoky," he answered, his eyes trying to reassure her. "If you want to make monthly installments to me—if you won't have it any other way—I'll even let you pay for it yourself."

"Oh, Tyler," she whispered, her voice plaintive as she tried to explain, tried to make him understand. "I wasn't just talking about the things you can give me." The tears started flowing down her cheeks. "That's not what I meant when I—"

His gentle, soft laughter interrupted her. "I've never been very good with symbols, sweetheart. But while I was trying to figure out what you were talking about today, I saw a family piling out of one of these things. It was a man and a woman with a whole passel of kids, all of them smiling and laughing while they unpacked their picnic gear. I swear, think even their big, floppy-eared dog had a smile on his face! And that's when it finally dawned on me what it was that a station wagon with wood on the sides meant to you."

He glanced out the window at the vehicle. "This one' exactly the same as the one I saw this afternoon...kind o a good omen, I thought...but if you don't like the color o the—"

"I—I like it just fine." Her fingers brushing at the moisture on her cheeks, Jerri tried to get her voice under control. "It's...just exactly what I had in mind."

"Well, Smoky, what do you say? Will you stay with me?" He tilted his head, ever so slightly, and gave her the most glorious, loving smile. "Will you marry me?"

Jerri stood up, swallowing the air that had been caught in her throat only a moment before. "Yes, Tyler," she said fresh tears of joy springing to her eyes. "Yes, I will. But only on one condition."

Tyler's eyes suddenly widened. "You don't—" he gestured toward the sofa behind her "—you don't want the couch, do you?"

"No!" she said, laughing and crying at the same time. "No, darling. I just want you to promise me something."

"Anything," he said, crossing the room, brushing away the wetness on her cheeks with the backs of his hands. "Just name it."

She reached up, her fingers tracing the faint line of his scar before she spoke.

"I want you to promise me that you'll never—" she put her arms around his neck, holding him close to the wild, ecstatic beat of her heart "—ever, *ever* try to get me out of your system."

"Not me, sweetheart," he whispered, his proud smile meeting hers as he held her against the length of his body. "You don't have a thing to worry about. The one time I tried it, my plan went right up in smoke."

Tyler's mouth came down on hers then. Surely, swiftly, tenderly. And in the midst of applause, Smoky kissed her bandit. The man she loved, the man she would be sharing a lifetime with, the man who made her feel like the *realest* woman in the world.

* * * * *

Silhouette Desire®

CHILDREN OF DESTINY

A trilogy by Ann Major

Three power-packed tales of irresistible passion
and undeniable fate created by Ann Major to
wrap your heart in a legacy of love.

PASSION'S CHILD — September

Years ago, Nick Browning nearly destroyed
Amy's life, but now that the child of his
passion—the child of her heart—was in danger,
Nick was the only one she could trust....

DESTINY'S CHILD — October

Cattle baron Jeb Jackson thought he owned
everything and everyone on his ranch, but fiery
Megan MacKay's destiny was to prove him wrong!

NIGHT CHILD — November

When little Julia Jackson was kidnapped, young
Kirk MacKay blamed himself. Twenty years later,
he found her...and discovered that love could
shine through even the darkest of nights.

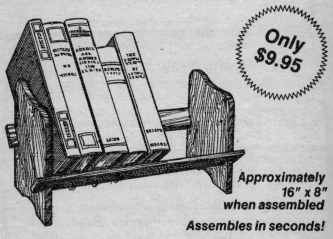

Silhouette Special Edition

COMING NEXT MONTH

#493 PROOF POSITIVE—Tracy Sinclair
Tough divorce lawyer Kylie O'Connor privately yearned for a happy
marriage and bouncing babies. But cynical Adam Ridgeway wasn't
offering either, and Kylie's secret couldn't keep for long....

#494 NAVY WIFE—Debbie Macomber
Navy officer Rush Callaghan placed duty above all else. His ship was
his home, the sea his true love. Could vulnerable Lindy Kyle prove
herself the perfect first mate?

#495 IN HONOR'S SHADOW—Lisa Jackson
Years had passed since young Brenna coveted her sister's boyfriend.
But despite recently widowed Warren's advances, Brenna feared some
things never changed, and she'd forever be in Honor's shadow.

#496 HEALING SYMPATHY—Gina Ferris
Ex-cop Quinn Gallagher didn't need anyone. Yet sympathetic Laura
Sutherland saw suffering in his eyes—and her heart ached. She'd risk
rejection if her love could heal his pain.

#497 DIAMOND MOODS—Maggi Charles
Marta thought she was over Josh Smith. But now the twinkling of
another man's diamond on her finger seemed mocking...when the
fire in her soul burned for Josh alone.

#498 A CHARMED LIFE—Anne Lacey
Sunburned and snakebitten, reckless Ross Stanton needed a
physician's care. Cautious Dr. Tessa Fitzgerald was appalled by the
death-defying rogue, but while reprimanding Ross, she began feeling
lovesick herself!

AVAILABLE THIS MONTH:

Silhouette Intimate Moments

JOIN BESTSELLING AUTHOR EMILIE RICHARDS AND SET YOUR COURSE FOR NEW ZEALAND

This month Silhouette Intimate Moments brings you what no other romance line has—Book Two of Emilie Richards's exciting mini-series Tales of the Pacific. In SMOKE SCREEN Paige Duvall leaves Hawaii behind and journeys to New Zealand, where she unravels the secret of her past and meets Adam Tomoana, the man who holds the key to her future.

In future months look for the other volumes in this exciting series: RAINBOW FIRE (February 1989) and OUT OF THE ASHES (May 1989). They'll be coming your way only from Silhouette Intimate Moments.
